Beyond Welfare

Beyond Welfare

New Approaches to the Problem of Poverty in America

Edited by
Harrell R. Rodgers, Jr.

M. E. Sharpe, Inc.
ARMONK, NEW YORK
LONDON, ENGLAND

Available in the United Kingdom and Europe from M. E. Sharpe, Publishers, 3 Henrietta Street, London WC2E 8LU.

Library of Congress Cataloging-in-Publication Data

Beyond welfare.

Includes bibliographies.

1. Poor—Government policy—United States. 2. Family policy—United States. 3. Child welfare—United States. 4. Family allowances—United States. I. Rodgers, Harrell R.

HV95.B49 1988 362.5'8'0973 87-28876

ISBN 0-87332-460-9

ISBN 0-87332-461-7 (pbk.)

Printed in the United States of America

Table of Contents

Acknowledgments

This book grew out of a conference on nonwelfare policies to alleviate poverty held at the University of Houston in the Spring of 1987. The Conference was sponsored by the University of Houston's Center for Public Policy, located in the College of Social Sciences. All the contributors to this volume attended the conference and presented early versions of the papers collected here.

Six University of Houston professors participated in the conference as discussants. Their insights contributed to a stimulating and rewarding conference, and to improved research papers. To George Magner, Professor of Social Work; Karen Haynes, Dean of the Graduate School of Social Work; Helen Rose Ebaugh, Chair of the Department of Sociology; Richard Hooker, Associate Professor of Education; John Antel, Assistant Professor of Economics; and Janet S. Chafetz, Professor of Sociology, we extend our sincere thanks.

We would also like to extent our thanks to Susan Hill, Operations Officer of the Center for Public Policy, who played a major role in organizing and managing the conference.

To our families we apologize for the late night and weekend writing binges, and express our love.

HARRELL R. RODGERS, Jr.
Houston, Texas

Introduction

The Role of Nonwelfare Social Policies in Reducing Poverty

Harrell R. Rodgers, Jr.

In recent years it has become increasingly evident that the nation's efforts to eradicate poverty are failing. In the late 1970s and early 1980s poverty increased quite significantly. It expanded most dramatically among families headed by a single parent (usually the mother), greatly raising the rate of poverty among children. Children in families headed by single women have the highest rate of poverty of any group in America. But poverty rates have risen for two-parent families as well. Since 1978 poverty among families with one or more full-time workers has doubled. Today, one-fifth of all American children live in poverty.

Why is poverty increasing?

In the first essay in this volume, "The Economy, Public Policy, and the Poor," Sheldon Danziger focuses on some of the major causes of recent increases in American poverty. Danziger points out that macroeconomic conditions since the early 1970s have refuted two key assumptions of the War on Poverty/Great Society planners: (1) that the business cycle could be controlled, and so poverty could be fought against a background of healthy economic growth; (2) that in an economy with low unemployment rates, and with antidiscrimination policies and educational and training programs in place, everyone—rich, poor, and middle class—would gain. Contrary to these expectations, the economy experienced several recessions and poverty and inequality increased, especially for families with children.

Over the 1973–1985 period, Danziger points out, the poor, especially the working poor, were adversely affected by all three of the main mechanisms by which income is generated and redistributed—the market, government income-support programs, and the tax system. Rising unemployment rates and declining real wages for many low-skilled workers raised poverty rates. The working poor—those with inadequate earnings—could have been helped by increased support from government income-maintenance programs. But, many benefits were eroded by inflation during the late 1970s. Then, despite back-to-back recessions, programs aiding the nonaged poor were cut during the retrenchment of the early 1980s. Deteriorating market incomes and reduced government benefits led to a sharp decline in pretax incomes. And to make matters worse, taxes on the poor increased steadily from the mid-1970s through 1986.

Danziger notes that, while the Tax Reform Act of 1986 eliminates taxes for most of the poor, it will do nothing to offset the declines in earnings and government benefits of the past decade. There is little evidence that the recent recovery has significantly benefited the working poor, much less those among the poor who are not expected to work. And, with unemployment rates projected to remain above 6 percent for the foreseeable future, the poor are not likely to find expanded employment and training opportunities in the private market.

What is clear, Danziger argues, is that poverty will not significantly decline unless and until its eradication is once again made a top priority of government.

An increasing number of scholars and public officials have come to agree that an antipoverty policy initiative is needed. Most also agree that it will take a combination of welfare reforms and new or improved nonwelfare social policies to strengthen families and greatly reduce poverty. The evidence, most agree, suggests that current welfare programs need to be better funded and the nation's major welfare program, Aid to Families with Dependent Children (AFDC), redesigned. Additionally, millions of families need assistance in the form of nonwelfare benefits or social services and legal protections if they are to escape or avoid poverty.

The essays in this volume provide in-depth analysis of many of the nonwelfare policies by which families could be economically strengthened and thus sheltered from poverty. One chapter also critically evaluates workfare, the primary reform of AFDC being debated in Congress and tested in some states and cities.

Integrating work programs into AFDC

There have been many proposals for reforming AFDC in recent years. The most prominent of them involve moving welfare recipients off AFDC by requiring or encouraging the parent to engage in a job search, enroll in job training, or accept a job. The proposals generally provide welfare parents with some supportive services that they will need to stay in the program or hold a job. The primary service many parents require is childcare. Under a variety of proposals based on the experiences of state and city programs, parents are to be provided with free or very low-cost childcare while they receive employment training or assistance and become established in the job market.

In "Workfare and Welfare Reform" Michael Wiseman provides an overview and recent history of work programs for welfare recipients. He begins by pointing out that the definition of workfare has changed: a term that at one time meant only requiring work in exchange for welfare payments has come to be used for any welfare reform that links income maintenance to employment programs. Wiseman next reviews the traditional arguments for and against exacting work in exchange for benefits and shows how the "work requirement" has gradually been changed to an "effort toward self-support" prerequisite. The catalyst for this change was a series of program options provided states by the Omnibus Budget Reconciliation Act of 1981 and subsequent related legislation.

Employing a model employment program as a base point, Wiseman examines three workfare programs. The first was a modest job-search/community-service-work requirement imposed upon new applicants for public assistance in San Diego, California in 1982. The second and third are the larger, much-publicized state workfare programs in Massachusetts (ET-Choices) and California (GAIN). Using data derived from studies by the Manpower Demonstration Research Corporation, Wiseman shows that while the San Diego program improved the work rate of recipients, increased their earning power, and reduced dependency, the actual effects of the program were modest. No evaluation data for the Massachusetts or California programs are available, but Wiseman cautions that although well-designed programs can produce positive results, workfare should not be oversold. Workfare is operationally complex, raises questions about equity, and its quantitative impact may be modest. Certainly workfare is not a panacea or a substitute for other social-welfare efforts. Still, in combination with other welfare programs, workfare might have a positive, incremental impact on poverty.

Family support policies

In "Reducing Poverty through Family Support," Rodgers's major thesis is that millions of families are in economic distress because social policy has failed to keep pace with major alterations in American family structure over the last two decades. The average American family is no longer a single-earner two-parent family. Rather, most families are headed either by a two-earner couple or by a single parent. To make ends meet, such families often need various types of supportive assistance, but quite often they find that the services are not available or cost more than they can afford. The result is that millions of families either cannot exercise options that would improve their economic conditions or they are seriously burdened by costly payments for essential services.

Rodgers discusses a variety of public policies that could be implemented to help families be economically and personally more viable. He starts with two options to enhance the take-home pay of low-income families: tax reform and modest alterations in the Earned Income Tax Credit (EITC). Next, two policies that play a major role in determining how well parents balance their dual role of parent and employee are examined. The first is childcare services. Four major problems with childcare services are examined and various policy options for overcoming these deficiencies are analyzed. Second, Rodgers discusses the need for maternity- and parental-leave policies. He points out that such policies are common in other western industrial countries, and are crucial if adults are to be encouraged to raise a family while pursuing a career. The policies that would have to be adopted to establish economically sound programs are examined.

Improving child support

A major contributor to the economic problems that afflict such a large percentage of female-headed families is the prevalence of flawed child-support systems. Most single parents are never awarded child support. Among custodial parents who are awarded support, only about half receive the full amount due them; about one-quarter receive nothing. In "Child Support and Dependency," Irwin Garfinkel, Sara McLanahan, and Patrick Wong critically examine the traditional private child-support systems that exist in most states, and the public program financed by AFDC. They then compare these approaches with the Child Support Assurance System (CSAS), a nonwelfare program currently being implemented and tested in the state of Wisconsin. The CSAS has three main features: (a) a standardized income-sharing rate reflecting the income of the noncustodial parent; (b) automatic income withholding; and (c) an assured child-support benefit that comes into effect when payments from the absent parent fall below a minimum level.

The authors also review recent federal efforts to strengthen state child-support systems. They conclude by comparing the economic consequences of adopting the CSAS approach as opposed to an improved private child-support system supplemented by public support. The analysis shows that, holding costs and reduction in poverty constant, CSAS shows a clear advantage in reducing the extreme dependence endemic to AFDC.

Improving the income of women

Another major cause of poverty among families is the low earning potential of most women. In "Labor Markets and the Feminization of Poverty," Jane Bayes isolates and analyzes the major factors that account for the low earning power of most female workers, and then examines some policies that might be implemented to enhance women's earnings.

As major causes of low earning power, Bayes focuses on the educational and market experience of women, the high rate of unemployment, occupational sex segregation, sex-related variations in pay within occupations, patterns of sex segregation between industries, changes in the international economy, and the evolving technological character and dual structure of the U.S. domestic economy.

As policy solutions Bayes considers comparable worth and a variety of methods of enabling more women to enter capital-intensive, core-economy industries and firms. She also discusses a wide range of family policies that would help parents to balance work and family roles. Bayes concludes that the economic policies reviewed can make incremental contributions to enhancing the earning power of women, but that to be effective they must be built on improved public policies for parents. Still, Bayes's primary conclusion is that achieving genuine economic equality will be a complex, difficult, and long-term project.

Reducing teenage pregnancy

There is a well-established link between teenage childbearing and poverty. In "Teenage Parenthood and Poverty," Richard Weatherley cites studies showing that early childbearing is associated with poor health outcomes for mothers and children, diminished educational, employment, and marriage opportunities, and an increased likelihood of public-welfare utilization. These findings make a compelling case for better preventive efforts to reduce teenage pregnancy and childbearing through sex education and family planning.

Weatherley reviews and evaluates the political and policy consequences of four approaches to teenage pregnancy prevention: (1) campaigns to discourage initiation of sexual activity; (2) sex education; (3) improving access to and use of contraceptives; and (4) policies to maintain and increase access to abortion. He also discusses two policies that would ameliorate the impact of teenage pregnancy: (1) greater utilization of adoption; and (2) education, childcare, and job-training programs for young parents.

Weatherley examines teen childbearing cross-nationally and shows that nations with similar levels of teenage sexual activity often have very different rates of teenage pregnancy and childbearing. A nation's approach to education and access to contraceptives have a significant impact on these rates. Income distribution policies may also have an influence. Teenage childbearing correlates significantly with poverty. Teenagers from low-income families, regardless of race, initiate sexual activity earlier and are more likely to become pregnant and carry a child to term. Weatherley, examining the correlation between teenage childbearing and poverty, concludes that poverty may be more a causal factor than an effect. Thus, while there are policies that can reduce teenage pregnancy and childbirth, dealing with the problem of poverty may be an essential part of this effort.

The role of education

In "Educational Programs: Indirect Linkages and Unfulfilled Expectations," Margaret LeCompte and Anthony Dworkin examine the educational innovations that have been directed at increasing the human capital of inner-city and low-income children. Too often, the authors point out, these programs have applied inappropriate standards and established contradictory as well as noncognitive goals for children. Compensatory programs have been badly underfunded, representing only 3 to 7 percent of educational expenditures. Moreover, funding is sometimes directed in such a way that those most in need do not receive the benefits.

Still, the authors note that it is possible to identify characteristics of educational programs that work to improve student learning and reduce dropout rates. Such strategies as early intervention (prekindergartens); teaching that prepares children for taking standardized tests; increasing "time on tasks," or a greater emphasis on assignments, especially in difficult subjects such as math and English; greater student-teacher interaction, facilitated by small student-to-teacher ratios; individualized educational plans along with structured instructional programs; and bilingual education, all have been found to be effective.

LeCompte and Dworkin argue that schools can be effective if the successful strategies discussed above are supplemented with the following reforms: individually tailored curricula; an end to the primarily remedial basic-skills focus of compensatory education; mainstreaming of potential dropouts; better and more standardized recordkeeping on dropouts; on-site daycare facilities for the children of student-parents; changing the anachronistic vocational orientation of programs for the disadvantaged; developing techniques for teachers to monitor their own behaviors; and affording to both students and teachers the opportunity to initiate educational planning.

Combining welfare and nonwelfare reforms

The isolated impact on poverty of any one of the reforms discussed in this book might be significant, but it must still be limited. The combined impact of reforms in all the policy areas, in conjunction with basic alterations in, and better funding of, the AFDC program could, however, be substantial.

In addition to the work programs analyzed by Wiseman, only two other reforms of AFDC have been seriously debated in Congress in recent years. One amendment given serious consideration would establish a minimum stipend level for all states. Currently, benefit levels vary greatly by state, with some being rather generous and others providing extremely inadequate benefits. Most reform proposals would require the low-paying states to increase benefit levels to 50 to 60 percent of the poverty level. The other major reform found in most recent proposals would require all states to extend AFDC payments to two-parent families when the father is unemployed. Currently only twenty-six states extend benefits to unemployed fathers. It is impossible to predict whether either of these reforms of the AFDC program will be passed by Congress.

Increased financial aid for supported work programs is a popular option in Congress and the most likely choice for increased congressional assistance. Supported work programs for poor parents combined with the other nonwelfare policies examined in this volume could have a substantial impact on American poverty. With enlightened policies the salaries of low-income workers could be enhanced, the availability, quality, and affordability of childcare could be improved, and parental-leave policies could enable more families to harmonize work and family responsibilities. Improved child-support policies would leave fewer single-parent families impoverished. Better sex education and family-planning services could reduce the number of unwanted pregnancies and births. A combination of policies could improve the earning power of women. A determination to design, fund, and implement instructional programs to give all children a quality education would enable more young people to maximize their talents and meet the needs of society.

The policies examined and critiqued in this book are not panaceas for poverty. They are incremental policy responses to obvious, and often changing, social and human needs. Most of these policies are of the type that enlightened societies employ to strengthen individuals and families so that they will never become poor. Such policies generally prevent more than they cure, and prevention is the most enlightened of all policy goals.

Beyond Welfare

The Economy, Public Policy, and the Poor

Sheldon Danziger

The antipoverty programs of the War on Poverty and the Great Society of the 1960s have come under frequent attack during the 1980s. In February 1986, in one of his Saturday radio addresses, President Ronald Reagan made this charge:

> In 1964, the famous War on Poverty was declared. And a funny thing happened. Poverty, as measured by dependency, stopped shrinking and then actually began to grow worse. I guess you could say, "Poverty won the War." Poverty won, in part, because instead of helping the poor, government programs ruptured the bonds holding poor families together.

This view is typical of a number of recent attacks (of which Charles Murray's *Losing Ground* [1984] is the most famous) on the programs of the War on Poverty and the Great Society.

Granted, there is much to criticize about the way we have attempted to reduce poverty, especially in the 1980s. But such attacks tend both to ignore the many successes of the War on Poverty and Great Society programs and to overlook the poverty problems caused by economic stagnation since the early 1970s.

The poverty rate in America remains high today not because of what government programs did, but because of what government programs did not do; not because we provided too much aid to the poor, but because we failed to aid many of them; not because of adverse economic and family effects created by public programs, but because of adverse and unexpected macroeconomic trends (see Danziger and Weinberg [1986] and Danziger and Plotnick [1986] for an elaboration of this view).

One of the biggest challenges faced by antipoverty policy today is that poverty, which was placed at the top of the policy agenda in the 1960s, is no longer a top-priority item. This change in priorities is one reason why poverty, which declined rapidly as the economy grew in the late 1960s and early 1970s, is declining so slowly during the current economic recovery. The War on Poverty, according to Robert Lampman (1974), led government agencies and Congress to ask, whenever new programs or policies were introduced, "What does it do for the poor?" This question remained in the mainstream of social policy discussions through at least the late 1970s.[1] But it was clearly off of the agenda by February 1981, when President Reagan introduced his Program for Economic Recovery:

> The goal of this administration is to nurture the strength and vitality of the American people by reducing the burdensome, intrusive role of the federal government; by lowering tax rates and cutting spending; and by providing incentives for individuals to work, to save, and invest. It is our belief that only by reducing the growth of the government can we increase the growth of the economy.

Rather than ask about a policy "What does it do for the poor?" government agencies and Congress were to ask "What does it do for incentives to work, save, and invest?"

In this essay my intention is, first, to provide a brief overview of recent trends in the economy and public policies that have affected family incomes and poverty, and then to examine the current economic situation of families with children. I emphasize poverty among children both because their poverty rates are higher than those of either adults or the elderly and because they are the target of most of the antipoverty reforms currently being discussed in Congress. I conclude that welfare programs have had little antipoverty impact on children. As a result, both welfare reform and expanded nonwelfare policies, as discussed in the other essays in this volume, will be needed if substantial declines in child poverty are to be achieved.

Factors affecting family incomes and poverty

The period since the early 1970s has been one of economic stagnation and increasing poverty and inequality, especially for families with

Table 1

Declining Incomes for Families with Children (constant 1985 dollars)

	Position in income distribution					Mean of all families	% poor[a]
	Lowest fifth	2nd fifth	Middle fifth	4th fifth	Top fifth		
1973	$9,639	$21,414	$30,020	$40,177	$65,509	$33,352	11.4
1985	6,529	17,469	27,724	38,399	65,702	31,167	16.7
% change 1973–85	−32.3	−18.4	−7.6	−4.4	+0.3	−6.6	+46.5

a. Percentage of all persons in these families with incomes below the official poverty line.

Source: Computations from March 1974 and 1986 Current Population Survey computer tapes.

children. Macroeconomic conditions have refuted two key assumptions held by planners of the War on Poverty and the Great Society. The planners thought that the business cycle could be controlled, and poverty could be alleviated against a background of healthy economic growth. They also believed that in an economy with low unemployment rates and with antidiscrimination policies and education and training programs in place, everyone—rich, poor, and middle class—would gain. At a minimum, it was expected that economic growth would be proportional and that all incomes would rise at about the same rate. At best, income growth for the poor would exceed the average rate.

History has proved these assumptions wrong. For the first two postwar decades, mean income for families with children, adjusted for inflation, grew at an annual rate of 6 percent per year. Between 1967 and 1973, annual growth rates were about 3 percent for two-parent families and less than 1 percent for female-headed families. Growth in mean family income between 1973 and 1985 (see Table 1) was actually negative, and in 1987 unemployment rates remained above 6 percent despite four years of economic recovery.

Changes in mean income indicate how the "typical" family has fared, but they obscure the differing experiences of families at different positions in the income distribution. The circumstances of the poor have altered dramatically over this time span. From 1949 through 1969 poverty declined rapidly and inequality lessened somewhat. In stark contrast, during the period 1973–1985 poverty increased substantially and the mean income of the poorest fifth of families with children declined by 32.3 percent (see Table 1). In 1973 the income of the richest fifth was about 7 times that of the poorest fifth; by 1985 it was about 10 times as large.

Throughout the 1973–1985 period, the poor, especially the working poor, were adversely affected by all three of the main mechanisms by which income is generated and redistributed—the market, government income-support programs, and the tax system. First, increased unemployment rates and declining real wages for many low-skilled workers raised poverty rates. In 1973, when the national poverty rate was at its historical low point, 12.7 percent of married men with children did not earn enough to keep a four-person family out of poverty ($211 per week in 1985 dollars); by 1985 this percentage had increased to 18.6.

The working poor with inadequate earnings could have been helped by increased support from government income-maintenance programs. This did not happen. During the late 1970s, many benefits were eroded by the high rate of inflation. Then, despite back-to-back recessions, most programs aiding the nonaged poor were cut during the retrenchment of the early 1980s. Programs for the working poor, such as unemployment insurance, Aid to Families with Dependent Children, and employment and training programs, were hit hardest. In 1985 only about half of poor families with children received welfare.

Deteriorating market incomes and reduced government benefits led to a sharp decline in pretax incomes. And to make matters worse, taxes on the poor increased steadily from the mid-1970s through 1986. The three devices in the personal income tax that aid the poor—the personal exemption, the zero bracket amount, and the earned income tax credit—were all eroded by inflation over this period. In 1975 a family of four with earnings at the poverty line paid 1.3 percent of its income in federal personal income and payroll taxes; by 1985 this had increased to 10.5 percent, an amount sufficient to offset the value of any food stamps the family might have received. Although the Tax Reform Act of 1986 eliminated taxes for most of the poor, it did not offset the declines in earnings and government benefits of the past decade (see Danziger 1986).

Poor children: a statistical profile

There has been much recent discussion of rising rates of poverty among children and falling rates of poverty among the elderly (Moynihan 1986), but one must be careful in drawing policy conclusions. Table 2 shows the composition of the population, the composition of the poor, the official poverty rate for children classified by the number of parents

Table 2

The Composition of the Population and the Poor, 1985 (in percent)[a]

	Composition of the population (1)	Composition of the poor (2)	Incidence of poverty (3)
All persons	100.00%	100.00%	13.98%
Children:			
In two-parent families	20.52	16.72	11.35
In one-parent families	6.39	22.80	49.90
Persons living in households where head is:			
Male, 18–64 years	50.36	28.57	7.88
Female, 18–64 years	11.08	21.28	26.78
Male, 65 and older	7.22	3.95	7.36
Female, 65 and older	3.93	6.69	23.13

a. In 1985, there were 236.59 million persons, of whom 33.06 million were poor according to the official poverty definition (see note 2).

Source: Computations from March 1986 Current Population Survey computer tapes.

with whom they live, and the poverty rate for adults classified by the age and sex of the head of their household.[2] The table suggests that the published poverty rates in 1985 for children and the elderly—20.1 and 12.6 percent, respectively—mask wide variations within each group.

For example, the poverty rate for children living in two-parent families, 11.35 percent, was actually below the rate for all persons, 13.98 percent, and the published rate for all elderly persons. The poverty rate for all children was high because the rate for children living in single-parent families was extraordinarily high, 49.9 percent. The poverty rate for all elderly persons was low because the rate for persons living in households headed by elderly men was low—7.36 percent.

However, the situation is more complex than Table 2 suggests, since data by race are not shown. Poverty rates among all minority children were very high—21.84 percent for those living with two parents and 64.34 percent for those living with a single parent. Similarly, the rates for elderly blacks and Hispanics were high—19.57 percent for persons living in households headed by black and Hispanic men, 39.17 percent for those living in households headed by black and Hispanic women.

A national poverty rate of 20 percent led Lyndon Johnson to declare war on poverty more than twenty years ago. Yet in 1985 the official poverty rates for minority children, white children in single-parent families, adult and elderly women heading households, and minority elderly all *exceeded* that rate.[3] Because analysts and policymakers rely on the published figures for large, general categories of people, they tend to neglect the diversity of the poverty problem. For example, it has been suggested that we need to shift public policies so that the elderly receive less and children receive more support. However, the disaggregated data indicate that one should not target antipoverty policies on the basis of age. The question that belongs at the top of our policy agenda is "What does this do for the poor?"—not "What does it do for the elderly?" or "What does it do for children?"

With this caveat, I now turn to a more detailed analysis of children in poverty because families with children are the main target group for the policies discussed in this volume.

Table 3, using data from 1985, classifies children living in two-parent and female-headed families into four mutually exclusive and exhaustive categories based on poverty status and receipt of government transfers. These data reveal those who received assistance from current programs and those who remained in need. Column 1 refers to children who were not pretransfer poor; children who were pretransfer poor are counted in columns 2, 3, and 4. Children living in families that did not receive enough money income from market and private-transfer sources (e.g., wages, dividends, child support) to raise them over the poverty line constitute the pretransfer poor (a more exact title would be pre–government-transfer poor). Pretransfer poverty reveals the magnitude of the problem faced by the public sector after the market economy and private-transfer system (e.g., private pensions, interfamily transfers) have distributed their rewards.[4]

Column 2 includes those children who were pretransfer poor, but who received enough in government transfers so that they escaped poverty and thus were not posttransfer poor.[5] The transfers considered in Table 3 include only those transfers with dollar values reported in the Current Population Survey data. These transfers—with the exception of medical-care transfers—account for the major programs that provide aid to families. They include social security, railroad retirement, unemployment insurance, workers' compensation, government employee pensions, veterans' pensions and compensation, Aid to Families with Dependent Children, Supplemental Security Income, general assistance, food stamps, and energy-assistance payments. Benefits from the last five programs are welfare transfers, as their receipt is contingent

Table 3

Poverty and Income Transfer Receipt among Children, 1985[a]

	Not pretransfer poor (1)	Pretransfer poor[b]: But not posttransfer poor (taken out by transfers) (2)	Pretransfer poor[b]: Received transfers, but not enough to escape poverty (3)	Pretransfer poor[b]: Received no transfers (4)	All children by category (5)
Two-parent families					
Number of children (millions)	41.91	1.40	3.08	2.16	48.55
% of (two-parent) children	86.33	2.89	6.34	4.44	100.00
Weeks worked by head	47.85	22.07	21.79	40.45	45.13
Weeks worked by spouse	28.14	11.50	8.08	14.69	25.79
Mean transfers	$ 644	$8,472	$4,911	0	$1,112
% receiving welfare transfers	4.69	60.84	87.34	0	11.35
Mean poverty gap[c]	0	0	$4,246	$4,831	$484
% receiving nonwelfare transfers	14.07	71.51	37.95	0	16.62
Female-headed families					
Number of children (millions)	5.38	1.04	5.84	1.12	13.38
% of (single-mother) children	40.22	7.76	43.65	8.36	100.00
Weeks worked by head	45.55	16.25	9.04	26.01	25.70
Mean transfers	$1,156	$8,727	$5,448	0	$3,521
Mean poverty gap[c]	0	0	$4,007	$5,229	$2,187
% receiving welfare transfers	14.24	69.54	94.65	0	52.45
% receiving nonwelfare transfers	20.01	58.97	18.64	0	20.76

a. About 3 percent of all children (1.89 million) live in single-parent families headed by males. They are excluded from this table.

b. Pretransfer income is determined by subtracting government cash transfers from a family's money income.

c. The poverty gap is the dollar amount needed to bring a poor family up to the poverty line.

Source: Computations from March 1986 Current Population Survey computer tapes.

on a family's having low income. The first six nonwelfare transfer programs provide benefits based on prior employment and contributions, not on the current income level of the family. The children in column 3 received government assistance, but not enough to pull them out of poverty, while those in column 4 received no transfers at all. The sum of columns 3 and 4 constitutes those who remained poor and are the target group for expanded antipoverty policies.

Consider, first, children living with two parents. Most—86.3 percent—were not pretransfer poor (column 1). Those who were not poor before transfers had parents who worked a substantial number of weeks during the year; their fathers averaged almost 48 weeks, their mothers, 28 weeks. Fewer than 5 percent received welfare transfers (AFDC, SSI, food stamps, energy assistance, general assistance); about 14 percent received nonwelfare transfers.

Pretransfer poor children aided by government programs, shown in columns 2 and 3, lived with parents who worked relatively few weeks during the year. Those who escaped poverty (column 2) received relatively large transfer amounts—averaging $8,472. About 60 percent received welfare transfers, and about 70 percent received nonwelfare transfers.

Those who failed to escape poverty (column 3) lived in families that received smaller transfer amounts, and tended to receive welfare (87 percent) but not nonwelfare transfers (38 percent). Their transfers averaged $4,911. This difference in the mean value of transfers for the children in columns 2 and 3 is not surprising, since the maximum benefits available in nonwelfare programs, such as social security and unemployment compensation, are well above maximum welfare benefits.

Column 4 shows that 2.16 million children living with two parents received no welfare or nonwelfare transfers and remained poor, even though their parents worked a significant number of weeks. Their mothers and fathers together worked 55 weeks on average during the year. These working poor families stand to gain the most from tax-based reforms, such as those discussed by Harrell Rodgers later in this volume. However, the large size of their mean poverty gap—$4,831—suggests that low wage rates are their primary problem, and such a gap cannot be closed through tax reform.

The bottom panel of Table 3 presents the same information for dren living with a female household head. These children comprised 21 percent of all children but 55 percent of all pretransfer poor children. Compared to children in two-parent families, many more were pretransfer poor—59.77 versus 13.67 percent (the sum of columns 2, 3, and 4 in row 2 of each panel of Table 3).

The largest group of children in female-headed families is found in column 3. These children lived with mothers with little attachment to the labor force and, despite almost universal welfare recipiency (94.65 percent), remained well below the poverty line. They are the group most likely to gain from workfare programs and child-support reforms, as discussed below by Wiseman and by Garfinkel, McLanahan, and Wong.

To sum up, the current system of welfare and nonwelfare transfers took about 2.5 million children out of poverty (17 percent of all pre-transfer poor children), and provided aid to about 9 million more, but left more than 12 million in poverty. The families who remained poor had incomes about $4000–$5000 below the poverty line, indicating that no single program or policy could significantly reduce their numbers.

Summary

The picture just presented is a gloomy one. There is little evidence that the economic recovery of the mid-1980s has significantly benefited the working poor, much less those among the poor who cannot work, such as the disabled or those with very young children. And, with unemployment rates projected to remain above 6 percent for the foreseeable future, the poor are not likely to find sufficient employment and training opportunities in the private market.

Given the extent of poverty and inequality and this gloomy forecast, I believe that antipoverty policy must be placed back at the top of the domestic policy agenda. Many poor families, especially those with both parents, do not receive welfare; consequently, they will not benefit from most of the current welfare-reform proposals. Thus, an effective antipoverty policy must be one that attempts to raise market incomes, either through macroeconomic policies or workfare/work opportunities, and to provide increased support through the income tax, child support reform, and other nonwelfare policies.

Notes

1. Following Lampman [1974], I define the War on Poverty and Great Society era broadly and categorize the Low Income Energy Assistance program enacted in the late 1970s as the last program of the era. When Congress decided to deregulate gasoline prices in order to promote greater production and efficiency, the question arose, "But what are its effects on the poor?" The result was the energy-assistance program, a

program that remains in place today. I do not claim that this program offset all of the problems of the poor related to higher energy prices, but simply that the question "What does it do for the poor?" was still on the national agenda in the late 1970s. There were no similar policy responses focused on a broad spectrum of the poor until the Tax Reform Act of 1986.

2. The federal government's official measure of poverty provides a set of income cutoffs adjusted for the household size, the age of the head of the household, and the number of children under age 18. (Until 1981, sex of the head of household and farm/nonfarm residence were other distinctions.) The cutoffs provide an absolute measure of poverty that specifies in dollar terms minimally decent levels of consumption. The official income concept—current money income received during the calendar year—is defined as the sum of money wages and salaries, net income from self-employment, social security income and cash transfers from other government programs, property income (e.g., interest, dividends, net rental income), and other forms of cash income (e.g., private pensions, alimony). Current money income does not include capital gains, imputed rents, government or private benefits-in-kind (e.g., food stamps, Medicare benefits, employer-provided health insurance), nor does it subtract taxes, although all of these affect a household's level of consumption.

So that they will represent the same purchasing power each year, the official poverty thresholds are updated yearly by an amount corresponding to the change in the Consumer Price Index. For 1985 the poverty lines ranged from $5156 for a single aged person to $22,083 for a household of nine or more persons. The average poverty threshold for a family of four was $10,989. According to this absolute standard, poverty will be eliminated when the incomes of all households are above the poverty lines, regardless of what is happening to average household income.

3. Care must be taken in interpreting the official poverty rates, which are based only on cash incomes. When the poverty thresholds were set in the mid-1960s, the poor received few in-kind transfers and paid little in taxes. Therefore, one could at that time legitimately compare *cash* income with the official poverty lines to obtain a fairly accurate picture of resources available to meet the families' needs. However, during the late 1960s and early 1970s noncash transfer benefits increased rapidly. While these noncash benefits represented only 12 percent of outlays on public assistance programs in 1966, this figure had risen to about 70 percent by 1983. Clearly a better measure of a family's ability to meet its needs would include the value of in-kind programs.

Likewise, taxes detract from the availability of resources to meet needs. If taxes had not increased very much since the mid-1960s they could be ignored, since the original poverty definition was based on income before taxes.

Unfortunately, we do not have a consistent time series for poverty which adjusts for both taxes and the value of in-kind transfers. The bulk of in-kind transfers fund medical care, mostly for the elderly. In addition, the valuation of these expenditures for poverty measurement is very controversial.

The Congressional Budget Office estimated that in 1985, in-kind food and housing benefits lifted from poverty 2.7 million persons living in families with children, but that federal income and payroll taxes added back 1.7 million. For those families, the official poverty rate was 16.9 percent, and the rate after adjusting for these selected in-kind transfers and taxes was 16.2 percent. Thus, the rates shown in Tables 1 and 2 should be considered as somewhat higher than the "true" poverty rates.

4. Pretransfer income is determined by subtracting government cash transfers from a family's money income. This definition assumes that transfers elicit no behavioral responses that would cause income without transfers to deviate from observed pretransfer income. However, transfers do induce labor-supply reductions, so recipients' net incomes are not increased by the full amount of the transfer; true pretransfer

income is likely to be higher than measured pretransfer income. Therefore, pre/post-transfer comparisons, like the ones made here, are likely to provide upper-bound estimates of antipoverty effects.

5. The posttransfer poverty rates in Table 3 differ somewhat from the official poverty rates shown in Tables 1 and 2 because these rates value the in-kind benefits of food stamps and energy assistance while the official rates do not.

References

Danziger, S. 1986. "Tax Reform, Poverty and Inequality." University of Wisconsin-Madison: Institute for Research on Poverty, Discussion Paper.

Danziger, S. and R. Plotnick. 1986. "Poverty and Policy: Lessons of the Last Two Decades." *Social Service Review*, March, 33–51.

Danziger, S., and D. Weinberg, eds. 1986. *Fighting Poverty: What Works and What Doesn't.* Cambridge, Mass.: Harvard University Press.

Lampman, R. 1974. "What Does It Do for the Poor?" *Public Interest*, No. 34, 66–82.

Moynihan, D. P. 1986. *Family and Nation*. New York: Harcourt, Brace, Jovanovich.

Murray, C. 1984. *Losing Ground: American Social Policy, 1950–1980*. New York: Basic Books.

Reagan, R. 1981. *America's New Beginning: A Program for Economic Recovery*. Washington, D.C.: Office of the Press Secretary, The White House.

Workfare and Welfare Reform

Michael Wiseman

Work has been a prominent issue in the national debate over welfare policy for more than twenty years. Most Americans seem to agree that adults who are capable of working should, if possible, contribute to the support of themselves and their dependents. But substantial disagreement arises over the way, if any, this obligation should be imposed by society, the extent to which those who are not self-supporting are capable of becoming so, and the ability of government to help in attaining this end. All of these questions have resurfaced in connection with discussions of "workfare," that is, welfare reforms that link income maintenance to employment programs.

Many of the issues in the workfare debate involve social values and not empirical problems. But workfare proposals also raise practical issues of policy, and here the outcomes of actual workfare programs and efforts at training poor people for jobs provide important lessons. In this essay, I discuss such issues in light of the results of current workfare programs. My conclusion is that welfare work programs offer a useful opportunity for incremental welfare reform, but unanswered questions about the organization and consequences of such programs necessitate a cautious approach to program development and merchandising.

The work requirement debate

Current workfare programs all involve somethıng more than a work requirement. Virtually all create a new sense of obligation to undertake some activity in exchange for benefits. Requiring work is the traditional way of doing this. In its simplest form, the work requirement is a standard of eligibility for assistance: unless the potential recipient is willing to work for some agency of the state, benefits are denied. Generally, the benefits involve more than wages, since most income maintenance schemes tailor payments to factors such as household size.

Making the poor work for relief has a long (and generally sordid) history going back to the English Henrician Poor Law of 1536 ("the Act for the Punishment of Sturdy Vagabonds and Beggars"). This history reinforces opposition to such policies.

The case for work requirements

Five interrelated arguments might be cited as support for requiring that needy persons work for benefits.

(1) *A work requirement is an effective test of need.* Most eligibility tests for public assistance involve current income, assets, or both. But need, at least in the abstract, is a matter not of what income is, but of what it could be. The willingness of the poor to work for benefits seems, for most people, to be a convincing demonstration of the absence of alternatives. This "needs effect" is ongoing. A work requirement creates incentives for job finding, or location of other resources, if opportunities arise. As such, it substitutes for the financial incentives that have been incorporated in welfare programs to encourage work.

(2) *Work requirements reduce welfare costs.* Costs are reduced in two ways. Work programs offset payments costs by the value of the product of the work recipients do. Costs are also lowered by caseload reductions that result from the "needs effect" already cited.

(3) *Work programs can preserve or enhance skills and contribute to employability.* The longer people are out of the labor force, the greater the difficulty they are likely to experience in obtaining and holding a job. Work, even in special jobs, may forestall this effect; and for recipients with no work history, workfare provides job experience.

(4) *Work requirements make welfare more equitable.* It has been an abiding principle of welfare reform efforts that persons who work should be better off financially than those who do not work.[1] But well-being involves both money income and time. While households of the working poor not receiving assistance may have higher money incomes than comparable welfare-dependent families without earners, they may be worse off, both because they do not get the in-kind benefits available to welfare recipients (such as Medicaid) and because welfare recipients

do not have to work outside the home. This differential may be particularly evident to single parents who struggle to find sufficient time for both work and childrearing.

(5) *Work requirements enhance political support for public assistance.* Survey data consistently indicate more generous public response to the the needs of the working than the nonworking poor. Recent research suggests that this attitude carries over to differentiation on the basis of how resolutely the unemployed recipients are trying to find a job.[2] Also, some studies indicate that the generosity of state welfare benefits is inversely related to expected total welfare costs.[3] Work programs thus lay the political foundation for higher basic benefit levels by assuring work effort and by reducing the caseload that will result from any given benefit standard.

The case against work requirements

Work requirements for welfare recipients are anathema to many persons concerned about social-welfare policy. Such programs, it is asserted, stigmatize the poor. Required work is therefore counter to the traditional focus of reform efforts, which has been on the development of systems of universal income support, such as the negative income tax, that provide nonintrusive cash assistance based on money income alone.

Opponents also deny the validity of the arguments that constitute the case for mandatory work requirements. The needs test argument may be rejected, it is claimed, because in welfare programs such as Aid to Families with Dependent Children (AFDC), eligibility already requires low or nonexistent income, very few assets, and, for many recipients, mandatory work registration and job search. The gains from eliminating a few persons unwilling to work from welfare rolls would be offset by the additional burden placed upon the majority of the genuinely needy and, in addition, upon the dependents of those who, for whatever reason, would refuse to accept mandated jobs. As for the skills argument, unless the jobs provided are skill-intensive (and therefore costly to provide), it seems unlikely that labor alone will enhance a recipient's job readiness.

Opposition to the incentives and equity arguments for work requirements turns in part on perceptions of the circumstances of welfare recipients. If welfare cases stay open only for relatively short periods of time and occur because of events beyond people's immediate control—

loss of jobs, for example—then welfare serves an insurance function, and the problem of dependency has its origin in the supply of jobs, and not recipients' unwillingness to work. Under these circumstances a work program might even lengthen welfare spells by interfering with the search for new, unsubsidized employment. Political support is a matter of education; if people correctly understand the circumstances of the needy, support will be forthcoming.

Opponents of mandated employment programs also tend to emphasize the cost of work-program operation. An effective work mandate requires a job-of-last-resort for all who are eligible. To guarantee the virtues of the program, such jobs must produce useful output (to offset costs), enhance skills (to improve employability), and be organized in the expectation of rapid employee turnover. These requirements call for considerable capital and managerial commitment as well as innovation. Without novelty, it is likely that the jobs, especially the more valuable jobs, will replicate work done by regular employees of public or private organizations and therefore incur charges of displacement. Attempts at implementation of small-scale work requirements in the 1970s in California, Massachusetts, and Minnesota were plagued with administrative problems and failed to achieve employment targets.[4] Given the institutional and social constraints under which welfare policy must operate, critics argue, such programs, even if desirable, are simply not administratively feasible.

Recent developments in the workfare debate

Despite reservations such as those outlined above, interest in workfare grows. This is a product of a more inclusive definition, opportunities created by legislation, and other developments.

What's in a name?

One of the most significant aspects of the evolution of thinking about work-welfare programs is the changing definition of workfare. In 1972, when then-Governor Ronald Reagan introduced the original Community Work Experience Program in California, workfare meant working in return for welfare payments. Fifteen years later the workfare designation has become much more broadly applicable, encompassing an obligation for job search or training, and not just work in public parks. The reason for this is in part political: some consider making needy people look for work a more palatable alternative than making them cut weeds. But the change also reflects the idea that the essence of a work requirement is not what you do, but whether you are *obligated* to do it. Thus it is now possible to combine under the general workfare label any program in which income maintenance is explicitly linked to employment preparation. Today, workfare programs are not simply systems that mandate that recipients work in exchange for benefits. Rather, they tend to entail processes, steps certain welfare-receiving adults are expected to take in connection with benefit receipt.

Legislation

The catalyst for new attention to workfare was the Omnibus Budget Reconciliation Act of 1981 (OBRA). OBRA allowed states to establish mandatory Community Work Experience Programs (CWEP). Adults receiving AFDC could be required to participate in CWEP training and "work experience" activities "to assist them to move into regular employment."[5]

In addition to CWEP, OBRA and subsequent legislation made other important additions to the toolkit for work-related welfare changes.[6] Many of these opportunities are related to the Work Incentive Program (WIN).

WIN was established by Congress in 1967 to furnish training programs and other employment-related assistance to welfare recipients. As originally designed, the program featured a dual administrative structure at both federal and state levels. On the one hand, the U.S. Department of Labor and the various state employment services handled work registration and training activities. On the other, the welfare application, approval, and payments system is the province of the U.S. Department of Health and Human Services and state income-maintenance units. WIN mandated that certain adult recipients—mothers without preschool children in single-parent families, and the unemployed principal earner (usually the father) in two-parent families—register with the WIN program as a condition of receiving welfare. In practice the participation requirement has not been meaningful, for shortages of staff and funds and coordination problems created by WIN itself have meant that two-thirds or more of those who register for WIN receive no services. In theory able-bodied adults without transportation problems or childcare problems who refused to accept job referrals generated through WIN or to participate in training could be "sanctioned'' by reduction of welfare grants. In practice this has rarely occurred. Some critics of WIN point to this as evidence of lack of effort. It is claimed that if WIN requirements were enforced for a larger share of recipients, performance would be improved.[7]

OBRA granted states the option of setting up WIN ''demonstrations'' in which the WIN program is administered solely by welfare agencies, which in turn contract with the state employment services for employment-related activities for clients. The option potentially allows states to avoid the administrative problems created by dual administration of the WIN program. Legislation passed in 1982 allows states to require AFDC applicants and recipients who meet WIN eligibility criteria to participate in a program of job search of up to eight weeks at the time of accession to AFDC, and up to eight weeks per year thereafter. States may target the requirement to subsets of the WIN registrant pool. The legislation includes federal support for transportation and other costs incurred. OBRA and the Deficit Reduction Act of 1984 authorized states to set up programs whereby AFDC funds could be used for limited periods to subsidize employment for welfare recipients placed in entry-level positions in nonprofit agencies and in private firms.

Other influences

While OBRA gave states the workfare toolkit, four other developments provided the ''building permit.'' One is resumption of growth of the AFDC caseload after the reductions brought about by other OBRA provisions.[8] Work programs, it is suggested, could reverse this trend. Burgeoning popular and scholarly concern over long-term welfare dependency and the associated development of a socially isolated underclass in the poorest areas of the nation's cities is a second influence.[9] Some argue that work programs are important for reintegration of this group with the rest of society.[10] The third is the growing attention given arguments that the AFDC system itself has contributed to poverty and welfare dependence by discouraging work.[11] As already discussed, work incentives are a major part of the case for work requirements. Finally, and perhaps of greatest importance, work and welfare programs have proved to be good politics, both for Republican conservatives such as Governor George Deukmejian of California and for new liberal Democratic leaders such as Governor Michael Dukakis of Massachusetts.

The new workfare

All of the new work-welfare schemes are amalgamations of AFDC and the old WIN with the tools presented by the new legislation. A representative program is set out in Figure 1, which charts steps that might be required of certain recipient-family adults in a new workfare program. These steps are as follows. First, on acceptance (sometimes on application) for welfare, the recipient registers for the workfare program and goes through a preliminary screening. Under arrangements fostered by the WIN demonstration office, this is done in immediate conjunction with welfare application. If a recipient is prevented from seeking employment for certain specified reasons, particularly because of lack of childcare, an attempt is made to provide the needed services in order to certify the recipient as employment-ready. Sometimes employment-readiness requires motivational counseling and training in interview techniques.

When the recipient is judged employment-ready, step two is an organized job-search effort. Organization varies, but a common approach involves "job club" techniques in which the adult joins other recipients at a regular time to make phone calls and plot job-finding strategies under the tutelage of a professional placement counselor.

If the job-search effort fails, the participant goes on to more intensive counseling and more detailed investigation of possible alternatives for employability enhancement. At this point the recipient gains access to a set of classroom or on-the-job training programs, becomes eligible for a subsidized job placement, or in some cases, may be assigned to community work. A plan is developed for recipient participation in some program. In general recipients are not paid for any of these activities, or where pay is received it is in lieu of the welfare payment. Funding for the services may come from a variety of sources; some of the training may be obtained from the local Private Industry Council using federal funds provided through the Jobs Training Partnership Act.

After program completion the recipient again participates in job search, followed by counseling, and so on.

Of course, actual workfare programs differ in detail from this model. Some states have been very slow in taking advantage of the new options. For example, in the spring of 1987 only 26 states were operating WIN demonstrations; 27 states were exercising the job-search option; 25 states had CWEP in at least one local area; and just 15 states

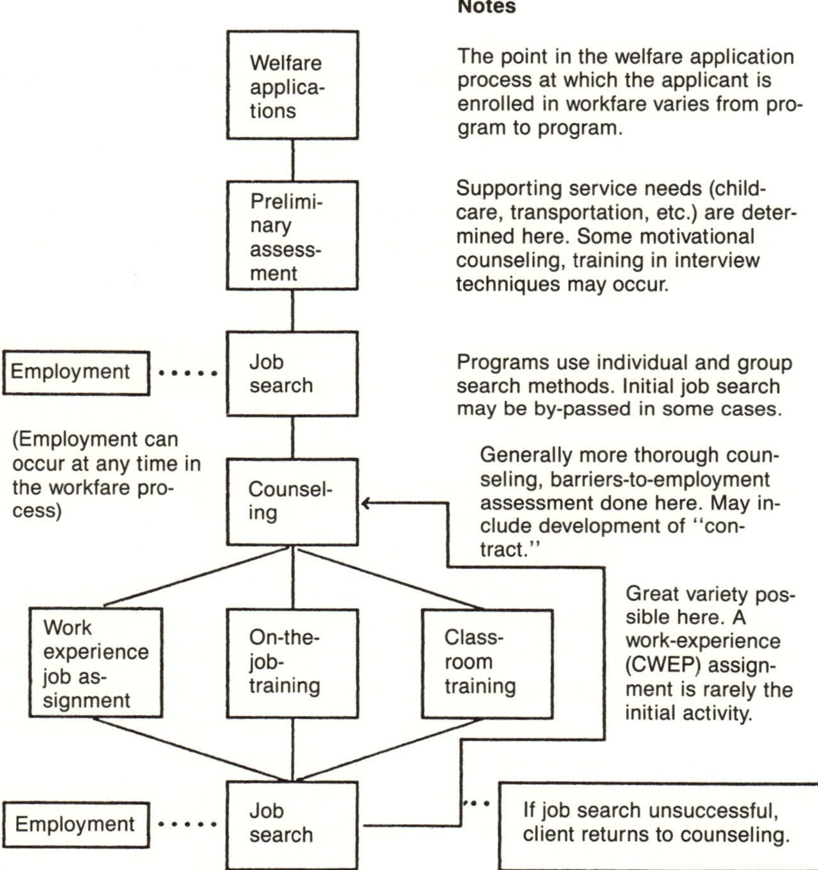
Notes
Welfare applica- tions
The point in the welfare application process at which the applicant is enrolled in workfare varies from program to program.
Prelimi- nary assess- ment
Supporting service needs (childcare, transportation, etc.) are determined here. Some motivational counseling, training in interview techniques may occur.
Employment
Job search
Programs use individual and group search methods. Initial job search may be by-passed in some cases.
(Employment can occur at any time in the workfare process)
Counsel- ing
Generally more thorough counseling, barriers-to-employment assessment done here. May include development of "contract."
Work experience job as- signment
On-the- job- training
Class- room training
Great variety possible here. A work-experience (CWEP) assignment is rarely the initial activity.
Employment
Job search
If job search unsuccessful, client returns to counseling.

Figure 1 **A Workfare Prototype**

were experimenting with grant diversion/work supplementation programs.[12] Nonetheless, interest in such programs, and the scale of proposals, was growing rapidly, and most programs appear to be evolving toward something like the model presented in Figure 1.

Experience with the difficulty of reforming welfare leads to skepticism about any policy posed as a solution to problems as diverse as reducing the long-time welfare dependency of the poor and assuring the long-time incumbency of politicians. Also, as critics are quick to point out, Figure 1 is a long way from the old-fashioned notion that the best welfare program is a job of last resort.[13] While the new programs often do incorporate work requirements, they also often commit substantial additional resources. Perhaps most importantly, they manifest a change in philosophy. Whereas employment-related activities have long been part of welfare, most programs have been small relative to the eligible population and, because of this, participation was largely optional for most recipients. The new workfare programs attempt to increase participation rates to the point where virtually all eligible adults meeting specified criteria participate. Workfare changes the nature of the welfare bargain. It does this not simply by conditioning welfare receipt on work, as in the simplest of work requirements, but by conditioning welfare receipt on an active program of preparation for self-support. Willingness to participate in such efforts in effect becomes a test of need for public assistance. The result is intended to make efforts at self-support an obligatory concomitant of receipt of public assistance, and delivery of employment-related services an obligatory concomitant of welfare system operation.

The sort of workfare program depicted in Figure 1 will impose significant costs on recipients and taxpayers. Accordingly, before committing income-maintenance policy to the workfare concept, it is important to gather as much information as possible on what they can accomplish.

Work and welfare in San Diego

In February 1986, the Manpower Development Research Corporation (MDRC) released the final report of a study of San Diego's "Job Search and Work Experience Demonstration."[14] It provides the best available data on the operation of a workfare program fashioned from parts of the workfare toolkit created by OBRA under an experimental design which allows assessment of its effects on recipient behavior and dependency. This project provides a point of departure for consideration of general programs in Massachusetts and California.

San Diego's program qualifies as "new workfare" because more than a work requirement was involved. Not all participants were at risk of CWEP assignments; and even for those who were, all job assignments were preceded by an intensive program of job-search assistance. Nevertheless, all aspects of the program were work-oriented: activity schedules were tight, and sanctions were imposed for failure to comply. The results show that it is administratively feasible to run a modified workfare program of this type; that such programs can improve recipient earnings, and thereby reduce dependency; that the mandatory aspect of workfare has important consequences; and that program effects differ among recipients according to household type and prior work experience. The results also show that the effects that can be expected from rudimentary work programs are relatively small.

Program design

The program created in San Diego was a very modest version of the general workfare scheme depicted in Figure 1. During the period October 1982–August 1983 new adult welfare applicants in the county for whom WIN registration was mandatory were assigned at random to one of three groups. Recipients in Group 1 were required to participate in a three-week intensive program of job search that included both "employment-readiness" training (how to prepare for interviews, etc.) and directed job search (JS). Group 2 recipients were also required to participate in the job-search program, but if the search was unsuccessful these people were assigned up to thirteen weeks of work in unpaid CWEP positions in local government or nonprofit agencies (JS/CWEP).[15] Group 3 was the "control"; recipients in this category participated in neither JS or JS/CWEP. While members of the control group were registered for WIN and nominally eligible for regular WIN job-search assistance and other services, less than 5 percent received any service during the first six months following application. This very low service-delivery rate suggests that the San Diego control group probably received slightly fewer WIN services than would be available under normal operation. All told, the three groups included 6,251 applicants, with 1,687 assigned to JS, 2,878 assigned to JS/CWEP, and the remainder serving as controls.

According to MDRC, "The programs were implemented without major administrative or other obstacles." This means that persons assigned job-search assistance received it, persons designated for the work-experience programs actually were given jobs, and the control group was established by genuinely random assignment. Significantly, implementation includes both delivery of services and the imposition of sanctions against recipients who did not cooperate; sanction rates were nine times greater for the experimental groups than was recorded for the controls. One shortcoming of the experiment was that JS/CWEP assignees were not warned of the job assignment that would follow if their job search was unsuccessful until after the job-search workshop was under way. This may have reduced the effects of the prospective work requirement on the behavior of people in this group.

Results

In evaluating impacts MDRC distinguishes between two groups of recipients. One recipient group (here labeled SP) is made up of heads of single-parent welfare households. The second (here labeled UPE) is the unemployed "principal earner" of two-parent welfare households. SPs are, for the most part, traditional welfare mothers. UPEs are generally jobless fathers. The results for various measures of welfare use and employment for the two groups are summarized in Table 1.[16] To conform with employer wage reports, all data were collected on the basis of calendar quarters. The first quarter includes the date of welfare application and usually covers some time before the family began receiving welfare. Since applicants for (and not recipients of) aid formed the target group for study (some 16 percent of the SP and 19 percent of the UPE groups), families in the sample never received welfare at all. Participant experience was followed for six quarters, and the numbers in Table 1 measure outcomes for the five quarters following application (for earnings data), or six quarters including the point of application (for welfare data).

Looking first at the impact on the single-parent group, the outcomes of the experiment are what workfare advocates would expect. Participants in the experimental programs were more likely to be employed than those in the control group; their earnings were greater; their use of welfare was less; and they received less in welfare payments. (Employment does not include the CWEP assignment.) In general the differential between the JS and JS/CWEP groups was in favor of the job-search-with-workfare group. Families in the JS/CWEP group reported 22 percent more earnings and received 8 percent less in welfare benefits over five quarters than did the controls. Members of the JS group also did better than the controls, but these differences are frequently not statistically significant. The difficulty encountered by MDRC in measuring experimental effects with precision reflects the large amount of random variation in earnings and work experience for people who apply for welfare; given the relatively small treatment effects, a larger sample size was needed for the JS group.

Four additional points about the outcomes for single parents should be made. First, for adults in this group there was a significant positive difference in employment rates and earnings between participants in the JS/CWEP combination and participants in the job-search–only programs. But this differential was accumulated principally because of

Table 1

Summary of Results, San Diego Job Search and Work Experience Demonstration

Recipient group and program outcome	Program groups		
	Control group	JS group	JS/CWEP group
Single parents			
For quarters 2-6:			
Ever employed (%)	55.4	60.5***	61.0***
Average no. of quarters with employment	1.7	1.9	2.0***
Total earnings,	$3,102	$3,353	$3,802***
For quarters 1-6:			
Average no. of months with AFDC	8.6	8.3	8.1*
Average total AFDC payments	$3,697	$3,494	$3,409**
SP sample size	873	856	1,502
Unemployed principal earners			
For quarters 2-6:			
Ever employed %	73.6	74.0	76.3
Average no. of quarters with employment	2.5	2.5	2.6
Total earnings	$7,145	$7,529	$7,361
For quarters 1-6:			
Average no. of months with AFDC	7.5	6.7***	6.6***
Average total AFDC payments	$3,653	$3,184***	$3,124***
UPE sample size	831	813	1,376

Note: Asterisks identify the results of application of (two-tailed) tests of significance to differences between experimental and control groups. The statistical significance levels are indicated as * = 10 percent, ** = 5 percent, *** = 1 percent. All other differences are not statistically significant at the 10 percent level.

Source: Barbara Goldman, Daniel Friedlander, and David Long, *Final Report on the San Diego Job Search and Work Experience Demonstration* (New York: Manpower Demonstration Research Corporation, 1986), pp. 54-55, 102-103.

relatively poor performance by late cohorts of assignees to the job-search component. Despite careful investigation by MDRC, the reasons for this outcome are unclear. The consequence, however, is that the experiment does not unambiguously indicate that addition of a work assignment makes a contribution to outcomes beyond what was accomplished by job search alone. What is conclusive is that something about an intensive and obligatory job-search/work-experience program can affect employability and employment. Second, the difference in earnings between the experimental and control groups came about solely because of differences in employment rates, not differences in wages. Both groups got the same types of jobs; job-search assistance seemed to help recipients in the experimental group find them more quickly. Third, program effects appear to have been greatest for recipients with little employment experience. Finally, the experiment produced no evidence that the employment experience component deterred people from continuing on welfare. However, as indicated above, this may in part be attributable to the fact that participants were not informed at an early point about the CWEP obligation that would follow an unsuccessful job search.

The consequences of the program for unemployed adults from two-parent families differ in important ways from those for single parents. As Table 1 indicates, no statistically significant effect on future earnings of unemployed principal earners was detected for either the JS/CWEP or JS-only approaches. However, both programs affected the incidence of postapplication welfare receipt and the amount of payments. The differences are statistically significant and important. Over 18 months, average welfare benefits received by applicants assigned to the JS-only component averaged 13 percent less than those received by control group members, and average benefits received by JS/CWEP assignees were over 14 percent less. The similarity of these figures points up another result: JS and JS/CWEP effects were virtually identical. Again, for the UPE group, effects were greatest for recipients with prior welfare history.

The apparent inconsistency between results for welfare receipt (which went down) and earnings (which showed no statistically significant effect) is an anomaly. Earnings data for the San Diego experiment were collected from state records for employer/employee contributions to the unemployment insurance benefits system. The results are consistent with the position that the work requirement caused some recipients to choose to forgo AFDC in favor of "underground" employment that produced no earnings report. Such activities are presumably also pursued when welfare does not require a commitment of time to job search or work. Thus, the San Diego results may confirm the contention that for some recipients even minimal work requirements lead to withdrawal from assistance because such obligations interfere with other activities. An upper-bound estimate on the proportion of San Diego UPE recipients falling into this category is 14 percent; this is not large, but neither can such an effect be taken as insignificant.[17]

Costs and benefits

The fiscal bottom line on the experiment depends critically on what is measured and for how long. Viewed strictly from the perspective of the taxpayer, and ignoring the value of whatever output recipients in CWEP produce, the present value of the benefits (measured over 5 years) of the JS/CWEP combination exceeded costs by about $950 per UPE participant; for SP cases, the difference was $1,160. For JS alone, benefits exceeded costs by $452 for single parents and by $1,239 per UPE recipient. Costs per participant were around $650. Most costs came before benefits, so that the immediate effect of introducing the San Diego program would be to raise costs without offsetting welfare savings and/or tax benefits from increased earnings. Like the impact effects, these results are small but important. The message is that programs of this sort will not reduce this year's deficit, but in the longer run they could make some difference.

Comments

The San Diego Job Search and Work Experience Demonstration makes an important contribution to our empirical knowledge about welfare policies. Five points deserve emphasis.

First, the San Diego program did not require onerous makework. MDRC attitudes surveys indicate that recipients viewed the jobs as meaningful and, more important, that most of them seemed to view the search/work obligation as fair. Many of the San Diego CWEP positions were provided through nonprofit organizations. This suggests that at least some of the difficulties that have plagued efforts at job creation within government agencies may be avoided by working with other organizations.

Second, the program was modest in conception and execution. The procedures followed were relatively straightforward and brief in impact. This minimized the likelihood of interfering with turnover that would have occurred in the program's absence. Data for the control groups indicate that 15–20 percent of cases that actually opened were closed within a quarter in the absence of any intervention. Well over half the cases were closed within a year.

Third, the program does not provide a clear-cut demonstration of the efficacy of work assignments. Although there is some indication that the addition of work experience added to program effects for single parents, no detectable additional effects appear in the data for principal earners.

Fourth, the program's obligatory elements appear to make a difference. In the absence of vigorous program monitoring, some recipients do appear to fall behind in the activities required for a rigorous job search. However, it is not clear that those persons most frequently out-of-compliance with the San Diego project's regulations, or those persons (if any) who may have been prompted to diligence by the threat of sanctions, were necessarily the same persons who benefited from the services provided. In other words, the sanctions may have had little or nothing to do with the outcomes. In a future experiment it would be useful to vary the degree of obligation in order to test the effect. This could be accomplished by eliminating sanctions for noncompliance for one experimental group.

Finally, both programs suggest that productivity will be enhanced by targeting on hard-to-employ cases. But the San Diego experiment did not include two groups that are the object of considerable interest: long-term dependents already on welfare (recall that the experiment used only new applicants) and single parents with children younger than age 6.

The new state initiatives

The San Diego Job Search and Work Experience Demonstration was relatively small. A number of states have embarked on much more elaborate programs. Two that have attracted considerable attention are the Massachusetts Employment and Training Choices (ET) Program and California's Greater Avenues for Independence (GAIN) initiative.

Emploment and Training Choices (Massachusetts)

Both the Massachusetts ET-Choices program and the GAIN program in California come much closer to the general model presented in Figure 1 than did the San Diego experiment. This may be illustrated by considering the path that would be followed by a single parent. For ET-Choices the initial step is to register.[18] This is mandatory for those meeting WIN requirements and optional for all other adult recipients. Step 2 is an appraisal session in which the recipient meets with an ET worker to develop an employment plan. In this session registrants are informed about ET options, which include career planning (an adjunct to the appraisal process), on-the-job training in supported work, various education and training programs, and direct job placement. In step 3 the recipient and worker agree on an employment plan based on recipient interests and available services. Simultaneously, a support services plan is developed which includes, as needed, provisions for daycare, arrangements for transportation, and assistance in developing healthcare alternatives if necessary once employment is attained. Finally the program is initiated.

ET-Choices has several important features. One is the importance attached to childcare. Most of this is delivered through a voucher system; availability of childcare support allows extension of the program to women with preschool children (a group exempted from the San Diego experiment). In fiscal year 1985, 35 percent of ET participants were women with preschool children. A second feature is the attention paid to planning for the period when employment is achieved and welfare eligibility is lost. By carefully describing to recipients the reduction of support once employment takes place, both uncertainty and adverse economic consequences are minimized. The change is facilitated by the extension of childcare support for one year past ET "graduation," i.e., job-taking. The third exceptional ET feature is that, aside from mandatory registration for WIN-eligibles, the program is *voluntary*. No sanctions are imposed. Once informed of the ET opportunity, recipients who choose not to participate need not do so. Finally, ET-Choices is surely the most publicized welfare program in the country. This publicity has two targets. One, of course, is the taxpaying public; because of the publicity, Massachusetts is one of the few states where a welfare program seems to be a political asset for state politicians. The other target is dependent adults. The publicity campaign serves to heighten awareness of the ET option, to create a popular presumption that welfare recipients are involved in efforts to achieve self-support, and, by placing emphasis on ET success stories, to arouse interest. In a sense Massachusetts has attempted to substitute expectation, and moral suasion, for rules.

Over the first two and one-half years of ET operation, the AFDC caseload in Massachusetts declined by 9.5 percent. Over the same interval the Massachusetts economy was very strong (the unemployment rate declined by over 4 percentage points), and this contributed to the ability of recipients to find jobs. But since other states experienced even greater changes in economic conditions without the same change in caseloads, ET officials were quick to attribute caseload trends to the program: "The successful job placement record of ET Choices has contributed significantly to the decline in the Massachusetts AFDC caseload."[19] Indeed, ET program reports claim that system expenditures are recovered within a year. These claims appear to be based on the assumption that ET placements accelerate welfare case closures by an average of one year.[20] But, as the evidence for San Diego indicates, closure rates for AFDC cases, especially those in the AFDC-U category, are substantial even with no employment program.

The Massachusetts approach to workfare operation makes MDRC-type evaluation problematic, since it emphasizes creation of an atmosphere of expectation regarding recipient work effort. If the media are filled with ET-Choices success stories, creation of an uncontaminated control group of randomly selected recipients who do not receive program services is virtually impossible. Indeed, to do so would compromise the philosophical basis of the program. Nonetheless, it is possible that oversell of ET-Choices may damage the credibility of what is a significant innovation. If the state attributes to ET virtually everything that happened to the caseload between 1983 and 1985, then it seems to follow that any reversals of trend are also to be laid at the feet of the program. Recent evidence indicates that the rate of caseload decline has attenuated and, despite continuing strength in the state's economy, welfare applications are up. It may be that by touting individual successes in the ET program as a marketing device, the state has created an incentive for those outside welfare to enter the system. Once in, they may stay longer than otherwise would be the case since, as indicated in Figure 1, in ET-Choices as in many other new workfare programs the reward for not finding a job is access to what are in some cases valuable services. The San Diego program did not have such a feature.

In 1967 Congress changed the procedures for calculating welfare benefits, so that earned income would not reduce welfare benefits dollar-for-dollar. This incentive applied only to earnings once welfare dependency was achieved; it could not be claimed by applicants. As a result, it was possible for some people, once on welfare, to increase earnings to the point where they would lose welfare eligibility were they to reapply. Others, in similar circumstances, who had never achieved welfare eligibility, would, with the same earnings, have lower incomes. This inequity was a major target of the Omnibus Budget Reconciliation Act in 1981. OBRA provisions reduced both the size and the duration of these features. ET and similar programs appear to create similar inequities. Why should some earners, by virtue of a spell of low income, be entitled to a substantial combination of supported education, childcare, transportation, and healthcare assistance, while others, whose current status is not objectively much different, are denied it?

Greater Avenues for Independence (California)

GAIN combines the San Diego and Massachusetts models: essentially the program splits the JS/CWEP system and inserts ET in the middle. While the core of GAIN is very similar to the generic new workfare scheme depicted in Figure 1, actual participant paths through the program can be quite complicated. Space permits only a cursory description here. As with ET-Choices and the San Diego demonstration, the GAIN program begins at registration. At this point job and welfare histories are evaluated and recipients are sorted on the basis of prior welfare history (whether or not they have been on aid more than twice in the preceding three years), labor-market connection (whether or not they have worked in the preceding two years), and need for remedial education. Those who have worked recently are routed into an individual job-search component; those deemed work-ready but without recent labor-market experience are routed to a job club for more intensive search assistance.

If after three weeks of job search the GAIN participant has not found a job, he or she meets again with a counselor to draw up a revised contract. At this point the participant is provided with a range of ET-type training and education services plus whatever support is necessary to achieve the goals of the plan. The contract binds the state to deliver the services, and the recipient to participate in the planned program. Services at this stage can include short-term (three-month) "pre-employment preparation" programs (workfare) to "provide work behavior skills and a reference for future unsubsidized employment," but only if such a program is consistent with the participant's plan. GAIN envisions two types of work program—"basic," oriented toward general work skills, and "advanced," intended to utilize specific participant skills.

Following completion of the services component, the participant reverts to job search. If still jobless, his or her next step is long-term (12 months) advanced preemployment preparation; then, if no job is found, a new contract is drawn up, and so on. Persons who fail to complete training or other ET–type programs may be assigned directly to long-term basic workfare. Workfare assignments are, as in the San Diego experiment, to be developed by public and private nonprofit agencies; the total hours of obligation for recipients are either 32 hours per week or roughly the family AFDC grant divided by $5.17 per hour (a figure derived by averaging wages for jobs listed by employers with the state employment service), whichever is less. At each stage the participant has a right to coverage of transportation and childcare costs and third-party arbitration of disputes over compliance with the individual employment plan. While failure to comply with employment-plan provisions can eventually bring sanctions, the sanctions imposed are moderate (elimination of benefits for the ET participant but not for the rest of the family) and appear to be difficult to enforce.

California's AFDC system is operated by counties, and it is anticipated that GAIN will not be implemented in all counties until 1988. There is little operating experience on which to judge the program. Nonetheless, several characteristics are clearly similar to ET-Choices. Like the Massachusetts program, GAIN is explicitly intended to include recipients with preschool children. GAIN also provides extensive support for participants, including childcare and transportation costs, with the childcare stipend extending at least three months beyond the point of job-taking. The foundation of the GAIN plan is a "contract" with the recipient. But here a subtle difference arises. For the California program recipients are required to develop a contract; in Massachusetts this is an option. And in California, if training services fail to produce employment, "preemployment preparation" work assignments are required. In publicity about the program, the obligational aspect has been emphasized, as has the major infusion of new resources provided by the legislature to support GAIN operations.

The GAIN obligations are not very strong, but they are there. The key problem is that the program is so elaborate that it is unlikely to be administratively feasible, at least in the beginning. Recipients are absolved from participation in job-search or employment programs while waiting for slots in training programs deemed appropriate by their own employment contracts. And it is not clear that the state will be able to mandate preemployment preparation for only some eligible participants if the total number of positions proves inadequate to meet demand.

GAIN includes a fallback. When available funds are insufficient to meet the requirements of the program for all recipients, recipients in various categories are excused. The first to be excused are new applicants for the AFDC-U program; the last are long-term dependents under AFDC-FG. This essentially reverses the targeting procedures in San Diego: it is on the principal earners in AFDC-U families that the search/work obligation in San Diego appears to have had the greatest effect.

GAIN places a remarkable burden upon its operating county agencies. The system calls for elaborate planning to assure that services are provided to meet recipient needs and that training programs match labor-market requirements. The system evinces great faith in the effectiveness of training programs for income enhancement at a time when the professional literature is at best ambiguous on this outcome.[21] One suspects that it is far easier to diagram a work program of this sort than to run one.

It is easy to criticize GAIN. But it is important to recognize what the legislation does. First, GAIN affirms application of the principle of employment orientation for the welfare system for virtually all recipients; this is a step beyond WIN. Second, GAIN attempts, albeit rather clumsily, to integrate a range of employment and training services fully with basic income maintenance; this, too, has not been attempted before on this scale. Third, the legislation makes an effort to target services on groups (young mothers, long-term dependents) thought to pose significant problems. Fourth, at least in public posture, the program is much more obligational than ET. Even with loopholes in the regulations, state and county welfare offices are likely to be held publicly accountable for the degree of obligation achieved. The public in California expects an operating work requirement, and this will certainly influence the character of the program that emerges from GAIN implementation. Perhaps most remarkable is the fact that, like the Massachusetts program, GAIN represents a major commitment of resources to the poor at a time when budgets are tight.

Conclusions

On balance, workfare in any of the three versions discussed above is an incremental welfare reform. Each program starts with the current AFDC system, and each changes the orientation of the program in the direction of increased emphasis on employment. The political popularity of the Massachusetts and California programs indicates broad public support for this type of initiative. The results of the San Diego job-search and work-experience demonstration indicate that relatively simple programs can have significant payoffs both for recipients and for taxpayers without creating hardships. ET and GAIN, however, go substantially beyond the San Diego model, with consequences that are still very uncertain.

The new aggressiveness and variety in welfare policy innovation at the state level is surely one of the benefits of a federal system, and it is a positive consequence of the provisions of OBRA. For the immediate future it is appropriate to continue these experiments and perhaps expand state latitude in innovation, as was recently recommended by the President's Domestic Policy Council.[22] But there are at least four reasons why it would be a mistake to argue that because states are becoming more active in welfare policy, the role of the federal government is substantially diminished.

The first is financial. Washington still provides at least half of state costs of AFDC (the federal share varies by state as a function of per capita income) and 90 percent of the costs of WIN up to a fixed total outlay. Good stewardship alone requires involvement in policymaking.

Beyond stewardship, a case can be made for larger federal financial participation in experimentation, on the grounds that successful innovation may have spillover effects. To the extent that any one state's experimentation produces effective innovations, other states can copy, and the federal government shares in the savings or program improvements achieved everywhere. This suggests that the federal share in financing innovation should be larger than the federal share in ordinary income maintenance. But for this argument to have validity, the federal government must assure that innovations are yoked with serious evaluation and testing, and that they focus on what are, by consensus, important issues in welfare system management. In designing such tests, high priority should be given to comparison of voluntary versus obligatory participation schemes and program effects for long-term dependents and mothers with young children.

Third, the federal government continues to play an important role in the collection of information. It is extremely difficult to investigate the targeting and other issues raised by workfare programs without having a better picture of the clients of the welfare system. Existing data-collection efforts concentrate on the characteristics of persons receiving assistance on some specific date. Yet, as is by now well known, the "point in time" caseload may differ quite significantly from the characteristics of newly opened cases. The latter group may be of greater importance for implementing workfare programs and studying the selection processes followed by those that exist. Procedures for designing surveys suitable for drawing inferences about the characteristics of newly opened cases are well understood;[23] they simply need to be implemented.

Finally—and this last point covers a lot of ground—workfare does not exhaust the agenda of policies designed either to reduce dependency or to improve the well-being of the poor. Workfare has no effect, for example, on the continuing gross inequity in levels of welfare benefits across states. This is a federal issue. Workfare policies work only within the welfare system, yet there is strong evidence that the most important opportunities for reducing welfare dependency lie outside the welfare system—for example, the Earned Income Tax Credit, systems for guaranteeing that absent parents pay for child support, and programs for reducing teenage pregnancy. The federal government should foster an assemblage of policies aimed at both encouraging movement to self-support by families receiving public assistance and sustaining self-support by those on the outside. Workfare cannot do both.

Notes

1. See, for example, the "goals of an income-tested welfare system" listed in Barth *et al.* (1974).

2. See, for example, Duncan and Ponza (1987). The Duncan-Ponza paper reports survey research in which a panel of respondents were asked to assign income transfers to various households described in simple vignettes. Characteristics of these households were varied at random across presentations in order to provide experimental evidence on the importance of various factors—family size, work effort, and so on—in

determining transfer assignments. In one evaluation single mothers with one child and weekly nonwelfare income of $50 were awarded transfers of $159 per week if they were "looking for work." If the mother was "not looking because available jobs only pay minimum wage," the average awarded benefit fell by over one-third (p. 16).

3. See Orr (1976). Similar results are obtained in Plotnick (1986).

4. See Gueron and Goldman (1983). Utah has been more successful in operating a welfare work program, but it may be a special case.

5. Public Law 97-35, August 13, 1981, Sec. 2307(a).

6. These changes are summarized in U.S. House of Representatives, Committee on Ways and Means (1987), pp. 391–400. See also U.S. General Accounting Office (1987), Chapter 2.

7. The strongest statement of this position appears in the work of Lawrence M. Mead. See Mead (1985) and "How to Make Sure Workfare Works" in *The Wall Street Journal*, April 15, 1987, p. 30.

8. For the General Accounting Office's evaluation of the effects of OBRA on the AFDC caseload, see U.S. House of Representatives, Committee on Ways and Means (1987), pp. 448–449. For detailed analyses of the effects of OBRA, see Hutchens (1984) and Moffitt (1984).

9. For a discussion of long-term welfare dependency, see and Ellwood and Bane (1983). Trends leading to underclass development are considered in Wilson (1985). An ingenious discussion of the spatial isolation of the underclass is presented in Ricketts and Sawhill (1986).

10. See Mead (1985).

11. The now classic exposition of the position that welfare discourages almost everything decent is Murray (1984). See also Kaus (1986).

12. Estimated from data in U.S. House of Representatives, Committee on Ways and Means (1987), pp. 295–6.

13. Mickey Kaus has made this point most forcefully. See Kaus (1968).

14. Goldman, Friedlander, and Long (1986). For a review of several MDRC workfare studies see Gueron (1986).

15. The CWEP program was actually labeled the Experimental Work Experience Program.

16. Estimates in Table 1 are derived from multivariate regressions that control for, in addition to experimental group, preapplication characteristics of sample members.

17. This rough estimate is calculated in the following way. For both experimental groups the maximum differential between average payments to families in the control and experimental groups occurred in the third quarter following application. In that quarter rates of welfare participation for unemployed principal earners were about 7 percentage points lower for the experimental than the control groups. Since by the third quarter following application only about 50 percent of applicants received any benefits at all, this implies that at most those who found the obligation imposed by the San Diego program unacceptable amounted to 14 percent (7/.5) of the caseload. This estimate may overstate the dissuasion effect, since the earnings differences between control and experimental groups reported in Table 1 show some positive effects on earnings. This could have produced some of the observed case closings and benefit reductions.

18. The description of the Massachusetts program that follows is based on conversations with staff of the Massachusetts Department of Public Welfare and Massachusetts Department of Public Welfare (1986).

19. Massachusetts Department of Public Welfare (1986), p. 6.

20. *Ibid.*, p. 16.

21. See Bassi and Ashenfelter (1986) and Barnow (1987).

22. See U.S. Office of the President (1986).
23. See Bawden, Erickson, and Davis (1984).

References

Barnow, Burt S. (1987) "The Impact of CETA Programs on Earnings: A Review of the Literature." *Journal of Human Resources* 22 (2), pp. 157–193.

Barth, Michael C., George J. Carcagno, and John L. Palmer, *Toward an Effective Income Support System: Problems, Prospects, and Choices* (Madison, Wisconsin: The Institute for Research on Poverty, 1974), pp. 39–42.

Bassi, Laurie J. and Orley Ashenfelter (1986). "The Effect of Direct Job Creation and Training Programs on Low-Skilled Workers." In Sheldon H. Danziger and Daniel H. Weinberg, editors, *Fighting Poverty: What Works and What Doesn't*. Cambridge, Massachusetts: Harvard University Press, 1986.

Bawden, D. Lee, Eugene P. Erickson, and Diana Davis (1984). *A New Survey to Study Duration on AFDC*. Final Report the the U.S. Department of Health and Human Services under Contract No. HHS–100–83–0048. Washington, D.C.: The Urban Institute.

Duncan, Greg J. and Michael Ponza (1987). *Public Attitudes Toward the Structure of Income Maintenance Programs*. University of Michigan: Survey Research Center. (Working Paper)

Ellwood, David T. and Mary Jo Bane (1983). *The Dynamics of Dependence: The Routes to Self-Sufficiency*. Cambridge, Massachusetts: Urban Systems Research and Engineering, Inc.

Goldman, Barbara, Daniel Friedlander, and David Long (1986). *Final Report on the San Diego Job Search and Work Experience Demonstration*. New York: Manpower Demonstration Research Corporation.

Gueron, Judith M. and Barbara Goldman. *The U.S. Experience in Work Relief*. New York: Manpower Demonstration Research Corporation, March 1983. (Discussion Paper)

Gueron, Judith M. (1986). *Work Initiatives for Welfare Recipients: Lessons from a Multi-State Experiment*. New York: Manpower Demonstration Research Corporation.

Hutchens, Robert (1984). *The Effects of the Ombnibus Budget Reconciliation Act of 1981 on AFDC Recipients: A Review of Reviews*. Madison, Wisconsin: University of Wisconsin Institute for Research on Poverty, Discussion Paper 763–84.

Kaus, Mickey (1986). "The Work Ethic State." *The New Republic*, July 7, pp. 22–33.

Massachusetts Department of Public Welfare (1986). *The Massachusetts Employment and Training Choices Program: Program Plan and Budget Request, FY87*. Boston: Department of Public Welfare, Executive Office of Human Services, Commonwealth of Massachusetts.

Mead, Lawrence M. (1985). *Beyond Entitlement: The Social Obligations of Citizenship*. New York: The Free Press.

Moffitt, Robert (1984). *Assessing the Effects of the 1981 Federal AFDC Legislation on the Work Effort of Women Heading Households: A Framework for Analysis and the Evidence to Date*. Madison, Wisconsin: University of Wisconsin Institute for Research on Poverty, Discussion Paper 742A–84.

Murray, Charles (1984). *Losing Ground: American Social Policy, 1950–1980*. New York: Basic Books.

Orr, Larry L. (1976). "Income Transfers as a Public Good: An Application to AFDC," *American Economic Review*, 66(3), 359–371.

Plotnick, Robert D. (1986). "An Interest Group Model of Direct Income Redistribution.'' *Review of Economics and Statistics*, November 1986, 594–602.

Ricketts, Erol R. and Isabel V. Sawhill (1986). *Defining and Measuring the Underclass*. Paper presented at the American Economic Association Meetings in New Orleans, December 28, 1986.

U.S. General Accounting Office (1987). *Work and Welfare: Current AFDC Work Programs and Implications for Federal Policy*. Report HRD–87–34.

U.S. House of Representatives, Committee on Ways and Means. (1987). *Background Material and Data on Programs within the Jurisdiction of the Committee on Ways and Means*. Washington, D.C.: U.S. Government Printing Office.

U.S. Office of the President, Domestic Policy Council Low Income Opportunity Working Group. *Up From Dependency: A New National Public Assistance Strategy*. Washington: The White House, December 1986.

Wilson, William Julius (1985). ''Cycles of Deprivation and the Underclass Debate.'' *Social Service Review*, 59, December, pp. 541–559.

Reducing Poverty through Family Support

Harrell R. Rodgers, Jr.

In recent years poverty in the United States has been on the increase. Table 1 provides an overview of the findings of the Bureau of the Census between 1959 and 1985. The data reveal that poverty declined from a high of almost 40 million poor in the early 1960s to a low of 23 million in 1973. But during the early 1980s the poverty count has expanded to over 30 million. In 1985 thirty-three million Americans, or 14.0 percent of the population, lived in poverty.

Scholars differ over the reasons for recent increases in American poverty, but, as Sheldon Danziger has indicated, considerable evidence points to a number of factors. First, unemployment has increased substantially since the mid-1970s. Second, the earning power of millions of workers, measured in inflation-adjusted dollars, has declined significantly over the last decade. Third, federal expenditures for social-welfare programs have declined. Another reason with important consequences is that an increasing percentage of all American families are headed by a single woman. Female-headed families suffer much higher rates of poverty than two-parent families.

Collectively these findings strongly suggest that poverty has increased because millions of families are in economic distress. Parents often earn too little to support a household adequately or are unemployed. This is true of single parents and often of families headed by a couple. Supportive family policies could help more adults obtain job training or a job, could enhance the take-home pay of low-income workers through tax-incentive programs, and could help parents stay in the work force by assisting them in balancing their dual role of parents and employees.

Table 1

Poverty Schedule: Family of Four (Nonfarm), 1959-85

Year	Standard	Millions of poor	% of total population
1959	$ 2,973	39.5	22.0
1960	3,022	39.9	22.0
1961	3,054	39.9	22.0
1962	3,089	38.6	21.0
1963	3,128	36.4	19.0
1964	3,169	36.1	19.0
1965	3,223	33.2	17.0
1966	3,317	30.4	16.0
1966*	3,317	28.5	15.0
1967	3,410	27.8	14.0
1968	3,553	25.4	13.0
1969	3,743	24.1	12.0
1970	3,968	25.4	13.0
1971	4,137	24.1	11.0
1972	4,275	25.4	12.0
1973	4,540	23.0	11.5
1974	5,038	24.3	12.0
1974*	5,038	24.3	11.5
1975	5,500	25.9	12.0
1976	5,815	25.0	12.0
1977	6,200	24.7	12.0
1978	6,662	24.7	11.4
1979	7,412	26.1	11.7
1980	8,414	29.3	13.0
1981	9,287	31.8	14.0
1982	9,862	34.4	15.0
1983	10,178	35.3	15.2
1984	10,609	33.7	14.4
1985	10,989	33.1	14.0

*Revision in Census calculations.

Source: Derived from U.S. Bureau of the Census, ''Money Income and Poverty Status of Families in the United States.'' Series P-60, various years.

This chapter will examine some of the family policies that could enhance the employability and income of millions of adults. We begin by examining in more depth some of the family types that need assistance the most, and the type of assistance they require.

Who needs assistance?

Female-headed families

In recent years scholars have focused a great deal of attention on the increase in female-headed families and the impact of this change in American family structure on increased rates of poverty (Rodgers 1986; Ways and Means 1985, Select Committee on Children, Youth and Families 1983; Burlage 1978; Cooney 1979; Pearce 1978). There is no doubt that the change has been dramatic. In 1960 only 9.0 percent of all families with children were headed by single women (Bureau of the Census 1984, p.146). By 1985, 22 percent of all children lived in such families (Bureau of the Census 1985).

The significance of this change is that female-headed families suffer a rate of poverty that is five times higher than that for two-parent families. In 1985, 34 percent of all female-headed families were poor. For families headed by women under the age of 25, the rate of poverty exceeds 74 percent. If the mother has never been married, the rate of poverty is over 70 percent. If the mother is a member of a racial minority, under the age of 25, and never married, the rate of poverty exceeds 85 percent. Given these rates of poverty it is not surprising that as the number of female-headed families has increased, the percentage of all the poor living in such families has grown from 27 percent in 1960 to 49 percent in 1985 (Bureau of the Census 1986).

One ominous consequence of the high rate of poverty for women who head families is the deprivation brought to their dependent children. As the number of female-headed families increased between 1973 and 1985, poverty among children grew by more than 50 percent. The result is that since the early 1980s the poorest age group in America has been children. One in five American children lives below the poverty level. In 1985 this included over 16 percent of all white children, 39 percent of all children of Spanish origin, and over 46 percent of all black children. The highest rate of poverty is among children living in a female-headed family: more than half of all children living in female-headed families are poor. Of all black children living only with their mother, over two-thirds live in poverty.

By all estimates the trend toward female-headed families will continue. In addition to rates of divorce, out-of-wedlock births (including births to teenagers) have increased significantly. In 1950, 4 percent of all children were born to unwed mothers; by 1980 the figure was 18.4

percent. In 1980, 666,000 children were born out-of-wedlock. Additionally, each year during the 1980s, 600,000 children have been born to teenagers. About half of the teen mothers are unwed and about half have not finished high school. Considerable research confirms a correlation between early childbearing, decreased educational attainment, poverty, and extended welfare dependency (Hogan and Kitagawa 1985; Moore and Waite 1981; Carlson and Stinson 1982; Bahr 1979; Danziger, Jakubson, Schwartz, and Smolensky 1982; Cramer 1980; Honig 1974).

A congressional committee recently calculated that the number of children under the age of 10 living in female-headed families would increase by 48 percent between 1980 and 1990. If this estimate is correct, the number of children in such families will increase from 6 million to 8.9 million. This would mean that by 1990 one of every four children under 10 would be living in a family headed by a single woman (Select Committee on Children, Youth and Families 1983, 27). Given these trends, without corrective social policy, poverty among children will significantly increase.

Female family heads suffer greatly elevated rates of poverty in part because they have high rates of unemployment and in part because, compared to men, they have lower earning power. In 1985, 66.0 percent of all poor female family heads were unemployed. The median income for families headed by women from all sources (wages, cash welfare, child support, etc.) was $13,660, compared to $27,735 for all families, and $31,000 for two-parent households.

Quite obviously, one path to poverty reduction among female-headed families would be supportive social policies that allowed more parents to complete educational and/or job-training programs and obtain and maintain employment.

Two-parent families

While poverty rates are very high among female-headed families, a slight majority of all the poor live in two-parent families. Two-parent families most often fall below the poverty level because of unemployment and low wages. Between 1980 and 1985 the national unemployment rate averaged 8.2 percent, leaving an average of nine million persons a month without a job (Social Security Administration 1986, 79). High unemployment rates have combined with a national shift from high-paying manufacturing positions to low-paying service- and trade-sector jobs (see Bayes). The result is that millions of the employed work at jobs that pay a very poor wage, sometimes even a poverty wage. In 1985 two million people who worked year-round at full-time jobs were still poor. In addition, 1.2 million poor families (16 percent of all poor families) were headed by year-round full-time workers (Bureau of the Census 1986).

The result of high unemployment and low wages, then, has been an erosion in family earning power. In inflation-adjusted dollars, median family income has risen by only 1.5 percent since 1970 (Bureau of the Census 1986). Many parents need either a job or a better-paying job. One option frequently chosen by parents to make ends meet is for both to work. Supportive social policies could make this an easier option for millions of families, and tax policies could enhance the take-home pay of low-income workers.

Women in the work force

For both economic and personal reasons, women have greatly increased their participation in the work force. As recently as 1960 there were 22 million female workers, comprising about one-third of the work force. By 1985 there were 47 million female workers, comprising 44 percent of all employees. Not only are more women in the work force, the marital status of women currently working has also changed. In 1940, 64 percent of all employed women were single, widowed, or divorced. By 1984, single, divorced, and widowed women were even more likely to be in the work force, but married women had increased their participation rate to the extent that they comprised 56 percent of all working women. Since 1980 there have been more families in the United States with both a husband and wife working than families with only the husband working (Bureau of the Census 1985, 413).

Increased employment rates have been greatest for women with children. In 1950 only about 20 percent of all women with children were in the labor force. By 1985, 68 percent of all mothers of children in the 6-17–year range were employed, as were 53 percent of those with children under six (Bureau of the Census 1986, 399). Nearly half of all mothers enter or reenter the work force soon after giving birth. By the time their youngest child is four, 60 percent of women are in the work force (Figure 1).

About 25 million children are in families where the mother is absent from home for part of the workday on a regular basis. In 1985, 65

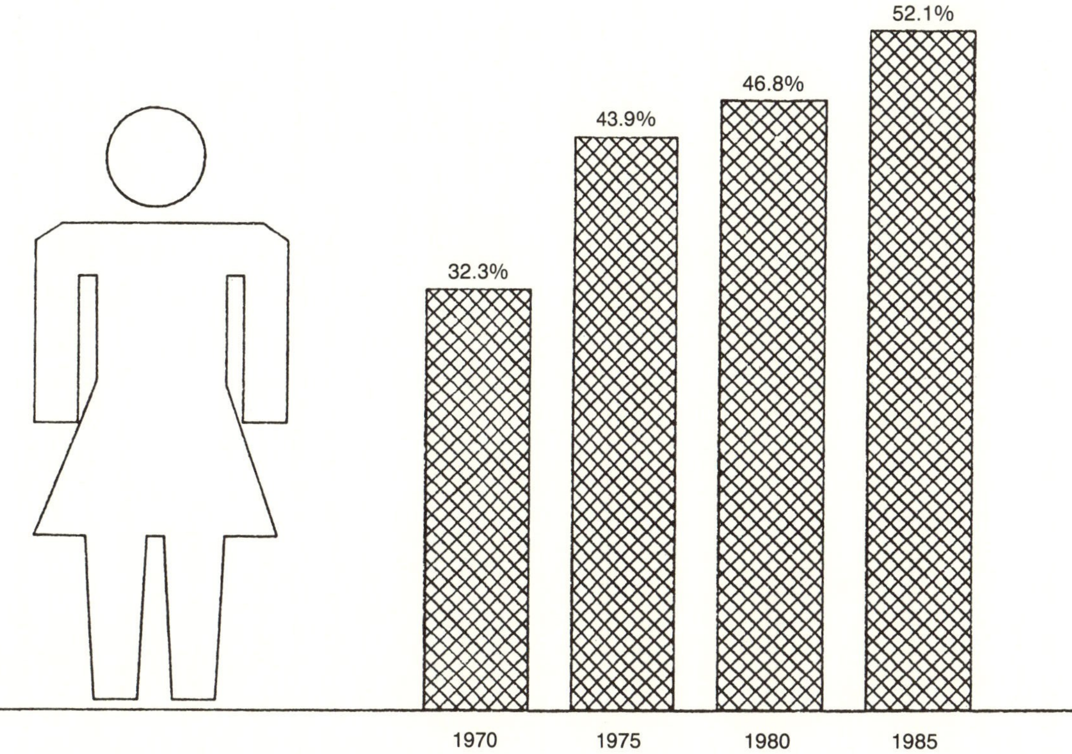

Figure 1 **Percentage of Women in Labor Force with Children under Age 6**

percent of the employed women with children under age 3 worked full time, as did 67 percent of those with children 3 to 5 years old, and 70 percent of those whose youngest child was between ages 6 and 17 (Hayghe 1986, 43).

The obvious social policies that would assist these families are childcare, parental leave to care for newborn, adopted, or ill children, and flexible work schedules.

Family policies

While the above statistics show that American society and American family structures have changed quite significantly over the last two decades, social policy has not kept pace. The millions of new single-parent families as well as families in which both parents work often fail to prosper because the parents cannot obtain the supportive services they need to balance their needs as parents and employees. As Kamerman (1984, 250) has pointed out, the United States lags behind the other major Western industrial nations in adjusting social policy to the needs of families. The United States is the only major western industrial country that has no statutory maternity benefits, no universal child-rearing benefits, and no universal healthcare benefits. The United States has also lagged behind many other western nations in expanding preschool and childcare programs.

Below we examine the family policies that would be most beneficial to American households and assess the possibility of implementing them in the United States.

Child or family allowances

Every western industrialized country except the United States provides a package of cash and in-kind programs to supplement the income of families with children (Kamerman and Kahn 1981). Many countries call this set of programs a "family benefit" package. A central component is the child or family allowance, found in at least sixty-seven countries (Kamerman 1984, 263). In most of these countries, including Canada, Belgium, and the Scandinavian countries, the allowances are universal and tax-free, regardless of income or family structure. In some countries (e.g., Great Britain and France) allowances are limited to families with two or more children, and sometimes they are means-tested (e.g., in West Germany). The allowances vary by the number of children in the family, and sometimes by the age of the children. France, for example, provides a larger supplement to families with young children. In all the major western countries single-parent families receive a special supplement. None of the countries excludes families from these benefits because they are intact or because a parent is in the labor force.

The allowances were originally designed to encourage higher birthrates. Whether the grants ever had a significant impact on childbearing is problematical, but they remain popular because they supplement the cost of raising children. By sharing the cost of children the society helps insure that basic needs are met. The general belief is that children raised in a more financially sound environment will be healthier, better educated, and more productive members of society.

The size of the grants is generally small, but the evidence suggests that they are a significant aid to low-income, especially single-parent, families (Kamerman 1984, 263). This is especially true since the allowance is larger when there is a lone parent.

Scholars who study social-welfare programs often argue that the United States should adopt a universal family- or child-allowance program fashioned after those found in the other western industrialized nations (Kamerman 1984, 270). Even conservatives like Gilder (1981, 153) have written in support of such an option. Yet Congress has never given serious consideration to a universal child or family allowance. In large part, this lack of serious attention results from the categorical, means-tested orientation of welfare programs in the United States. American policymakers are not inclined to give consideration to a program that would aid all parents or children without regard to economic need. The means-tested child-allowance programs found in nations such as West Germany might have more appeal. This type of program, however, could be established most easily through some reforms of the AFDC program or the Earned Income Tax Credit (EITC).

The EITC is, in fact, a version of a family allowance, which with some revisions could approximate the programs found in Europe. The EITC was added to the Internal Revenue Code in 1975. It provides an annual earnings supplement to parents who maintain a household for a child, provided they have an adjusted gross income below a set level. In 1986, for example, the credit equaled 11 percent of the first $5,000 of earnings, or a maximum of $550. Between $5,000 and $6,500 the EITC remained constant at $550. Between $6,500 and $11,000 the credit phased out, with a reduction of 12.3 cents per dollar above $6,500.

The EITC is the only tax credit that is refundable. If the parents do not owe any taxes, or have a tax obligation lower than the credit, they receive a payment from the IRS. This program was adopted to give low-income parents a "work bonus" or incentive to work, and to compensate for the regressive impact of the Social Security tax.

The EITC gives low-income families with dependent children some financial assistance, but analysts have argued that the tax credit, as originally designed, was flawed. The most significant criticisms included: (1) The credit is not indexed to inflation. Congress has made adjustments in benefits every few years, but the changes have never kept up with inflation. Thus, a much smaller number of families received assistance in 1986 than in earlier years. (2) A low-income parent does not qualify for the credit unless he or she earns enough income to provide at least 50 percent of the support of the children in the family. A single mother receiving 50 percent or more of her income from AFDC would not qualify for the credit. (3) The credit does not vary by the number of children in the family. (4) Even the families that qualify for the credit receive it only at the end of the year in a lump sum. (5) Many low-income families are unaware of the program. If the family's earnings are so low they do not file a tax return, they often do not realize that they qualify for benefits.

In its 1986 revisions of the tax code, Congress raised the credit and corrected a couple of the program's major flaws. Congress raised the tax credit to 14 percent of the first $5,714 of income, to a maximum of $800, plus an adjustment for inflation. The credit is phased out between $9,000 and $17,000. These changes take place in 1988, and the credit will be indexed to reflect all inflation since 1984. The law also requires the Secretary of the Treasury to notify persons with low incomes that they may be eligible for the program.

Congress debated more extensive reforms of this program, but compromised on those discussed above. Since the EITC is on the books, and since there are many options for making it a better program, it provides Congress with a means for improving the earnings of low-income parents.

The revisions in the EITC are enhanced by the fact that Congress, in its 1986 revisions to the tax code, significantly raised the amount of money a family has to earn before it incurs a tax obligation. The revisions will remove about six million poor families from the tax rolls.

Combined with the EITC, most poor families with dependent children will not only be exempt from federal taxes, they will receive a refund equal to most of their Social Security taxes. For example, a couple with two children earning a poverty-level income of $12,368 in 1988 will owe no federal taxes and will receive an EITC refund of $663. This refund represents 71 percent of the family's $929 Social Security tax, leaving it with an effective tax rate of 2.2 percent.

Congress's revisions of tax rates and the EITC will provide poor families with tax obligations equal to those in effect in the early 1970s. This will not, however, fully compensate for the erosion in real wages or for the cuts in welfare programs imposed during the Reagan years.

Childcare

A critical need of parents who want or need employment or educational or job training is quality childcare at affordable rates. The demand for childcare is now very high and will increase in the future. The population of children under six is expected to increase from 19.6 million in 1980 to 22.9 million in 1990. The number of children under 10 in single-parent households is also expected to increase during this period, from 6 to 9 million. And, as noted above, a majority of both married and unmarried women are in the work force.

A recent study by the Bureau of the Census (1982, 15–19) revealed that even more women would seek employment if they could obtain the required childcare. This included 26 percent of all mothers not in the job market. The figure increased to 36 percent of women in households with an annual income below $15,000, and 45 percent of single mothers. Additionally, 21 percent of all mothers working part-time said that they would increase their work hours if they could obtain childcare.

The four major problems. A comprehensive reform effort would have to deal with four separate childcare problems: an inadequate supply, a lack of knowledge about options, quality control, and cost barriers.

Most parents find a shortage of childcare options; in some parts of the country daycare centers have six-to-twelve month waiting lists. Parents also frequently find it difficult to obtain good information about childcare options, including publicly or privately subsidized childcare programs for low-income families. Cost is a major problem for many families. Studies indicate that care for one child ranges from

$2,000 to $6,500 a year, with the average cost being about $3,000. Obviously, these costs are prohibitive for many families, especially those headed by a lone parent.

Quality control is a very difficult problem because childcare is so diversely provided. As Figure 2 shows, a majority of children in childcare are in care outside their homes, with the largest percentage being in family daycare facilities. In 1985 a congressional committee estimated that 70 to 90 percent of these facilities are unlicensed (SCCYF 1985). A number of national surveys of daycare facilities have concluded that the quality of care provided by both family and center daycare is generally of average to low quality (Department of Health and Human Services 1982; Clarke-Stewart 1982; Fosburg and Hawkins 1981; Keyserling 1972).

The problems may be even worse where infant care is concerned. A recent study (Young and Zigler 1986) found that forty-seven states do not meet minimal standards for staffing daycare centers for infants. The three major problems the study uncovered were: little if any training for workers, minimal qualifications for staff, and high ratios of infants to adults. This study was restricted to licensed daycare centers. Most infants, however, are cared for in unlicensed homes and centers. The authors point out (p. 52) that conditions in unlicensed facilities are most likely even worse.

The federal role. There are many ways that these four issues could be addressed. In designing any solution, however, it is inescapable that the federal government will have to significantly increase its commitment to childcare. The major federal program that supports childcare is the Social Services Block Grant, generally referred to as Title XX. Until 1981 the federal government required the states to set aside $200 million of all Title XX funds for childcare. In fact, the states spent about 18 percent of all Title XX funds on childcare, totaling about $720 million in 1980. In 1981 Congress cut funding for Title XX by 20 percent, and the states were given the option of deciding how much they wanted to spend on childcare. Since 1981 the states have spent less on childcare, but Title XX still provides the largest direct federal support for these services. About 20 percent of the $2.7 billion allocated for Title XX in 1986 went to childcare, although state spending varies considerably. In inflation-adjusted dollars, 29 states spent less for childcare funded through Title XX in 1986 than in 1981 (Blank and Wilkins 1986, 4).

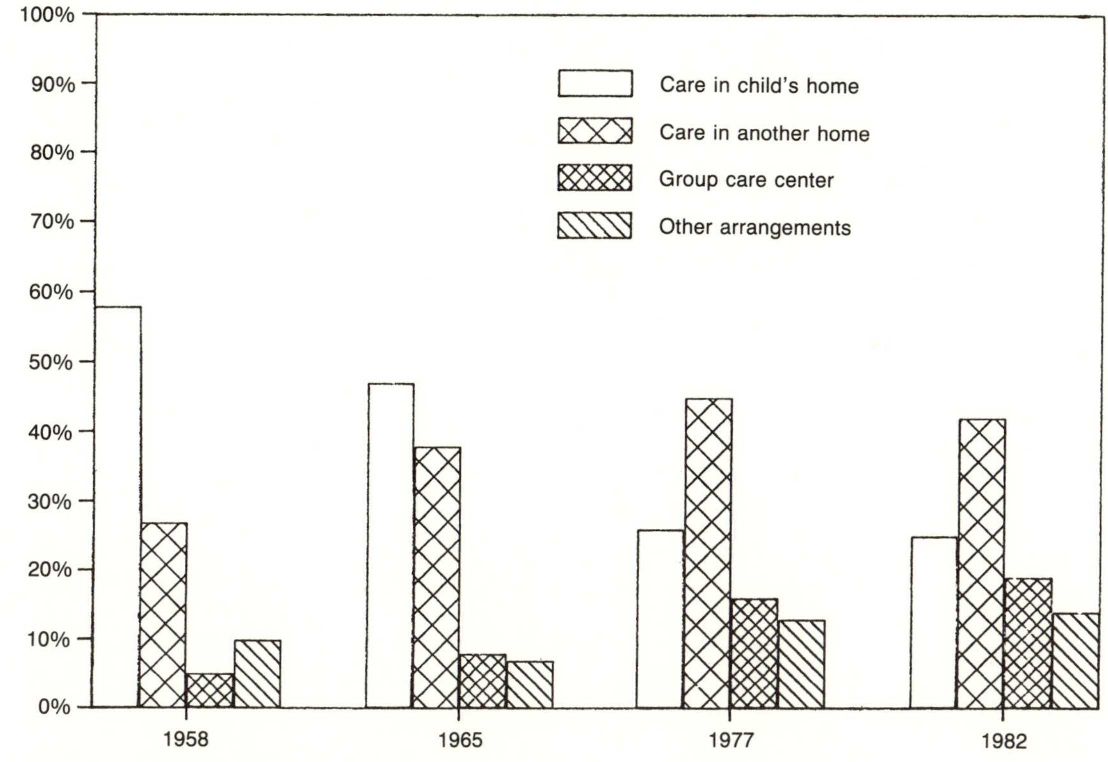

Figure 2 **Childcare Arrangements (for preschool children with mothers working full time)**

Source: U.S. Bureau of the Census.

The federal commitment to childcare funding needs to be increased. The states are spending less because they are receiving less, and because the set-aside was eliminated. An obvious option would be to increase funding for the Social Services Block Grant, and require the states to use the new funds for childcare services. The states could use these funds in a variety of ways. For example, the states might use some of the funds to subsidize providers of childcare services to low-income families. The states would have the option of providing more lucrative incentives to public or private agencies offering childcare services to specific low-income parents, such as single parents. To make certain that low-income parents could afford the services, daycare providers receiving subsidies could be required to use sliding-fee scales. Some of the money might be used to match state expenditures on full-day kindergartens in public schools. States might also qualify for matching funds to improve childcare-monitoring systems. The states would also have the option of providing subsidies and technical assistance to partnerships between public and private organizations committed to providing more childcare for low-income families.

Another option would be for the states to fund start-up costs for umbrella organizations that would provide training and certification to providers of family daycare services. The umbrella organization ideally would also monitor family daycare, provide financial assistance, and develop methods of sharing resources. The providers of family daycare can be provided with many incentives to cooperate with the umbrella organization, including certification for participation in the Child Care Food Program. Participation in this program ensures that the nutritional and health needs of the children receive some attention.

Young and Zigler (1986) recommended two additional methods by which the federal government could play a role in improving the quality of childcare. First, they propose establishment of a national daycare clearing house within the federal bureaucracy. The clearing house would provide public officials, parents, and care providers with the latest and best information available on the characteristics, impact, and operation of quality childcare. Second, they recommend developing a model for daycare programs based on Head Start models, which emphasize an educational partnership between parents and providers. A central component of these model programs would be a parental right to unlimited access to their child's program, and a responsibility on the part of the provider to furnish parents with periodic progress reports (Young and Zigler 1986, 53).

Congress has responded to recommendations for expansion and improvements in childcare in only very modest ways. In 1984 Congress passed a bill allocating $20 million to the states to expand the availability of childcare services. Forty percent of the funds were earmarked to fund organizations that provide information about services for children, the elderly, and the handicapped. Sixty percent was designated to establish before- and after-school childcare in community centers and school facilities. However, as of mid–1987, the program has not been funded by Congress.

At least seven bills concerning childcare were introduced by members of Congress in 1986. None passed, but most were reintroduced in 1987. The most comprehensive is a bill (H.R. 1001) reintroduced by George Miller (Dem., Calif.), Chair of the Select Committee on Children, Youth and Families. Miller's bill would increase Title XX funding from $2.7 billion to $3.3 billion, earmarking the increase for childcare services. The new funds would be designated for pilot programs to encourage the private sector and government entities to improve childcare resources, including upgrading standards, training childcare professionals, funding full-day kindergartens, and aiding groups with special needs such as single and low-income working parents.

The childcare tax credit. Another method by which the federal government could increase the availability and affordability of childcare is by changes in the dependent-care tax credit. As currently written, this program provides little assistance to low-income families. Currently, working parents who pay for childcare receive a nonrefundable tax credit for each child. For example, for one child the credit applies to the first $2,400 of costs, for two children it increases to $4,800. The credit decreases with income, with a minimum of 20 percent of outlays for families with a gross income above $28,000.

Most of the families using the tax credit have incomes over $25,000. Only 6 percent of all the families using the credit in 1982 had incomes below $10,000 (Ways and Means 1985, 374). Low-income and poor families receive little benefit from the credit because they generally do not have enough federal tax liability to use this option. This will be even more true when the 1986 Tax Reform Act, which lowers, or even abolishes, the tax liability of millions of low-income families, takes full effect in 1988.

This program could be amended to increase childcare options for many families. The credit limits could be raised so that childcare expenses could be reduced for most working families. Second, the program could be altered to give larger credits to low-income parents. Last, the credit could be made refundable, so that low-income families with little or no tax obligation could receive the full value of the deduction. This last option would provide more assistance to low-income families than to the really poor, because the credit would not be received until the end of the year. The poorest of families generally cannot benefit from tax credits because they have no way to meet out-of-pocket expenses, even if they might be reimbursed.

Representative Nancy Johnson (Rep., Conn.) has introduced legislation (H.R. 4787) that would amend the tax credit in another way. Her bill would exclude families with adjusted gross incomes of $50,000 or more from eligibility for the tax credit. The $200 million saved by this amendment would be given to the states to provide daycare vouchers for families with incomes less than 200 percent of the poverty threshold. This amendment would reverse the irony of the current law: the richest families qualify for the credit while the poorest earn too little to qualify.

Latchkey children. Another issue that has to be faced is the growing problem of latchkey children. A latchkey child is one left unattended before or after school or during holidays because the parent or parents are at work. Estimates of the number of latchkey children vary from two to seven million (SCCYF 1984, 24). Some states use Title XX funds to finance care for latchkey children, but most Title XX funding is reserved for preschool programs. A recent study by the Children's Defense Fund reported that there were publicly or privately supported programs in about half the states (Blank and Wilkins 1986, 49–54). Often the public schools and community groups form a partnership to provide care for children after regular school hours or during holidays. Volunteer and charitable groups often provide "warm" phone lines that latchkey children can call to help them deal with fear and loneliness. Most of the states with programs meet the needs of only a small proportion of the children in need of care and often exclude poor families by cost barriers. The programs should be expanded considerably, and they need to be based on a sliding-fee schedule, with exemption from fees for the poorest families.

After-school care can do more than provide children with supervision and companionship. Studies reveal that children attending after-school programs show marked academic improvements and increased self-esteem (SCCYF 1984, 30).

Preschool programs. One trend that might decrease the need for childcare while assisting low-income families is the growing popularity of preschool programs for three-to-five-year-olds. By 1982 over 36 percent of all three- and four-year-old children were in preschool, up from 20.5 percent in 1970 (*Times* 1984, 12). In 1985, 94 percent of five-year-olds attended kindergarten, up from 80 percent in 1970 and 71 percent in 1965. The popularity of prekindergarten and kindergarten programs reflects a growing appreciation of the educational advantages of earlier education. Growing evidence supports the conclusion that early education has long-term educational benefits, especially among disadvantaged students (Schweinhart and Weikart 1980; Consortium for Longitudinal Studies 1978).

Increasingly states are passing laws to require earlier schooling. For example, Mayor Ed Koch of New York City recently appointed a commission of early-education experts to study a proposal to establish a universal school program for all four-year-olds (*New York Times* 1986, 18). In endorsing the proposal the panel noted that ''appropriate intervention at this formative stage of development is known to build educational, social and psychological foundations critical to future success in school and life—foundations that cannot be as effectively built at a later time'' (*New York Times* 1986, 18). The commission reported that the program would cost about $2,750 per child. While expensive, this is less than the $3,000 the commission estimated that it costs to hold a child back a grade, or the $5,000 it costs to provide special education. If this program is adopted, New York would be the first major city to offer universal preschool education.

The House Select Committee on Children, Youth and Families recently recommended that Congress pass legislation providing incentive grants to public and private nonprofit agencies to assist in establishing educational programs in the public schools for four-year-olds. The committee recommended that special grants be established for districts that establish enrichment programs for disadvantaged children. The programs, the Committee concluded, should be based on sliding-fees so families from all income levels can participate (SCCYF 1984, 18).

AFDC families. One group of parents with special needs is AFDC parents. Unfortunately, the childcare provisions for AFDC parents are seriously deficient. Because Title XX funding is so modest, most parents receiving AFDC simply cannot obtain adequate childcare assistance. The result is that most AFDC mothers are unemployed. Even programs like WIN (Work Incentive Program) do not provide enough childcare assistance to allow all the AFDC mothers who qualify for job training to enter the program. AFDC parents who are in the work force have to qualify for assistance under a privately financed program, qualify for some limited special programs under Title XX or other federal programs, or use the Child Care Disregard. Under the disregard, the parent pays the cost of childcare and a maximum of $160 per child is disregarded from her income in calculating AFDC benefits.

This approach is seriously flawed. First, the actual cost of care may exceed $160 per child. Second, the parent locates the childcare provider, with no requirements for the quality of the care. The children may be left in homes or centers with no special programs for disadvantaged children. Third, the parent must first pay the costs of the care and then be reimbursed. Since most AFDC mothers have minimal or no discretionary funds, this requirement can be a serious barrier to employment.

In fact, most poor mothers cannot complete their high-school education, obtain job training, or get established in the work force without long-term childcare assistance. The AFDC program and many state programs limit childcare to a certain length of time or terminate assistance when the family income exceeds a modest level. Such policies punish poor family heads who attempt to become self-sufficient, often forcing them to choose between employment and adequate care for their children. A more productive policy would provide vouchers that AFDC mothers could use to obtain free or inexpensive childcare from qualified providers while they get established in the job market. Additionally, these families need quality childcare based on sliding-fee schedules so they can afford to stay in the work force.

An innovative approach that recognizes the need to give low-income mothers and their children support has been launched in a large public housing project in Chicago. In six of the 28 buildings that comprise the Robert Taylor Homes, all pregnant teenagers and their newborns will be enrolled in the Center for Successful Child Development. The center is located in the project, and staffed by residents. The staff includes a nurse and several educational specialists. The staff will provide comprehensive care, including healthcare for pregnant mothers and their children, lessons in mothering, daycare, and counseling and support to encourage the mothers to stay in school, in job training, or in the work force. The children will be assisted by the Center until they enter elementary school.

The intent is to allow the children to enter school on an equal footing with peers from more financially secure families, and to help the mothers escape poverty. The project has been called a Marshall Plan for preschoolers (*New York Times* 1986, 12).

The private sector role. A positive trend in childcare is that more corporations are getting involved. The most recent figures (Friedman 1986) indicate that about 3,000 corporations are providing childcare assistance of some type to their employees. As recently as 1978 only 110 corporations had childcare programs. While corporations are showing more awareness about the childcare needs of their employees, a great deal remains to be done. In 1986 there were approximately 44 thousand corporations with 100 or more employees.

Corporations are increasingly involved in childcare because a very large percentage of their employees are women with children, or fathers whose wives are also employed. Sixty percent of all married men now have a working wife, and presumably a more stressful home life. Studies conducted by or for corporations indicate that childcare services reduce employee stress, improve employee morale, lower absenteeism, and increase the recruitment advantage of the company (Perry 1982; Magid 1983; Burud, Aschbacher and McCroskey 1984). The studies tend to be more impressionistic than rigorous, but the findings seem credible (Miller 1984).

The assistance being provided by corporations takes a number of forms including childcare information and referral services, grants to state agencies involved in training and certifying childcare providers, voucher and cash-grant benefits to employees that can be used to pay for childcare, company contracts with centers to obtain discounts for employees, and on-site childcare centers financed by corporations.

About 150 corporations have established on-site childcare centers for employees. Employees usually pay for this childcare on a sliding-fee basis. Some corporations have individually or jointly elected to support and subsidize one or more centers for their employees. Other companies have helped organize and train personnel to run home or family daycare centers. Businesses have also collaborated with school districts and community agencies to run before and after-school programs in schools, churches, and storefronts. A few companies have established summer day programs on or near company property. To deal with absenteeism, a number of companies provide nurses to stay with sick children or subsidize centers that specialize in looking after children who are ill.

One common form of corporate childcare service is information. Corporations either gather information on childcare facilities or they hire agencies that specialize in this service to assist their employees. IBM, for example, established a national contractor called Work/Family Directions to identify referral services and providers for employees in its 200 offices across the country.

As one option to help parents deal with the costs of daycare, many corporations now offer their employees flexible benefits. The employee is offered a choice of benefits, one of which is a childcare subsidy. One option is encouraged by the tax code and is the fastest growing form of federal childcare assistance. The employee can opt to have the employer reduce his or her income by an agreed-upon amount. The employer pays the employee's childcare costs directly from this fund. The value to the employee is that his or her taxable income is reduced. As long as the value of the assistance is less than $5,000, it is a nontaxable benefit. Because of the tax rate, this option is of little benefit to families that earn less that $20,000 a year. For higher-income families, however, it will provide substantial assistance.

Some corporations are also introducing job sharing, flexitime, part-time work, and personal or sick child leave to reduce employees' needs for childcare.

Maternity and parental leaves

The United States is far behind the other major western industrial nations in the development of maternity- and parental-leave policy. The United States, in fact, is the only major western industrial nation without a national policy covering maternity leaves. In the other major western nations women at childbirth are given a paid employment leave with assurance of job protection and retention of seniority and pension entitlements (ILO 1974, 1978, 1979).

Other western industrialized countries. In most of these nations maternity benefits have been national policy for at least a couple of decades. The benefits were originally designed to protect the health of mothers and their newborn children. But as Kamerman (1980, 13) has pointed out, in recent years the policies have been expanded to include protecting the economic contribution of women and helping workers, especially women, balance their family and employee responsibilities.

In 1980 Kamerman counted seventy-five countries, including all the industrialized nations except the United States, that had a maternity policy. The paid maternity leave ranged from a low of twelve weeks in Israel to a high of nine months in Sweden; the average was six months. All of the countries extend the benefits for difficult pregnancies or births, and some of the countries provide extended paid leaves for second or subsequent children, multiple births, or for single mothers.

In these nations the social-security or social-insurance system provides the new mother with a cash grant equal to all or part of the wage that she would have received from employment. In most countries the benefit level is 90–100 percent of the maximum wage covered by social insurance. Generally, the benefit is tax-free and available to all women who have been employed for some minimum period before childbirth, regardless of income. Sweden, Norway, and Finland have expanded benefits to cover both parents, making them the only countries with genuine parental-leave policies.

All of the countries that provide maternity leaves also assume responsibility for medical and hospital coverage at birth, plus prenatal and postnatal care. Almost all the countries provide one-time benefits such as a small cash grant or infant clothing and furniture. The cash or in-kind grants are often contingent on the mother having one or more prenatal examinations.

As maternity policies have evolved and expanded to meet the needs of working couples, many nations have added optional supplemental leaves for mothers who want to remain at home with their children for longer periods. These leaves start after regular maternity benefits are exhausted and usually provide a flat grant under the unemployment insurance system or under sickness insurance. These leaves are usually for a year or until the youngest child is two. Many countries allow a mother to opt for a longer, unpaid but job-protected leave if she wants to stay home with her young children.

The United States. The Pregnancy Discrimination Act of 1978 required employers to treat pregnancy like any other disability or illness. In practice this means that company insurance must cover the same share of costs that is normally paid for an illness, and that the employer must give mothers a short disability leave. The law does not require the employer to extend the leave beyond the immediate recovery period, or guarantee the job security of the mother if she opts for a leave beyond the immediate recovery period.

In January 1987, in its first major interpretation of the Pregnancy Discrimination Act, the Supreme Court (*California Federal Savings and Loan Association* v. *Mark Guerra*, 93 L Ed. 2nd 613) upheld a state law that requires employers to grant special job protection to employees who are physically unable to work because of pregnancy. In a 6–3 decision the court upheld a California statute that requires employers to grant an unpaid leave of up to four months to women disabled by childbirth, even if similar leaves are not granted for other disabilities. The majority on the court argued that the Pregnancy Discrimination Act established a floor of benefits for pregnant women, not a ceiling. Justice Thurgood Marshall in the majority decision said: "By taking pregnancy into account, California's pregnancy disability leave statute allows women, as well as men, to have families without losing their jobs."

The Supreme Court's decision is a major victory for women, but the California law does not establish a universal maternity policy. It is, in fact, quite restrictive. It limits leaves to women physically disabled by pregnancy, childbirth, or related medical conditions. The full four months of leave would not be given unless there were special medical problems. The employer is obligated to give a woman back her job or an equivalent position, but only if economic conditions make this possible.

The states of Hawaii, New Jersey, New York, and Rhode Island have passed laws that are comparable to the California statute. The court's decision will undoubtedly stimulate other states to pass similar legislation. It will also provide ammunition to those members of Congress who have been trying to pass legislation establishing a national maternity policy. The author of one proposal, Pat Schroeder (Dem., Colorado), reacted to the opinion by saying: "The California decision has opened the doors for us. It says the Supreme Court recognizes there are women in the work force who are there to stay and that the demands of family have to be addressed by society" (*New York Times* 1987, 10).

Only a week after the California case, the Supreme Court ruled (*Wimberly* v. *Labor and Industrial Relations Commission*, 93 L Ed. 2nd 909) that a 1976 Federal unemployment-compensation law prohibited discrimination against pregnant women, but did not require preferential treatment. In this case a woman took a leave without guarantee of reinstatement to have a child. Within a few weeks of having the child she informed her employer that she would like to return to work. Upon being informed that no job was available, she applied for unemployment compensation. The state of Missouri refused her request under a neutral statute that denies unemployment compensation to any worker who leaves a job voluntarily.

The court's support of the Missouri law is in one sense of limited importance. Only three other states have unemployment-compensation laws as restrictive as Missouri's. The importance of the case, however, is that it clarifies the court's view that while Congress has prohibited discrimination against pregnant women, it has neither required that they be given preferential treatment nor prohibited preferential treatment.

It is unlikely that the maternity issue will be resolved very well in the United States unless the cost is spread among employers. Only the larger corporations are likely to accept the costs of paid leaves, and in fact many small employers probably could not afford to give their employees paid maternity leaves. Currently only about half of all women in the work force have some type of maternity benefit. Many of the nation's largest corporations provide a 12-16–week leave to new mothers, most guaranteeing job protection. Some of these corporations also allow leaves for fathers, although corporate norms are not supportive of men who take this option. Many smaller companies extend maternity leaves, but guarantee the mother her job or a comparable position only if favorable business conditions prevail. Most American companies that offer leaves do not give the mother any cash benefits after the immediate recovery period. Some corporations do allow the mother the option of returning to work on a part-time basis, and some allow mothers to adopt a flexitime schedule.

The bill (H.R. 4300) that Representative Pat Schroeder has introduced into Congress would require all companies to provide unpaid and job-protected leaves for 18 weeks to new parents (including adoptive parents), disabled workers, and those needed at home to care for an ill child. Additionally, an employee could take up to 18 weeks of unpaid leave over a 12 month period to recover from a serious health condition. Preexisting health benefits would continue during the leave. The employee would have a right to the same or an equivalent position upon returning to work. Both men and women are covered under the proposal. The bill would apply only to public or private employers with fifteen or more employees. This program would be modest by Western standards, but prospects even for its passage are problematical because a well-organized opposition is arguing that it would be too expensive for small-to-medium-size companies.

Schroeder's bill might have better prospects if it required employers to pool their funds in an insurance plan that would cover the cost of parental leaves. There are several insurance options. One option would use the federally supervised unemployment-compensation program to cover parental leaves. A second would be state-managed insurance funds modeled on plans currently run by New York and New Jersey. A third option would require employers to obtain private insurance. Hawaii is currently the only state with such a law. Unless maternity/parental leaves are financed through some type of insurance program, the protection and benefits that most parents receive in the immediate future will most likely depend upon the policies and wealth of the company they are employed by.

An additional argument for establishing a national parental-leave policy in the United States is one of cost. Two experts on early child development and childcare, Gamble and Zigler (1985), have estimated that the cost of high-quality infant and toddler daycare is about $150 per week. Few families could afford these costs. If high standards are maintained, either employers or public agencies will have to supplement the costs for most families. A policy that allowed a parent to remain at home until a child was two might be less expensive. This would clearly be the case for parents with more than one preschooler.

Elements of a parental-leave policy. Kamerman and Kahn (1987) conclude that there are five steps in making parental leave a right without imposing a burdensome financial hardship on employers:

1. All states should require employers to provide disability benefits to employees, including employees disabled by pregnancy and childbearing, and those required at home to care for an ill child. Coverage should be for a minimum of 14 weeks every 24 months.
2. All parents not covered by private medical insurance should be covered by public plans.
3. Allow all employees to take a "parenting" or "childcare" leave, unpaid but job-protected, to devote time to childrearing.
4. Encourage employers to develop more part-time, flexitime, and phased-in work for new parents who want to balance childrearing with employment.
5. Develop insurance "pools" to lower the costs of disability insurance for employers.

Summary and conclusions

Poverty has increased substantially since the late 1970s. Four factors that have contributed to increased poverty are high rates of unemployment and subemployment, a national shift from an industrial to a service economy with fewer high-paying jobs, cutbacks in social-welfare expenditures, and a great increase in the percentage of all families headed by a single woman. Women, both married and single, have tried to deal with family economic problems by entering the work force in record numbers. Today most women of working age, including those with children, are in the labor force. The entry of millions of additional women into the work force has undoubtedly kept the poverty rate from rising even higher, but it has not had an optimal impact, because the nation has failed to adapt and expand its social policies to meet the changing needs and roles of families.

This essay has reviewed a range of policy issues that must be resolved if American social policy is to be made compatible with current family needs. Millions of American families need supportive social programs to help parents better balance their dual roles as parents and employees, and to deal with the financial challenge of supporting their families. Millions of women who head AFDC families need the same type of support to enable them to complete educational or job-training programs, and to enter and maintain themselves in the workplace.

The policies that would meet the needs of families are very obvious. Families need decent childcare and preschool educational programs at affordable prices, tax programs that allow them to retain more of their earnings, and maternity- and parental-leave policies. Childcare services are now so deficient that there is little chance that supply will be adjusted to need without substantial additional intervention by federal and state agencies and private employers. Poverty among female-headed families will never be adequately addressed without childcare services that allow the mothers to become economically independent. Well-designed programs could also deal with many of the needs of children from poverty households, allowing them to enter public school on an equal footing with other children.

Recent tax reforms have eased the financial burden of millions of low-income and poor families, and rather modest revisions in the EITC and the childcare tax credit could give them substantially more assistance.

Maternity- and parental-leave issues have only recently attracted serious scrutiny by employers and public officials. A small percentage of all employers, mostly larger corporations, have adopted enlightened policies, a few states have passed laws requiring employers to address the issue, and progressive legislation has been introduced for consideration by Congress. This issue will not be adequately addressed until a method is found by which the costs can be shared. An insurance plan, perhaps subsidized by the federal and state governments, seems the most promising option.

Until American social policy is reformed to make it supportive of families, women will continue to be penalized, and even impoverished, for bearing children. Millions of families will be unable to cope with their responsibilities positively or even adequately, which will mean more family stress and continued dependence on welfare programs that maintain the poor at poverty levels without dealing with the problems that impoverished them.

References

Baldwin, W. and Presser, H. B. 1980. Child Care as a Constraint on Employment: Prevalence, Correlates, and Bearing on the Work and Fertility Nexus. *American Journal of Sociology*, 85: 1202-13.

Bahr, S.J. 1979. "The Effects of Welfare on Marital Stability and Remarriage." *Journal of Marriage and Family*. 41 (August): 533-60.

Blank, H. and Wilkins, A. 1986. *State Child Care Fact Book 1986*. Children's Defense Fund: Washington, D.C.

Bureau of the Census. 1986. "Money Income and Poverty Status of Families and Persons in the United States: 1985." *Current Population Reports*, Series P-60, no. 150. Washington, D.C.: GPO.

Bureau of the Census. 1986a. *Statistical Abstract of the United States: 1985*. 105th edition. Washington, D.C.:GPO.

Burlage, D. 1978. "Divorced and Separated Mothers: Combining the Responsibilities of Breadwinning and Child Rearing." Unpublished Ph.D. Dissertation, Harvard University.

Burud, S., P. A. Aschbacher, and J. McCroskey. 1984. *Employer-Supported Child Care: Investing In Human Resources*. Boston: Auburn House.

Carlson, E. and Stinson, K. 1982. "Motherhood, Marriage Timing, and Marital Stability." *Social Forces*. 61 (September): 258-67.

Clarke-Stuart, A. 1982. *Daycare*. Cambridge, Mass.: Harvard University Press.

Consortium for Longitudinal Studies. 1978. *Lasting Effects After Preschool*. Final Report of DHEW Grant No. 90C-1311. Washington, D.C. U.S. Administration for Children, Youth and Families (OHDS<DHEW).

Cooney, R.S. 1979. "Demographic Components of Growth in White, Black and Puerto Rican Female-Headed Families: Comparison of the Cutright and Ross Sawhill Methodologies." *Social Research* 8: 144-58.

Cramer, J.C. 1980. "Fertility and Female Employment: Problems of Causal Direction." *American Sociological Review*. 47 (August): 556-67.

Danziger, S., Jakubson, G.,Schwartz, S. and Smolensky, E. 1982. "Work and Welfare as Determinants of Female Poverty and Household Headship.'' *The Quarterly Journal of Economics.* (August): 519–534.

Emlen, A. C. and Koren, P.E. 1984. *Hard To Find and Difficult to Manage: The Effects of Child care on the Workplace.* Portland, Oregon: Portland State University Press.

Emlen, A.C., J. Kushmuk, P. Koren, and Faught, L. 1985. *Community Shares: Corporate Financing of a Child Care Information Service.* Washington, D.C.: Department of Health and Human Services.

Farrell, G. 1980. *On Site Day care: The State of the Art and Models Development.* Albany, New York: Welfare Research Institute.

Fosburg, S. and Hawkins, P. 1981. *Final Report of the National Day Care Home Study,* Vol 1., Cambridge, Mass.: ABt Books.

Friedman, D.E. 1986. ''Child Care for Employees' Kids.'' *Harvard Business Review,* March-April:28–34.

Gilder, G. 1981. *Wealth and Poverty.* New York: Bantam.

Hayghe, H. 1986. ''Rise in Mother's Labor Force Activity Includes Those With Infants.'' Monthly Labor Review, February:43–45.

Hogan, D.P. and Kitagawa, E. M. 1985. ''The Impact of Social Status, Family Structure, and Neighborhood on the Fertility of Black Adolescents.'' *American Journal of Sociology.* 90:825–855.

Honig, M. 1974. ''AFDC Income, Recipient Rates, and Family Dissolution.'' *Journal of Human Resources.* 9 (Summer): 303–322.

International Labor Organization. 1974. *Equality of Opportunity and Treatment for Women Workers.* Geneva, Switzerland.

International Labor Organization. 1978. *Employment of Women with Family Responsibilities.* Geneva, Switzerland.

International Labor Organization. 1979. *Equal Opportunity and Equal Treatment for Men and Women Workers: Workers with Family Responsibilities.* Geneva, Switzerland.

Kamerman, S. B. 1980. *Maternity and Parental Benefits and Leaves.* New York: Columbia University Press.

Kamerman, S. B., and A. F. Kahn 1981. *Child Care, Family Benefits, and Working Parents.* New York: Columbia University Press.

Kamerman, S. B., A. J. Kahn, and Kingston, P. 1983. *Maternity Policies and Working Women.* New York: Columbia University Press.

Kamerman, S.B. 1984. ''Women, Children, and Poverty: Public Policies and Female-headed Families In Industrialized Countries.'' *Signs: Journal of Women in Culture and Society,* vol. 10, no.2:249–271.

Kamerman, S. B. and A.J. Kahn, 1987. Quoted in *Ms*, March, p. 44.

Keyserling, M. 1972. *Windows On Day Care.* New York: National Council of Jewish Women.

Magid, R. Y. 1983. *Child Care Initiatives for Working Parents: Why Employers Get Involved.* New York: American Management Association.

Miller, T. I. 1984. ''The Effects of Employer-Sponsored Child Care On Employee Absenteeism, Turnover, Productivity, Recruitment or Job Satisfaction: What is Claimed and What is Known.'' *Personnel Psychology,* 37: 277–289.

Moore, K. and Waite, L. 1981. ''Marital Dissolution, Early Motherhood and Early Marriage. *Social Forces.* 60 (September): 20–40.

New York Times, 1987. ''Job Rights Backed By Supreme Court In Pregnancy Case.'' January 14: pp. 1 @ 10.

New York Times, 1984. ''Earlier Schooling Is Pressed.'' December 17: 1 @ 12.

Nollen, S. D. 1979. ''Does Flexitime Improve Productivity?'' *Harvard Business*

Review, September/October: 4–8.

Pearce, D. 1978. "The Feminization of Poverty: Women, Work and Welfare." *Urban and Social Change Review*.

Perry, K.S. 1982. *Employers and Child Care; Establishing Services Through the Workplace*. Washington, D.C.: Women's Bureau, U.S. Department of Labor.

Rodgers, H.R. 1986. *Poor Women, Poor Families: The Economic Plight of America's Female-Headed Families*. Armonk, New York: M.E. Sharpe.

Schweinhart, L. J. and Weikart, D. P. 1980. *Effects of Early Childhood Intervention on Teenage Youth: The Perry Preschool Project, 1962–1980*. Monographs of the High/Scope Educational Research Foundation, No. 7.

Select Committee on Children, Youth and Families. 1983. "U.S. Children and Their Families: 1983: Current Conditions and Recent Trends." 98th Congress, 1st Session. Washington, D.C.: GPO.

Select Committee on Children, Youth and Families. 1984. "Families and Child Care: Improving The Options. 98th Congress, 2nd Session. Washington, D.C.: GPO.

Social Security Administration. 1986. *Social Security Bulletin*. Washington, D.C.: U.S. Department of Health and Human Services.

United States Department of Health and Human Services, 1982. *Comparative Licensing Study: Profiles of State Day Care Licensing Requirements for Day Care Centers*. Washington, D.C.

Ways and Means. 1985. *Children In Poverty*. U.S. House of Representatives, 99th Congress, 1st Session. Washington, D.C.: GPO.

Young, K. T. and Zigler, E. 1986. "Infant and Toddler Day Care: Regulations and Policy Implications." *American Journal of Orthopsychiatry*, 56: 43–55.

Zigler, E. and Gordon, E. (eds) 1982. *Day Care: Scientific and Social Policy Issues*. Boston: Auburn House.

Zigler, E. and Muenchow, S. 1983. "Infant Day Care and Infant-Care Leaves." *American Psychologist* 38: 91–94.

Child Support and Dependency

Irwin Garfinkel, Sara McLanahan,
and Patrick Wong

The economic well-being of a large and growing percentage of children in the United States is partly dependent upon the nature of our child-support institutions. At present one of five children is potentially eligible for child support, and nearly one of every two children born today will become eligible for child support at some point before reaching age 18 (Bumpass 1984). Given that such a large proportion of the next generation will be affected, the quality of our child-support institutions is of vital interest to the nation.

The first part of this paper describes the traditional child-support system, documents its shortcomings, and summarizes recent federal efforts to strengthen it. The second section outlines a new Child Support Assurance System (CSAS) currently being implemented in the state of Wisconsin. The third section presents estimates of the benefits and costs of implementing such a system nationwide, and compares the Wisconsin CSAS with an alternative reform that supplements welfare income with private child support. The alternative allows welfare mothers to "disregard" a portion of child-support income in calculating their welfare grant and has the effect of increasing welfare benefits and dependence. The paper concludes with a brief summary of the differences between a child-support-assurance system and welfare.

Shortcomings of the current system and developments in federal reforms

The traditional child-support system consists of two major parts: the family court system and the welfare system. The former establishes responsibility for payment of private child support, sets the amount of support to be paid, and enforces the parent's obligation to pay. The latter provides public cash and in-kind benefits to poor children and their custodial parents. Because of recent federal initiatives, these two systems have become increasingly intertwined. In the following section, we examine both the private and the public systems. The current problems and limitations of each system will be discussed along with recent reforms by the federal government.

The private child-support system

The private child-support system in this country has historically been a state prerogative implemented through the judicial branch. Under the traditional family court system, two steps are involved in obtaining private child support: (1) determination by a court of the amount of child support to be paid by the noncustodial parent on an individualized basis; and (2) payment of that support obligation directly by the noncustodial parent.

Several problems can arise in establishing awards and setting amounts of child support. First, there is often a failure to establish any award at all. Nationally, only 58 percent of mothers eligible for child support are awarded it (U.S. Bureau of the Census 1985). The proportion awarded support varies dramatically with the marital status of the mother. Whereas about eight out of ten divorced mothers receive child-support orders, less than half of separated mothers and less than one in five never-married mothers have orders.

Second, the setting of an award on a case-by-case basis by a judge in a judicial hearing is very expensive, both in time and cost to the parents and in delays for the children needing support. The time of judges and other court personnel makes the procedure expensive to the public as well. As the number of child-support determinations continues to increase, concern has been expressed as to whether these costs are justified. Unfortunately, information is not available on the cost of the present individualized system.

Third, the case-by-case determination of the amount of the award often results in unfairness. The great variation in the size of awards is evidence that the system treats equals unequally. Data for Wisconsin indicate that child-support awards range from zero to over 100 percent of the noncustodial father's income. Table 1 shows that in 20 percent of the cases, child-support awards for one child were less than 10 percent

Table 1

Child Support Order as a Percentage of Gross Income (by number of children)

Order as % of noncustodial parent's income	Percentage of cases by number of children 1 N = 1,087	2 N = 829	3 N = 277
0–10%	20%	10%	6%
11–20	50	36	27
21–30	21	30	33
31–40	5	15	20
41–50	3	5	9
More than 50	2	5	6

Note: This table covers custodial families with a child support award and with three or fewer children. Cases with 4 or more children (N = 102) are not tabulated because the sample size is too small for reliable estimates. Of the 3,806 cases meeting the sample requirements, income information is missing in 1,536 cases. In addition, 77 cases have zero reported income and are also excluded. This results in a final N of 2,193.

Source: Family Court record data file from Wisconsin Child Support Reform Demonstration Project, 1985, Institute for Research on Poverty, University of Wisconsin, Madison.

of the noncustodial father's income. In 50 percent of the cases, awards were between 11 and 20 percent. The data also indicate that average award levels as a percentage of the noncustodial parent's income vary substantially across counties. The average for one child varies from 12 percent to 24 percent. For two and three children respectively, the ranges are 18 percent to 36 percent and 13 percent to 37 percent (Nichols-Casebolt *et al.* 1985, Table 3).

The present system is also regressive. Child-support obligations represent a greater proportion of the incomes of low-income parents than of those who are well off. In Wisconsin, orders decline as a percentage of income as the noncustodial father's income increases (Table 2). For one child, orders range from a high of 32 percent for those with incomes less than $5,000 to a low of 12 percent for those with incomes between $30,000 and $40,000.

Aside from the difficulties associated with the establishment of an award and the setting of an amount, the system also has problems when it comes to collection of support once the award is made. The standard procedure has been for the court to order the noncustodial parent to pay, with the enforcement of the order left to the beneficiary of the order, the custodial parent. This means that if the absent parent fails to

Table 2

Relationship between Noncustodial Parent's Income at the Time of the Child-Support Order and Level of Child-Support Awards (by number of children and gross income category, selected Wisconsin counties)

Income category of noncustodial parent	N	Percentage of income by number of children 1 N = 1,087	2 N = 829	3 N = 277
Less than $5,000	151	32%	41%	33%
$5,000–10,000	538	20	27	28
$10,000–15,000	506	18	25	31
$15,000–20,000	443	15	22	30
$20,000–30,000	450	13	21	24
$30,000–40,000	107	12	20	32
$40,000 or over	100	16	19	14
Weighted average	2,295	18	24	27

Note: There is an upward bias in the estimates for child support as percentage of gross income. Because of coding error, net income is used for about 280 cases for which gross income is not available. Current work is in progress to separate those cases.

Source: Family Court record data file from Wisconsin Child Support Reform Demonstration Project.

pay, the custodial parent has to initiate legal proceedings to enforce the court's support order, usually by citing the nonpaying parent for contempt. This proceeding is fraught with difficulties for both parties. For the custodial parent, it requires legal counsel—a substantial financial burden for a parent already not receiving support—and often involves difficult fact determinations because of the lack of adequate records of direct payments to the custodial parent. For the noncustodial parent, the sanction imposed for willful nonpayment can be drastic—imprisonment in jail (Krause 1981; Chambers 1979). Generally, the legal system for collecting child support is regarded as ineffective (Garfinkel and Melli 1987; Krause 1981; Chambers 1979). Nationally, only half of the parents with awards receive the full amount due them and about one-quarter receive nothing (U.S. Bureau of the Census 1985).

The failure of the private child-support system in the United States to provide adequately for the needs of children in single-parent households is not new. In the early part of this century it had become sufficiently acute to attract the attention of the National Conference of Commissioners on Uniform State Laws, which in 1907 directed its Committee on Marriage and Divorce to study the problem.[1] However, the enforcement of private child support was viewed as strictly a state and local problem until four decades ago.

In the late 1940s congressional interest in absent fathers grew in response to the upward trend in divorce, separation, desertion, and out-of-wedlock births. Because of this trend, children with living but absent parents replaced orphans as the most numerous dependents on the public child-support system, Aid to Families with Dependent Children (AFDC), to which we will turn later. Congress enacted the first federal legislation regarding private child support in 1950, requiring state welfare agencies to notify law-enforcement officials when a child receiving AFDC benefits had been deserted or abandoned. Further legislation, enacted in 1965 and 1967, allowed states to request addresses of absent parents from the Department of Health, Education, and Welfare (HEW) and from the Internal Revenue Service (IRS). States were also required to establish a single organizational unit to enforce child support and establish paternity.

The most significant federal legislation was enacted in 1975, when Congress added Part D to Title IV of the Social Security Act, establishing the Child Support Enforcement (IV-D) program. The legislation established an Office of Child Support Enforcement in HEW and required each state to establish a corresponding agency to help enforce child support in all AFDC cases and, on request, in non-AFDC cases. It also required states to maintain a parent-locator service which tied in with a federal service. In short, the 1975 act created the public bureaucracy to enforce private child-support obligations. By 1985 collections had increased to $2.7 billion, including $1 billion for AFDC recipients. In the four-year period between 1976 and 1980, nationwide collections of child support for AFDC recipients increased by 111 percent, and in the five-year period between 1980 and 1985, collections again increased by 81 percent (U.S. Department of Health and Human Services 1980, Table 2; 1985, Table 1). There is good reason to believe that child-support collections will continue to grow, for the 1985 figures do not reflect the effects of the strongest federal child-support legislation to date.

That legislation was passed in 1984 by a unanimous Congress. It addressed the three major shortcomings of the private child-support system: failures to obtain child-support awards from the courts; the inadequacy of the amount of the awards that are made; and failures to collect delinquent support payments.

On the issue of obtaining orders, the states were required to adopt expedited procedures for obtaining support orders either in the judicial system or in an administrative agency. On the issue of adequate support orders, all states must establish child-support guidelines to be available for use by October 1, 1987, by judges and other officials who set child support. And on the issue of effective collection of child support, the 1984 amendments required the states to adopt automatic income withholding for child support to take effect after one month of nonpayment.

The public child-support system

Public support is a significant feature of the child-support system. Public transfers in the United States to poor families with children eligible for child support substantially exceed private child support transfers to all U.S. children. Whereas about $7 billion in private child support was paid in 1983, AFDC expenditures on families eligible for child support were equal in 1985 to about $8 billion. If the costs for Medicaid and food stamps are included, public transfers equaled nearly $21 billion, or three times private child-support transfers.[2] In general, the public system substitutes for the private system where the latter has broken down. About half of all children living in female-headed households are on welfare, and only 10 percent of these receive any financial support from their fathers.

The AFDC program was established in 1935 for quite different purposes from those it now serves. It was intended to provide support for the families of deceased fathers in a society in which it was considered undesirable for mothers with children to work. Today the program is primarily for children who have a living absent parent legally liable for their support and a custodial parent who increasingly is expected to work.

As structured, the current public system of child support encourages welfare dependency. It imposes a high tax on the earnings of welfare mothers, which discourages work, and it offers nothing outside of welfare to supplement the incomes of poor single mothers who have a low earnings capacity. Like any welfare program, AFDC is designed to aid only the poor, and therefore benefits are reduced when earnings increase. After four months on a job, a woman on AFDC faces a benefit reduction of a dollar for every dollar of net earnings. That is equivalent to a 100-percent tax on earnings. It is not surprising that the majority of mothers on welfare do not work during the months they receive benefits.

Welfare mothers have a very low earnings capacity, and even if they were fully employed, one-half could earn no more than the amount of their annual welfare grant. Another quarter could earn only up to $1,000 more (Sawhill 1976). This suggests that it is unreasonable to expect these women to be totally self-supporting and that some form of public assistance is necessary to provide an adequate standard of living for their families. The only way to alleviate their poverty without creating total dependency is to supplement rather than replace the earnings of poor custodial mothers. Some of this money can come from improved collections of private child support; the rest must come from public transfers.

We have already described a number of federal reforms designed to strengthen the enforcement of private child-support obligations. Increased child-support payments from parents of children on AFDC will generate savings in AFDC expenditures. These savings can be used to reduce taxes or to increase the economic well-being of children eligible for child support, or some combination of both. In view of the fact that children potentially eligible for child support and the mothers who care for most of them are among our poorest citizens, using these funds to improve the economic well-being of these families is at the very least the compassionate thing to do. It is also wise. One-half of our next generation will be eligible for some child support before reaching adulthood. Investing in them is therefore investing in our future. Furthermore, sharing some of the increased revenues with these families will encourage the mothers to cooperate in establishing the paternity of noncustodial fathers—one of the weakest links in the current system. Congress has already approved two alternative methods of sharing some of the AFDC savings with families eligible for child support. All states are now required to ignore the first $50 per month of child support (a $50 set-aside) in calculating the amount of the AFDC benefit. One state, Wisconsin, is permitted to use the federal share of AFDC savings to help fund an assured child-support benefit. The savings in Wisconsin will be used to take women outside the welfare system. Which method is preferable: sharing the gains inside or outside of welfare? To prepare for an answer, the next section first describes the Wisconsin program.

The Child Support Assurance System

The Child Support Assurance System (CSAS) being developed in Wisconsin proposes changes in both the private and the public components of the present child-support system.

Under CSAS, all parents living apart from their children would be obligated to share income with their children. The sharing rate would be specified in the law and would depend only upon the number of children owed support. The obligation would be collected through payroll withholding, as in the case of social security and income taxes. Children with a living noncustodial parent would be entitled to benefits equal to either the child support paid by the noncustodial parent or a socially assured minimum benefit, whichever was higher. Should the noncustodial parent pay less than the minimum, the custodial parent would be subject to a small surtax up to the amount of the subsidy. Any remaining difference would be financed out of general revenues. To summarize, the reform provides the following:

1. The use of a standardized income sharing rate, based on a percentage of the income of the noncustodial parent;
2. The use of a system of automatic income withholding to collect the amounts of child support awarded;
3. The establishment of an assured child-support benefit, accompanied by a custodial parent surtax.

The contents of and rationale for each of these features are described in the next three subsections, which will be followed by a brief discussion of the objections that have been raised to CSAS.

The percentage standard

The term "percentage standard" is used to describe a set formula that determines the amount of the child-support obligation by taking a percentage of the gross income of the noncustodial parent, based upon the number of children for whom that parent is responsible. The 1984 federal amendment requires states to establish guidelines for setting child-support amounts. The Wisconsin reform, on the other hand, uses a legislated percentage of income as the standard.

There are several reasons for basing the amount of the support award on a predetermined percentage of income instead of an individualized judicial determination. To the extent that nonlegislated guidelines would not be binding upon—and therefore could be ignored by—local judges, they would be less effective than legislated standards. It is also the best method of achieving equitable parental financial responsibility (i.e., making child-support awards more uniform), and it is more efficient and economical than the present system. A percentage standard is "horizontally" equitable in that absent parents with the same income and the same number of children would pay the same amount. At the same time, the current regressiveness in child-support obligations would be corrected by using a proportional formula. Further, the formula would reduce one of the principal conflicts between former spouses by eliminating the possibility of disputes over the size of the child-support payments. A final justification for the transfer of jurisdiction from the judiciary to the legislative branch is simple: taxpayers, who now provide for the large number of children whose absent parents do not pay sufficient support, have a large stake in the determination of how much child support noncustodial parents should pay.

The percentage standard, which has been published for use by courts in Wisconsin as part of the child-support reform, was developed by the state's Department of Health and Social Services. It was based roughly on studies of the cost of raising children in terms of the percentage of parental income devoted to that purpose.[3] The standard set 17 percent of gross income for one child, 25 percent for two, 29 percent for three, 31 percent for four, and 34 percent for five or more children.

The standard is increasingly used to establish the initial child-support order; but as yet it is infrequently used as a way of automatically adjusting the order as the noncustodial parent's income changes. County clerks of courts currently have no way of monitoring income changes. This problem should disappear when immediate income withholding is implemented, when employers are required to report earnings along with withheld child support, and when the computer capabilities of the child-support system are updated.

Beginning July 1, 1987, a court is required to use the percentage standard unless it finds, by clear and convincing evidence, that application of the percentage would be unfair to the child or one of the parents. The court must state, in writing or on the record, the reason for that finding and for setting another amount based upon a list of factors specified in the statute. These factors include such items as extraordinary travel expenses for visitation, the need of both parties for self-support at a subsistence level, and the presence of other legal dependents of either parent (Wis. Stat. 767.25 (lj) and (lm) effective July 1, 1987; 1985 Wisconsin Act 29).

Automatic income withholding

Automatic income withholding refers to a system of collecting child support by having the employer of the noncustodial parent—or the state, if, for example, the noncustodial parent's income source is unemployment compensation—withhold the amount of that order from the parent's pay.

Withholding for income and payroll taxes attests to the effectiveness of withholding in general. This type of collection has also been used rather extensively in response to default on the part of the supporting parent. As noted, the 1984 federal Child Support Amendments require that all states provide for income withholding when the paying parent is one month in arrears in support payments (42 U.S.C.A. 666[b] [1986 West supp.]). What distinguishes the Wisconsin proposal is that it provides for withholding from income effective automatically on entry of the support order. By not requiring default in payment as a basis for triggering the income withholding, the Wisconsin proposal not only assures more stable support for the child but also eliminates stigma for the paying parent. Withholding is no longer an indication of a remiss parent; it is a routine, legally required method of payment.

Automatic income withholding has been extensively piloted in the last two years. As of early 1987 over 40 of 72 Wisconsin counties, including Milwaukee, had begun implementing universal immediate income assignments. Beginning July 1, 1987, all counties in the state will be required to use immediate assignments (Wis. Stat. 767.265(1) effective on effective date of 1987–89 biennial budget act; 1985 Wisconsin Act 29).

The assured child-support benefit and custodial parent surtax

Under CSAS all children will receive the amount that is collected from their noncustodial parent using the percentage standard and automatic income withholding. In addition, eligible children are entitled to receive no less than an assured child-support payment, regardless of the amount paid by the noncustodial parent. This assured level of support is based on the number of eligible children in the custodial unit and is payable to the custodian of the children. Child-support benefits as a whole are not income-tested: all eligible children are entitled to receive benefits, whatever their economic circumstances. However, when the absent parent pays less than the assured benefit, the custodial unit will be subject to a special surtax withheld during the course of the year through payroll withholding or assessed at the end of the year through the state income tax. The effect of the surtax is that well-off custodial parents will have to pay back the state-subsidy portion of the assured benefit.

To be eligible for the Child Support Assurance System, a child must first be a resident of the state of Wisconsin. Second, the child must be one to whom a duty of support is owed.

Under the laws of Wisconsin, therefore, the child must be under the age of 18 (or, if still attending high school or its equivalent, under the age of 19). Third, the child must have a legally liable absent parent. This means that the child must have an absent parent who has been ordered to pay child support. That parent does not have to be a Wisconsin resident. Children with a deceased parent are not included; they are usually eligible for social-security payments provided by the deceased parent's work-related social-security tax. Children of unmarried parents are also not eligible unless paternity has been established. If paternity is not established, they must depend on the income-tested benefits of AFDC.

The argument for a socially assured benefit is fourfold. First, it reduces the risk to children whose noncustodial parents became unemployed or unable to work. In such cases, child-support payments fall only to the socially assured benefit level, not to zero. Second, the assured benefit, when combined with earnings, lifts many single-parent households out of poverty and removes them from welfare. Custodial parents going to work need not face a dollar-for-dollar reduction in their child-support payments, as they do under AFDC. Reduction in their payments is small and occurs only if the absent parent pays less than the assured benefit. Thus custodial parents have the usual incentive for acquiring jobs—the knowledge that by so doing they enhance the well-being of their families. Third, an assured child-support benefit creates an incentive (outside of welfare) for unwed custodial mothers to identify and help locate the fathers of their children. Fourth, benefits are no longer seen as welfare for the poor alone, but as more akin to social insurance to which all children eligible for child support are entitled. Therefore, the Child Support Assurance System, like Survivors Insurance, preserves the concept that the child is supported by the parent.

There are two related arguments for the custodial-parent surtax in the event that the noncustodial parent pays less than the assured benefit. First, in the absence of a custodial-parent charge, a few well-to-do custodial parents may receive a public subsidy. Second, a custodial-parent charge will reduce the cost of the program.

The assured benefit is the only segment of the Child Support Assurance System that has not yet been implemented in Wisconsin or elsewhere. Because the public monies that will fund it are the federal and state appropriations now used for AFDC, it was necessary to obtain permission from the federal government and specific authorization from the state of Wisconsin. In the 1984 Child Support Amendments, Congress expressly provided for the use of AFDC funds from September 30, 1986, to October 1, 1994, for the purposes of the Wisconsin Child Support Initiative (U.S. Pub. L. No. 98–378 Sec. 22 [1984]). In 1985 the Wisconsin legislature authorized expenditure of these funds for the purpose of the Child Support Assurance Program (Wis. Stat. 46.257; 1985 Wisconsin Act 29). The assured benefit is scheduled to be piloted in two counties beginning in mid–1988.

Objections raised to CSAS

Each of the three major provisions of a Child Support Assurance System is controversial.

The percentage-of-income standard has been criticized for not taking account of (1) unusual debts encumbering the obligor; (2) remarriage and start of a new family by the noncustodial parent; and (3) the income or remarriage of the custodial parent. It has also been criticized for being inflexible, for eroding judicial discretion, and for diminishing the ability of the parents to negotiate individual child-support arrangements geared to their unique circumstances. Furthermore, this provision results in administrative rather than legal procedures being used to modify support obligations. That is, under the standard approach, the obligation would adjust automatically as the obligor's income changes. Some argue that all changes in support orders should continue to be based upon a judicial review of relevant factors.

We have already alluded to the advantage of a legislated standard over a judicial one. The reduction in judicial flexibility is in our opinion a trade-off well worth taking. As for the standard's lack of responsiveness to the noncustodial parent's current economic needs, it is really a matter of society's view of parental responsibility. If poor fathers in intact families are expected to share their income with their children, it is hard to defend treating absent fathers differently.

The immediate income-withholding provision has also evoked opposition. Some construe this provision as an unnecessary intrusion of government into a private transaction, a variant of the "big government'' argument. Opponents also view it as penalizing obligors who intend to meet their obligations and as eliminating the personal touch associated with paying child support. And finally it has been argued that employment-related problems will ensue, either because employers object to costs associated with administering the wage assignment or because employees experience embarrassment vis-à-vis their employer.

Regarding whether immediate withholding is necessary, we simply refer to the tax system. Does anyone imagine that income- and payroll-tax collections would be as high if we withheld them only for delinquents? As a matter of fact, empirical evidence indicates that 70 percent of absent fathers become delinquent within 36 months. Uniform automatic withholding just renders the system more efficient.

Some have argued that the enforcement provisions of CSAS will lead to greater conflict over child custody and to ''father flight'' into the underground economy. This argument has some merit, in that the CSAS program promises to redistribute some of the economic responsibility for raising children from the custodial to the noncustodial parent.

Note that this argument applies not only to CSAS, but to all reforms aimed at increasing awards and strengthening collection. Since women have traditionally assumed the custodial-parent role, such a redistribution will favor women over men. In order to protect their economic position, men may be expected to respond in one of two ways. They can reduce their financial obligation either by decreasing their ''legitimate earnings'' (i.e., by disappearing into the underground economy) or by increasing their custodial responsibilities. In the latter case, such action would reduce the control over children that women have enjoyed for the past century. While not all noncustodial fathers will take such drastic action, stricter enforcement of child-support obligations will undoubtedly increase fathers' demands for decision-making rights. Greater economic participation implies greater social and psychological participation. Thus, the redistribution of financial obligations implies a redistribution of parental control as well.

Since the assured child-support level has had the least public exposure, little is known about public reaction to this provision. Several possible objections can be identified. Some object to the concept of publicly guaranteed child support as an unwarranted extension of government responsibility. According to this view, government should reduce, not increase, the number of benefit guarantees. Others are concerned about potential costs, particularly with respect to how large an increase (if any) the public would accept. Finally, many may view the assured benefit as an extension of welfare under a different name. We will address cost concerns in the next section and cover the welfare question in the conclusion of this paper.

The benefits and costs of a child-support assurance system

Objections to CSAS must be weighed against its possible social benefits. In this section we consider several quantifiable criteria in evaluating the reform: its net government cost or savings, its effect on poverty, and its effect on AFDC dependency.

Both the benefits and the costs of a child-support assurance system will depend upon the level of the assured benefit, the income-sharing rates on noncustodial and custodial parents, and the effectiveness of the new collection system. In this section we will first present estimated effects of the reform for the nation at different assumed levels of collection effectiveness. Then, the relative merits of CSAS and the recently legislated child support set-aside in welfare will be examined.

Estimated effects on the national level

Table 3 presents estimates of net savings or costs, and reductions in poverty and AFDC caseloads, for the nation, on the basis of four different assured-benefit levels. The assured benefits for the first child range from $2,000 to $3,500. Assured benefits for the second, third, fourth, fifth, and sixth child are equal to $1,500, $1,000, $500, $500, and $500, respectively. The tax rates for noncustodial parents are 17 percent for one child, 25 percent for two children, 29 percent for three children, 31 percent for four children, 32 percent for five children, and 33 percent for six or more children. Tax rates for custodial parents are equal to one-half those for noncustodial parents. The estimates in the top panel of Table 3 assume 100-percent collection effectiveness.

The most striking finding in Table 3 is that three of the four child-support assurance programs would actually save money, assuming 100-percent collection of the noncustodial parents' child-support obligation. That is, the extra dollars paid out under the new program would be more than offset by increased child-support collections and consequent reductions in welfare expenditures. Even the most generous plan costs

Table 3

Estimated U.S. Costs or Savings, and Effects on Poverty and AFDC Caseloads, of Alternative Child Support Assurance Programs (in 1983 dollars)

Assured benefit for first child	Net savings or costs (billions)	Reduction in poverty gap	Reduction in AFDC caseloads
	100-percent collection effectiveness		
$2,000	$ 2.37	39%	48%
2,500	1.72	43	54
3,000	0.87	48	59
3,500	−0.18	53	64
	80-percent collection effectiveness		
$2,500	$ 0.59	40%	49%
3,000	−0.33	45	56
	70-percent collection effectiveness		
$2,500	$−0.06	38%	48%
3,000	−1.83	43	54

Note: The estimates are derived from the "1979 Current Population Survey–Child Support Supplement" (CPS-CSS). The CPS-CSS is a match file that contains data from both the March annual demographic and income survey and the April 1979 Child Support Supplement. On the basis of the March survey 3,547 women who were eligible to receive child support were identified and interviewed in April. In order to estimate savings or costs and reductions in poverty and AFDC caseloads, it was necessary to impute noncustodial-parent incomes. Estimates of the noncustodial-fathers' income are derived from regressions relating wives' characteristics to husbands' incomes. For a more detailed description of the data and methodology, see Oellerich and Garfinkel 1983.

less than a quarter of a billion dollars.

At the same time, all the programs would reduce the poverty gap—the difference between the income of a poor family and the income that family would need to reach the poverty line. The number of families on welfare would be reduced as well. Reductions in the poverty gap for families eligible for child support are quite large, ranging from a low of 39 percent to a high of 53 percent. Similarly, reductions in welfare caseloads are very large, ranging from 48 to 64 percent.[4] In short, all of the child-support assurance programs would substantially reduce poverty and welfare dependence, and three of the four would actually save money.

No matter how efficient the collection system is, however, less than

100 percent of potential revenue will be collected. Consequently, the second and third panels in Table 3 present estimates of the effects of collecting only 80 percent and 70 percent, respectively, of the noncustodial parents' child-support obligations. If we collected only 80 percent of potential revenue, the $2,500 assured-benefit plan would still save $0.59 billion, whereas the $3,000 assured-benefit plan would cost an additional $0.33 billion. If we collected only 70 percent of potential revenue, both plans would cost more, although the extra cost of the $2,500 plan would be very small. Note also that collecting less than 100 percent of the noncustodial parent's obligation reduces the effectiveness of a child-support assurance program in reducing poverty and welfare dependence. These effects are not so large as the effect on costs, however, because for poor families the assured benefit makes up for most of the loss in private child support.

Comparison with alternative strategies

We noted earlier that recent reform at the federal level has provided for the sharing of the increased child-support collections with custodial families within the welfare system. This "$50 set-aside" rule for computing AFDC benefits is in contrast to the CSAS being piloted in Wisconsin, which calls for the use of savings to take custodial families out of welfare through the assured benefit. The impacts of these two strategies differ in important ways.

Table 4, like Table 3, presents estimates of alternative child-support assurance systems. Unlike Table 3, however, the numbers in Table 4 pertain to Wisconsin rather than to the nation as a whole. This inconsistency is necessary because we have to yet incorporate the $50 child-support set-aside into our national estimates. The estimates of the Child Support Assurance System in Table 4 also include a work-expense subsidy of $1 per hour worked for families with one child and $1.75 for families with two or more children. This subsidy is designed to help single mothers pay for daycare and other work expenses. Because Wisconsin has one of the highest welfare-benefit levels in the country, the work-expense subsidy was added to make the CSAS more competitive with welfare. All of the estimates in Table 4 assume that child-support collections improve substantially but still fall far short of perfection; the improvement would be somewhat equivalent to the 70-percent collection rate in Table 3 (see Garfinkel, Robins, and Wong 1987).

Finally, unlike the national estimates, the estimates for Wisconsin incorporate a labor-supply response on the part of AFDC beneficiaries. This is very important because increased private child-support payments make work more attractive and AFDC less attractive. Unlike AFDC, neither private child support nor the assured benefit is reduced dollar-for-dollar as earnings increase. Private child support is not affected by either the work status or the income of the custodial parent, and the assured benefit is taxed at a low rate—and only to the extent that it subsidizes the payment made by the absent parent. A set-aside for child support within welfare, however, has the opposite effect. By increasing the amount of income that a family can receive on welfare, it adds to the attractiveness of welfare and reduces the attractiveness of work. The labor-supply estimates used in our model are taken from the Seattle-Denver Income Maintenance Experiment and represent rather conservative estimates (Garfinkel, Robins, and Wong 1987).

The first column in Table 4 shows the effect of increased collections in the absence of either an assured benefit or a set-aside within welfare. AFDC savings would equal $62 million. The poverty gap would be reduced by 16 percent and AFDC caseloads would fall by 8 percent. These effects suggest that increased public enforcement of private child-support obligations would reduce poverty and welfare dependence even if nothing else were done.

The next two columns present the effects of increased child-support collections in the presence of the current $50 set-aside and a set-aside of $100 per month ($600 and $1,200 per year). With the $50 and $100 dollar set-aside, the reduction in the poverty gap increases from 16 percent to 24 and 30 percent respectively. Correspondingly, savings decline from $60 million to $33 million and $6 million. Finally, the set-asides within welfare lead to slightly smaller reductions in welfare dependence compared to no set-aside. Instead of an 8-percent decline, the declines are only 7 percent and 5 percent respectively.

The last three columns show the effects of a Child Support Assurance System with assured benefit levels of $2,000, $2,500, and $3,000 for the first child. The assured benefit reduces savings, poverty, and welfare dependence. The most interesting comparison is between the fifth and second columns—an assured benefit of $2,500 compared to the $50 per month set-aside. The assured benefit ties on two outcomes, and dominates substantially on the third! Savings and the poverty-gap reduction are identical, but the reduction in AFDC caseloads is four times greater.

Our estimates should be replicated with national data and the effects of the assured benefit should be distinguished from those of the work-expense subsidy. We are confident that the qualitative picture will be similar to that conveyed by the estimates presented in Table 4. If so, there is a powerful case for the elimination of the $50 child-support set-aside and its replacement by an assured child-support benefit.

Conclusion: welfare *vs.* an assured benefit

Some have asked, "Isn't CSAS just welfare by another name?" The answer is no.

Welfare programs are based on the widely accepted concept that it is a governmental responsibility to aid the poor. Like Survivors Insurance, a child support assurance system is based on the widely accepted concept that to parent a child is to incur a responsibility to support the child. Like Survivors Insurance, CSAS provides more to the poorest beneficiaries than their poor fathers could have provided on their own. But that does not make CSAS a welfare program any more than Survivors Insurance is a welfare program. The architects of our social security system said, "A Democratic society has an immeasurable stake in avoiding the growth of a habit of dependence among its youth." So they urged adoption of a Survivors Insurance system, which required workers to insure themselves in order to reduce future dependence on AFDC and to "sustain the concept that a child is supported through the efforts of the parent. . . ."

Unlike the welfare system, the Child Support Assurance System is not just a program for the poor. Like our social-insurance and public-education systems, it serves children from all income classes. Unlike the welfare system, it supplements rather than replaces earnings. There is no benefit for the custodial parent and the benefits for the children are not eliminated as the earnings of the custodial parent increase. In our study of the change in labor supply among custodial families in Wisconsin, the 28 percent of the AFDC caseload that leaves AFDC under the Child Support Assurance System works an average of 1,126 more hours per year and earns an average of $3,548 more per year than they would in the absence of a CSAS. Their average level of dependence on government, as measured by the ratio of income from government to total income, declines from 69 percent to 28 percent. In the face of these differences it is hard to argue that child-support assurance is simply welfare by another name.

Notes

1. The Committee concluded that family desertion should be treated as a crime. Therefore, it proposed a Uniform Desertion and Nonsupport Act to make desertion and nonsupport extraditable offenses.

The law, which was approved in 1910, was not effective. On the one hand, it was too drastic because it provided no civil remedies, only criminal prosecution; on the other hand, it was inadequate because it provided no interstate enforcement procedures for an increasingly mobile population.

2. Estimates of private child support are taken from U.S. Bureau of the Census, "Child Support and Alimony 1983." Estimates of public child transfers were derived from Garfinkel and McLanahan 1986, Table V–2. Though the estimates are not exactly comparable—private child-support payments are for 1983 and include those to remarried mothers whereas the public transfers are for 1985 and are limited to female heads—the orders of magnitude are right.

3. The percentages selected were lower than the proportions that absent parents would have spent on their children had they lived with them. Judgments on appropriate amounts balanced conflicting objectives of providing well for the children, minimizing public costs, and retaining incentives and a decent standard of living for the noncustodial parent. For an explanation of how they were calculated see Nichols-Casebolt, Garfinkel, and Wong 1985, 33–34.

4. Actually, the welfare caseload reductions are too high because they are based on annual data whereas eligibility is based on monthly income. On the other hand, they are too low because they do not take account of the increases in work that would result from the improved incentives of a child support assurance system.

References

Bumpass, Larry L. 1984. "Children and Marital Disruption: A Replication and an Update," *Demography*, 21 (February): 71–82.

Chambers, David L. 1979. *Making Fathers Pay: The Enforcement of Child Support* (Chicago: University of Chicago Press).

Garfinkel, Irwin, and Sara McLanahan. 1986. *Single Mothers and Their Children: A New American Dilemma* (Washington, D.C.: Urban Institute).

Garfinkel, Irwin, Philip Robins, and Patrick Wong. 1987. "The Wisconsin Child Support Assurance System: Estimated Effects on Participants," IRP Discussion Paper, #833–87.

Garfinkel, Irwin, and Marygold Melli, "Maintenance through the Tax System: The Proposed Wisconsin Child Support Assurance Program," *Australian Journal of Family Law*, January 1987, 152–68.

Krause, Harry O. 1981. *Child Support in America: The Legal Perspective* (Charlottesville, Va.: Michie, 1981).

Nichols-Casebolt, Ann, Irwin Garfinkel, and Patrick Wong 1985. "Reforming Wisconsin's Child Support System," Institute for Research on Poverty Discussion Paper no. 793–85, University of Wisconsin, Madison.

Oellerich, Donald, and Irwin Garfinkel, "Distributional Impacts of Existing and Alternative Child Support Systems," *Policy Studies Journal* 12(1) (September 1983), 119–29.

Sawhill, Isabel. 1976. "Discrimination and Poverty among Women Who Head Families," *Signs*, 2, 201–211.

U.S. Bureau of the Census 1985. "Child Support and Alimony, 1983," Current Population Reports, Series P-23, No. 141.

U.S. Department of Health and Human Services, Office of Child Support Enforcement 1980. *Child Support Enforcement, Fifth Annual Report to the Congress for the Period Ending September 30, 1980*, (Rockville, Md.: National Child Support Enforcement Reference Center).

U.S. Department of Health and Human Services, Office of Child Support Enforcement 1985. *Child Support Enforcement Statistics Fiscal Year 1985*, Vol. II.

Labor Markets and the Feminization of Poverty

Jane Bayes

Two seemingly contradictory trends describe the economic status of women in the United States in the 1980s. The first trend shows that increasing numbers of women, along with their children, have incomes that fall below the poverty line (officially less than $10,989 per year for a family of four in 1987). The total number of people living in poverty has been increasing consistently since at least 1969, and reached a high of 15.3 million in 1983, and women have constituted a larger and larger percentage of all those classified as being in poverty (Sidel 1986, 11). A 1978 study documented the fact that for each year between 1969 and 1978, 100,000 additional women with children fell below the poverty line. In 1983 two of every three poor adults were women. Women headed over half of all poor families (Stallard, Ehrenreich, and Sklar 1983).

The increasing impoverishment of some women exists simultaneously with dramatic changes in the participation of women in the labor force during the last 20 years. In 1948 women constituted only 29 percent of the labor force. By 1985 women's share of the total labor force had increased to 45 percent. The labor-force–participation rate for women rose from 33 to 55 percent during this period while the participation rate for men declined from 87 percent in 1948 to 77 percent in 1985. The women-to-men ratio of money income almost doubled from 1959 to 1983, growing from 0.22 in 1959 to 0.40 in 1983 for persons in the labor force aged 25 to 64 (Fuchs 1986, 460).

Although women remain predominately in sex-segregated occupations and earn only two-thirds of what men earn, increasing numbers of women have been breaking into previously all-male professions such as law (20 percent in 1987 vs. only 5 percent in 1970), medicine (18 percent in 1987 vs. only 10 percent in 1970), and computer science (28 percent in 1987 vs. only 14 percent in 1970). Women have been slower at moving into other male-dominated occupations including fire fighters (1 percent women), construction workers (2 percent women), mechanics (3 percent women), and police officers (6 percent women). Overall, the sex segregation of occupations seems to be declining (Bianchi and Rytina, 1986) as more women move into managerial, professional, and technical occupations. However, women also continue to move into occupations that are over 95-percent female such as receptionists, typists, childcare workers, nurses, and dental assistants. In spite of the decline in the sex segregation of occupations, the expected increase in the ratio of median annual earnings for full-time female workers compared to those of full-time male workers has remained remarkably stable. During the late 1950s, this ratio waivered between 0.61 to 0.64. In 1960 it was 0.61; in 1970 it was 0.59; in 1980 it was 0.60; and in 1984 it was 0.64 (Bloom 1986, 27).

How is this seemingly contradictory set of trends to be explained? In what ways do the patterns of women's participation in the labor force and the level of women's wages contribute to the poverty of women in the United States? Finally, how are we to assess the wage and employment policy responses that attempt to address the interrelationship between economic and equity issues for women?

Some of the factors responsible for the relatively low wages of women in comparison to men are the same as the factors that have caused women to compose an increasing proportion of those who are living in poverty. For example, the difference in the "human capital" in terms of education and labor-market experience that men as opposed to women bring to the labor market has a causal impact on both issues. Major changes in the structure of the economy have also had an impact on both phenomena. Other causes of one of these trends, however, have not had a particular impact on the other trend. For example, the high divorce rate has had a role in pushing women with no previous labor market-experience into poverty, but it has little direct relationship to the female-to-male wage ratio. The unemployment rate is another factor that increases the poverty levels of both men and women, but has little direct impact on the wage gap. In 1980 the unemployment rate was 6.2 percent. By 1983 it had risen to 10.8 percent. It fell to around 7 percent in 1987.

Of particular importance in pushing women into poverty have been the severe cutbacks in low-income programs by the Reagan Administration beginning in 1982. Programs like Aid to Families with Dependent Children, the school lunch program, the food stamp program, housing subsidies, employment and training programs, and child welfare programs were reduced by 40 percent between 1981 and 1982. In 1983 they were cut 19 percent more (Stallard, Ehrenreich, and Sklar 1983). Between 1982 and 1986, twenty national studies on hunger were made by groups such as the U.S. Conference of Mayors, the National Council of Churches, the U.S. Department of Agriculture, and the Physician Task Force on Hunger in America based at the Harvard School of Public Health. All found that the problem of hunger, which had been virtually eliminated by governmental programs in the 1960s and 1970s, has once again become a serious national problem in the 1980s. Hunger is a problem that brings with it a host of consequences especially for the elderly, for children, for pregnant women, and for unborn children. Increased rates of infant mortality, impaired growth in children, learning disabilities in children, and even brain damage in children are some of the consequences of nutritional deficiency (Brown 1987). Caring for these nutritionally damaged children places still another burden on low income women that can easily push them and their children into poverty and keep them there. This is not an uncommon situation. One study found that slightly over 25 percent of all Americans had received some form of welfare during the period between 1969 and 1978. Approximately 12 percent received help for less than two years, 8.5 percent received some form of welfare for 3 to 7 of the 10 years, while only 4.4 percent received welfare payments for more than 8 of the 10 years. In short, a quarter of the population of the United States required some help from the safety net provided by the government for low-income families during the 1960s and 1970s. For most the need was temporary, to help surmount some catastrophic problem such as a death, a divorce, unemployment, or a major sickness (Duncan 1983). The dismantling of the safety-net programs for low-income families during the 1980s has meant that many who might have been able to keep their incomes above the poverty line with the help of these programs have become poor. Furthermore, many of those who might have been in poverty only temporarily if low-income programs had continued to operate, find themselves unable to escape poverty level status for much longer periods in the 1980s.

In much of the literature concerning women and poverty, the sex segregation of occupations is named as a contributing factor to the poverty of women. Occupational sex segregation of the labor force has remained at a depressingly high and constant level for over 50 years, and occupations dominated by women consistently pay less than occupations dominated by men. The relationship of occupational sex segregation and poverty occurs because occupational sex segregation limits the employment opportunities open to women (even those who are well educated and highly skilled such as nurses) to low-paying, low status jobs, thereby keeping large numbers of full-time working women near the poverty line and extremely vulnerable to any untoward development such as a recession, a death, a divorce, sickness, childcare problems, or any other hardship. More complicated is the relationship between occupational sex segregation and the female-to-male wage ratio. Recent studies suggest that more variation in pay may exist between the sexes within occupations that crosscut type and size of establishment and/or industry than may exist between the sexes within any one establishment or even within one industry (Beck *et al.* 1987; Hodson and England 1986; Bayes 1986). Large establishments and core industries pay higher wages to all occupations. In this situation, conclusions drawn from the aggregation of occupational wage data across establishments and industries may be misleading (Bayes 1986, 1987).

In an attempt to address and discuss some of these questions, this paper will consider first some of the major changes in the structure of the economy and in the labor force during the last 20 years. Next the paper will discuss some of the major factors that contribute to the wage gap between men and women and the extent to which these factors are responsible for increasing the proportion of women in poverty. Finally, the paper will describe and evaluate some of the policies and policy proposals that seek to remedy this situation.

Changes in the economy of the United States

Many observers believe that the United States is on the verge of a second industrial revolution that will move the country from an economy based primarily on heavy industry with its smokestacks and heavy equipment to an economy dependent primarily on the innovations of complicated and sophisticated high technology (O'Toole 1981; Bluestone 1982). Others argue that this major change is characterized primarily by the fact that third world wages dramatically undercut the wages of workers in industrialized countries. Between 1975 and 1983,

3.7 million manufacturing jobs left the high-wage countries of the United States, Canada, Great Britain, France, and West Germany and 3.67 million manufacturing jobs were created in Asia. The average wage for a U.S. worker in 1983 was 12.26 an hour. In comparison, the average hourly wage (including benefits and payroll taxes) was $1.29 in Korea, $1.40 in Hong Kong, and $1.45 in Mexico (Mead 1987).

The speed with which the technological change occurs will depend on the strength of the economy as it moves into the future and on the availability of investment capital. Whether economic growth is strong or weak, problems of unemployment and job displacement will persist for many workers in the United States. A weak economy will mean chronic high unemployment while a rapidly changing economy will mean high displacement and unemployment for certain categories of workers. In either case, demand will be high for programs that will provide a safety net for low-income individuals and families. Already the consequences of this shift are in evidence in the labor force of the United States. Many manufacturing industries have moved away from what is becoming known as "the rust bowl" of the midwestern industrial cities to third world countries where labor is cheaper. Meanwhile, the high-technology and service sectors of the economy have been growing.

High technology affects the work force in two ways. First, the use of computers, automation, robots, and electronic communications will make many current jobs obsolete. Just as elevator operators have become practically extinct, jobs such as bank tellers and telephone operators are diminishing in rapid numbers. A Massachusetts Institute of Technology study reported that at one St. Louis bank, automatic teller machines and computer technology permitted 35,000 more transactions to be handled each day with 10 percent fewer tellers (Treadwell and Redburn 1983).

The second way in which the switch to high technology affects the work force is in the demand which it creates for a particular type of worker. The basic heavy manufacturing industries that are leaving the United States in the 1980s required blue-collar skilled and unskilled laborers. Some jobs required heavy lifting, some involved working in unpleasant or dirty surroundings. Most jobs were fairly repetitive and did not require high levels of education. In contrast, high-technology firms require highly educated workers, workers who are self-motivated, and capable of constant and continuous on-the-job education to meet the demands of rapid change in a very competitive industry.

Workers must be flexible and willing to assume whatever job the company assigns them. Given the relatively small pool of people in the general population who are capable of filling high-technology jobs, the inclusion of women practically doubles the (male) labor supply for such occupations. Clearly, the demand for high-technology labor will open opportunities for women in nontraditional occupations.

Recognizing that the supply of labor suitable for high-technology jobs is limited, many large firms such as IBM and Hewlett-Packard, as well as smaller high-tech firms like Materials Research Corporation in Orangeburg, New York, have instituted a no-layoffs policy. Such a policy not only generates high morale, it contributes to a firm's ability to maintain a stable, highly trained labor force and reduces some of the high costs associated with the continual recruitment and training of high-tech employees.

In contrast, the blue-collar workers who have been the backbone of the industrial might of the United States are finding their lives becoming increasingly precarious. In 1953 blue-collar employment in the steel industry reached its zenith at 620,000. Foreign competition and technological innovations reduced the employment figures by over half to 290,500 in 1982. In the automobile industry, the number of blue-collar jobs decreased by 30 percent between 1978 and 1982. These "displaced" blue-collar workers often are unable to find new jobs that pay as well as the jobs they left. Many of them do not have the skills that are needed to fill the skilled jobs that are available for industrial machinery repairmen, computer operators, mechanics, and licensed practical nurses. Furthermore, many of these "displaced" workers do not have the ability to acquire these new skills. Others are unwilling to move to new locations where new jobs exist.

Many have argued that the decline in family income for these workers, coupled with inflation, has been an important factor encouraging women to enter the labor force to supplement the sagging incomes of their families. While high-technology firms are prospering and manufacturing industries are declining, white-collar occupations such as managers, administrators, teachers, professional and technical workers, clerical and sales personnel, and people in the retail trades are growing. In 1950 these white-collar jobs constituted 36 percent of the labor force; in 1981 they constituted 52 percent of all jobs. Labor economists project that in the 1980s, the largest growth in positions available will be in the low-status, low-paying service sector. The U.S. Bureau of Labor Statistics estimates that 37 occupations, mostly in the low-paying service sector, will account for 50 percent of all new jobs in the 1980s (Treadwell and Redburn 1983). The occupations of secretary, nurse's aide, janitor, sales clerk, cashier, truck driver, fast-food worker, office clerk, and waiting tables are all projected to have large numbers of positions available in the 1980s. It is this sector of the economy that is most open to women without education and labor-market experience. However, it would probably require two incomes from service-sector occupations such as these for a family to maintain itself much above the poverty level.

The overall consequences of the above changes in the economy and in the work force suggest that the future of the middle class in the United States is in jeopardy. Income inequalities are increasing as wealth concentrates in the hands of a few, and increasing numbers of people become poor. The Center on Budget and Policy Priorities, a Washington-based research and advocacy group, reported in 1985 that in the previous year the poorest 40 percent of families in the nation received only 15.7 percent of the national income, while the top 40 percent received 67.3 percent of the national income; the share for the middle 20 percent decreased to 17 percent (Ehrenreich 1987). Furthermore, the median income for the families in the poorest 40 percent of the population dropped by $470 between 1980 and 1984, while the median income for the families in the richest 40 percent rose by $1800 between 1980 and 1984. (Sidel 1986, 11). Put another way, the average earnings for nonsupervisory personnel reached a high in 1973: $201 per week; by 1986 these earnings had fallen 15 percent to $171 (using constant 1977 dollars) (Mead 1986).

What these trends have meant for women is that, aside from the fact of the sex segregation of occupations and employment problems connected with childbearing and childcare, the number of middle- and high-income jobs available in the economy is decreasing. A limited number of women who have the intellectual and organizational capacities and skills that are in demand in the middle- and high-paying white-collar occupations will be able to compete with men for these jobs if they can offset or avoid the career disruption that childbearing and childcare usually bring. However, most women (and most men) will be drawn into the labor force primarily in low-status, low-paying service jobs. To the extent that the additional burdens of childcare, housekeeping, and care for the elderly fall on the shoulders of working women, their tendency to fall into poverty is higher than that of a man with the same level of market skills.

The wage gap, its causes, and comparable worth

The statistic that women earn approximately 0.64 of what men earn, and the fact that this relationship has remained relatively constant over 50 years, has become an issue for women in the 1980s. Finding issues that will unite rather than divide women has been a priority for organizers in the women's movement, and few issues have as much unifying appeal as economic-equity issues. The fight over ratification of the equal rights amendment did not unify women. The abortion issue has been divisive. Childcare has limits as an issue, since most women need childcare assistance for only a few years of their lives, and many women believe that early childcare by someone other than the mother is undesirable. Even economic-equity issues can be divisive if they are seen to challenge existing protective legislation for women. Women who believe that women should be treated in the same way as men are opposed by other women who believe, for example, that the law should not force a woman to choose between having a child and losing her job (California Federal Savings and Loan Assn. *v*. Guerra, 1986). The Equal Pay Act of 1963 was not opposed by any women's group, although some groups wanted it to provide "equal pay for comparable work" rather than just "equal pay for equal work" regardless of sex (McGlen and O'Connor 1983, 170).

While the Equal Pay Act of 1963 has not made any substantial difference in the wage gap between men and women, many activists have identified the comparable-worth issue as an extension of the economic-equity issue, one that is particularly valuable because of its unifying effects for the women's movement. As a policy, comparable worth attempts to rectify the undervaluation of primarily female sex-segregated occupations. Advocates of a comparable-worth policy argue that predominantly female occupations do not require less education or cognitive skill than male occupations (Treiman and Terrell 1975; England and McLaughlin 1979; England *et al.* 1982). While women exhibit lower levels of education and experience than men, due to their relatively recent entry into the paid labor force, women's reduced level of "human capital" can explain only about one-half of the sex gap in earnings (Corcoran 1979; Mincer and Polachek 1974, 1978; Mincer and Ofek 1982; Polachek 1975). The remainder of the difference between men's and women's wages generally is attributed to the sex segregation of occupations and the observed fact that, with all other factors held constant, *both* men and women earn more in occupations that have a higher percentage of males.

In the implementation of a comparable-worth policy, female-dominated jobs are compared with jobs dominated by males on the basis of certain criteria. Usually, benchmark jobs are chosen and assigned points on the basis of educational, training, and skill requirements, working conditions, and responsibility. Jobs having equal or similar numbers of points are assumed to be of comparable worth. Comparable-worth policies seek to mandate equal pay for jobs of comparable worth. Normally, this means raising the wages of female-dominated occupations. Lowering wages for male occupations is politically difficult, as it attracts little support from needed male allies.

The public sector tends to be the arena where comparable-worth policies have had an impact. In large part, this is due to the public availability of wage data for public employees and the fact that the wages of public employees are the public's business (private firms generally will not make personnel and salary data available). Also important is the fact that 25 percent of the female labor force works in the public sector. Not surprisingly, the union that seeks to organize public employees, the American Federation of State, County, and Municipal Employees (AFSCME), has been one of the most active organizations advocating comparable worth in city and state legislatures, in collective bargaining, and in the courts.

At present, the comparable-worth movement is in its beginning stages. By 1983 state legislators had introduced comparable worth legislation in 13 states, and two years later the number had increased to include another 25 states. Most of these actions, initiated and supported by women's groups within the respective states, called for task forces or commissions to study the implementation of a comparable-worth policy. Some states, such as Minnesota, Washington, Iowa, Connecticut, Massachusetts, New York, and Ohio, and some local governments such as the cities of Los Angeles and San Jose, have implemented such policies with varying degrees of success (Chi 1986; Kelly and Bayes 1986). Minnesota is the only state that has mandated comparable-worth pay equity for all employees of local governments.

Comparative studies of the women-to-men wage ratio in the 50 states have shown that, contrary to the expectations of some, the sex/wage gap is the greatest in the more progressive states that pay higher wages to their state employees. In states with relatively low wages for all employees, the wage gap is much smaller (Vertz 1987). For example, preliminary studies have shown that New Jersey and Michigan had sex/wage gaps of 28 percent and 21 percent respectively. In 1982 Minnesota had a wage gap of 20 percent, which was reduced to less than 10 percent after two years of comparable-worth implementation. Indiana, Iowa, and Kentucky had wage gaps ranging from 15 to 17 percent. In contrast, North Carolina had only a 5–6 percent wage gap (Chi 1986; Vertz 1987). Figures from the U.S. Census Bureau indicate that when state and local governments are compared with other entities with regard to the average wages of women as a percentage of average male wages, the average female wage in state and local governments in 1980 was 72 percent of the average male wage. In the federal government, women's average wage was 63 percent of the average male wage. In the private sector, females earned 56 percent of what males earned. For all sectors in 1980, the average female wage was 59 percent of the average male wage (Chi 1986, 810).

Altogether, the comparable-worth issue has been and continues to be extremely important strategically as a unifying issue for the women's movement. In addition to being an extension of the pay-equity movement, which appeals to large numbers of women, comparable worth is also an issue that lends itself readily to action on the state and local levels. This has been particularly important in the 1980s, as the Reagan Administration has been totally unsympathetic to women's issues and the movement has had to focus its energies elsewhere. The strategic importance of comparable worth as an organizing issue is somewhat different from the impact of comparable-worth policies on the sex/wage gap, on the operation of labor markets, and on the issue of poverty, however. To explore this question, it is helpful to review what is known about the various factors that contribute to the fact that women earn only about 0.64 of what men earn.

Factors that contribute to the sex/wage differential

Human capital factors, work history, and motherhood

A number of economists have argued that the differences between the wages of men and women are due to sex differences in education, training, work experience, work history, health, and labor-force attachment. Women do not invest in developing their own human capital to maximize their potential earnings in the ways that men do. Studies assessing the relative contribution of these various factors have found that these "human capital" items account for as much as, but no more than, 50 percent of the earnings gap between men and women. Corcoran and Duncan (1979), for example, found that they could account for 44 percent of the wage differential using such factors. The most important of the factors they measured were years with current employer prior to current position (12%), and years of training on the current job (11%). Other slightly less important factors were proportion of total working years that were full-time (8%), years out of the labor force since completing school (6%), and years of work experience prior to current employer (3%). Surprisingly, years of school completed accounted for only 2 percent of the wage difference, and variables measuring attachment to the workforce (hours of work missed due to illness (0%), hours of work missed due to the illness of others (-1%), and limits placed on job hours or location (2%) accounted for only 3 percent of the total wage differential.

Another recent study that supports the Corcoran and Duncan finding that work-history variables are the most significant single determinant of the women-to-men wage ratio argues that motherhood is the foremost reason for job segregation and for the wage differentials between men and women (Fuchs 1986). The effect of having children on women's occupational choices and on their subsequent earnings occurs in a variety of ways. Most babies (76%) are born to mothers who are under 30 years of age. Insofar as women leave the workforce during and/or after pregnancy, they interrupt their work-force experience at a time that is crucial to labor-market earnings in later years. Even if new mothers remain in the workforce after having their children, their choice of occupation tends to be restricted by their childcare responsibilities. Lower earnings and lower potential earnings become an acceptable trade-off for shorter hours, flexible time schedules, limited travel, and location near the home. Managing the burden of primary responsibility for childcare and associated housework, many women are unable or unwilling to compete with men (who usually do not have primary responsibility for this second workload) for high-paying, high-pressure jobs that demand maximum effort and often long hours of overtime. As evidence for this argument, Fuchs uses regression analysis to show that the hourly earnings of white women who worked at least 1000 hours in 1983 varied in relation to the number of children they had. More specifically, for women between the ages of 30 and 34 who had similar education, those who had no children earned approximately 5 percent more than women who had one child; approximately 18 percent more than women who had two children; approximately 22 percent more than women who had three children; and approximately 27 percent more than women who had four children.

This negative correlation between relative hourly earnings and number of children obtained for similar regressions for 1959, 1969, and 1979. The pattern persists, although not quite as dramatically, for women aged 35 to 39. The female-to-male wage ratio decreases rather dramatically with age. In 1979 white female workers between the ages of 27 and 30 earned 70–74 percent of what white males earned. White female workers who were 35 years old earned approximately 60 percent of what males earned, and those 40 years old earned only about 55 percent of what their male counterparts earned. By 1983 the female-to-male wage ratio had increased by about 5 percentage points for all white workers under 40 years of age. Significantly, the average number of children in the household for each female worker aged 35 had also decreased from about 1.75 in 1979 to 1.50 in 1983 (Fuchs 1986).

All of this evidence suggests that the fertility rate and the age at which women have children is of major importance in determining the wage gap between men and women. Approximately 70 percent of women born between 1935 and 1939 had their first child by age 25. Only 53 percent of the women born between 1950 and 1954 had their first child by age 25 (Westoff 1986). This massive postponement of childbearing inevitably means that larger numbers of women will not have children or will have only one child. In 1985 the average number of children ever born to women aged 35 to 44 was 2.15 for whites and 2.56 for blacks. In 1960 the corresponding averages were 2.42 for whites and 2.85 for blacks (Westoff 1986). If current trends in delayed childbearing and declining fertility continue, the women-to-men wage ratio should rise accordingly. To the extent that these trends do not apply to ethnic subgroups such as blacks and Hispanics, women in these groups will be disadvantaged in the labor market in comparison to white women and in comparison to all males. Hispanic women aged 35 to 44 in 1985 had a mean number of children equaling 2.85, a figure higher than that for blacks of the same age (Westoff 1986).

The sex segregation of occupations and industries

The pervasiveness of occupational sex segregation in the United States has been well documented as has the positive correlation between the percentage of female workers in an occupation and low wage rates for that occupation (Bianchi and Rytina 1986; Bayes 1986). In 1981, 80 percent of all working women worked in only 150 of the 420 occupations listed by the Department of Labor. The National Committee on Pay Equity reported that over 50 percent of all employed women worked in occupations that were at least 75 percent female in composition. In 1980 almost 60 percent of female workers would have had to be in different occupations if women were to be as widely distributed throughout the occupational structure as men are (Bianchi and Rytina 1986). The weekly earnings for the twenty occupations having the highest percentage of female workers in full-time wage and salary work in 1981 range from $79 for household workers to $275 for stenographers. The percentage female for these 20 occupations ranged from 87 percent to 100 percent female. In contrast, the weekly earnings for the twenty occupations having the highest earnings for full-time employed men ranged from $507 for civil engineers to $619 for aerospace and aeronautical engineers. Of these twenty high-paying occupations, only 6 were not male sex segregated (defined as being 70 percent or more male) (Bayes 1986).

The "queue theory" or "overcrowding" is the explanation often given for the existence and persistence of occupational segregation. The queue theory holds that employers rank employees in relation to the perceptions of the employees' productivity and desirability and in relation to the wages the workers demand. The best and highest-paying jobs will go to the most productive and most desirable workers. As employers move down the queue they will fill the less desirable jobs with employees that they perceive to be either less productive or less desirable. Insofar as women are perceived to be less productive because of human-capital factors or less attached to the labor force on account of childbearing or childrearing, women will stay at the bottom of the queue. In many cases, this perception by employers, combined with discrimination according to the employer's taste, will crowd women into certain occupations, depressing the wages for these occupations even further.

The inverse correlation of indices of female occupational segregation with the female-to-male wage ratio, however, is not a simple one. If occupational sex segregation is straightforwardly related to lower pay for women, then a decrease in sex segregation should result in a decrease in the wage gap between men and women. During the decade of the 1970s, this relationship did not materialize. Several studies have documented the decrease in the sex segregation of occupations during the 1970s using different methodologies to arrive at the same conclusion (Bianchi and Rytina 1986; Beller 1984; Bayes 1986). Using an index of dissimilarity that measures the percentage of either male or female workers that would have to change occupations if both were to become equally distributed among occupations, Blau and Hendricks (1979) estimate that the index of dissimilarity declined by three percentage points between 1960 and 1970. Bianchi and Rytina (1986) calculate that this index declined by another 7.4 to 8.5 percentage points between 1970 and 1980. In spite of this change in the distribution of sexes among occupations, the wage gap remained the same, with women earning approximately 0.60 of what men earn.

The complexity of the relationship between occupational sex segregation and the female-to-male wage ratio can be better understood by looking at the segmented or dual structure of the economy (Averitt 1968; Bluestone 1968, 1974; Edwards 1979; Doeringer and Piore 1971; Reich *et al.* 1973). From this perspective, the United States has a dual economy. The two segments exhibit very different characteristics and tend to be defined somewhat by industry. The industrial core, which accounts for about 70 percent of the gross national product, is composed of about 500 to 800 large oligopolistic firms primarily in the extractive, construction, petrochemical, transportation, and communications industries and in portions of the durable-manufacturing, wholesale-trade, and professional industries. These core-sector firms are characterized by large size, high market concentration and control, high profit margins, high concentration of capital, extensive unionization, well-developed internal labor markets, relatively high wages, high job-skill requirements, good benefits for employees, and low employee turnover. The periphery is composed of the thousands of remaining medium-to-small firms in the economy. Firms in this sector compose portions of the nondurable-manufacturing industry, portions of the wholesale- and retail-trade industry, portions of the real-estate, finance, and insurance industries, portions of professional and technical industry, and most of the service industry. Periphery firms generally are smaller, competitive, and not highly capital-intensive. They have low profit margins, fewer internal labor markets, and they pay lower wages and offer few benefits.

Accompanying the dual economy is a dual or segmented labor market with primary, intermediate, and secondary sectors. Occupations in the primary labor market are the most highly paid and the most highly skilled in the economy. Barriers to entry are high. Internal labor markets operate with well-understood job sequences for career advancement. On-the-job training tends to be constant. Examples of occupations in the primary labor market would be executives, top managers, highly skilled engineers, some doctors, some lawyers, technical experts of various sorts. The intermediate labor market would include a variety of white-collar and skilled blue-collar jobs. Barriers to entry are lower than in the primary labor market; pay and skill requirements are less. The secondary labor market is characterized by low barriers to entry, low skill levels, tendencies toward personal and arbitrary supervision, high job turnover, and low pay. Jobs in the secondary labor market would include most unskilled jobs involving unskilled assembly-line or factory work, household work, some clerical jobs, many food-service jobs, cashiers, many retail-sales workers.

Occupations are not confined to one segment of the economy or of the labor market, although some occupations may be concentrated in one sector of the economy and one sector of the labor market. The chief executive of an industry would be classified as being in the primary labor market whether that person worked for a core-economy firm or for a smaller, periphery-sector firm. A secretary working in a core-industry firm probably would be classified as being in an intermediary labor market because of relatively higher pay, good benefits, and relatively low turnover. A secretary with the same skills might well be operating in the secondary labor market if she works for a firm in the periphery economy that pays comparatively low wages, has few benefits, and has high employee turnover. Both core- and periphery-economy firms provide jobs for secondary labor-market workers. However, the exodus of U.S. manufacturing firms from the United States to the Third World indicates that many of the core firms are drastically reducing, if not eliminating, both secondary-market jobs and many intermediate-labor-market jobs that required skilled blue-collar labor.

These changes in the industrial composition of the U.S. economy and consequently in labor demand helps to explain why the wage differential between men and women workers has remained approximately the same in spite of decreasing levels of occupational sex segregation. The explanation comes in the fact that during the decade of the 1970s, while occupational sex segregation was declining, industrial sex segregation was increasing (Bayes 1986). Industries in the core sector were losing blue-collar manufacturing jobs, which were heavily male-sex segregated. Meanwhile, women were moving into the labor force in large numbers and were joining firms primarily in the peripheral economy. In a study using 1975 Current Population Survey data of the Census Bureau, Beck, Horan, and Tolbert (1980) found that both "males and females with moderate schooling and experience in the core sector have greater dollar returns on human capital investments than do their periphery sector counterparts." Females, however, had greater returns in the periphery than they did in the core firms. Beck, Horan and Tolbert found that 77 percent of the women employed in core firms were concentrated in two occupations; clerical (56.4%) and operatives (20.5%). In periphery firms the percentage of females in these two occupations was only 33 percent. The conclusion to be drawn from these findings is that the occupational movement of women out of primarily female sex-segregated occupations is occurring primarily in the lower-paying peripheral sector of the economy and not in the higher-paying core sector. Beck, Hogan, and Tolbert estimate (p. 119) that an equal distribution of males and females in both core and periphery sectors of the economy would generate a reduction of about 9 percent in the wage gap.

In another, more recent study, Hodson and England (1986) used 1970 data from the Bureau of the Census and elsewhere to study the sex/wage differential in 188 industries. After classifying these industries according to core and periphery criteria, Hodson and England developed controls for occupational skill level in each industry, for human capital of the industry's employees, for the percentage of workers in each industry employed year-round, and for median hours worked per week. Finally, they used the sex composition of the industries "to assess how much the industrial placement of men and women affects the sex gap in wages through mechanisms other than crowding or 'comparable worth' wage discrimination." Hodson and England conclude that men and women are differently distributed across industries. Men are located in industries "that are more unionized, have larger companies, have greater foreign dividends, are more capital intensive, and have greater productivity. Women are concentrated in industries which experienced a rapid growth in employment between 1960 and 1970" (p. 22). Another important finding regarding the differences between men and women is that more men work year-round and longer hours than do women. Furthermore, women are more likely to work in industries "that employ a higher percentage of female workers and that have a greater proportion of office jobs" (p. 22). Women tend to work in industries that are not unionized and in industries that have low capital intensity. Both of these factors were responsible for about 15 percent of the wage gap, according to this analysis. The factor of greatest importance to the wage gap, however, was the prevalence of year-round employment and, especially, the average number of hours worked. These two factors accounted for almost 40 percent of the wage differential (p. 28).

On a variety of other variables, Hodson and England found no differences between men and women by industry. For example, very small differences existed between the age and average education of men and women. Men and women did not differ according to the economic concentration, government purchases, or profit rate of the industries in which they were employed. A surprising finding of this study was that the sex composition of an industry did not have any impact on the sex/wage gap. This would suggest that the industries where women are concentrated do not have low pay because of "crowding" or because of comparable worth type discrimination.

Several overall general conclusions concerning the impact of the sex segregation of industries in the U.S. economy follow from the above discussion. While human-capital factors, occupational sex segregation, and occupational skill demands have long been identified as important determinants of the sex/wage gap, industrial structure is an equally important variable to add to the list. An understanding of the segmented industrial structure of the economy and the operation of segmented labor markets within that structure is critical to an understanding of all other information about the sex/wage differential. More specifically, occupational sex segregation seems to be breaking down somewhat in the peripheral sector of the economy; however, in the capital-intensive, highly unionized core sector, women continue to be confined to relatively low-paying, low-status clerical and operative jobs. Among human-capital factors, the most important determinants of the sex/wage gap seem to be those that measure work history. Variables such as the number of hours worked and the opportunity for year-round work help explain the wage differences between men and women. Among women, age at birth of first child, and total number of children are inversely related to weekly earnings. In short, the double burden that motherhood creates for women in the United States means that women work in the paid labor force less continuously and for fewer hours than do men. The inability to compete with men in this area means that women are not able to obtain on-the-job experience that is critical for moving up internal labor-market chains. Second, even when women have the same jobs as men, if they work fewer hours, they will bring home less pay.

Human factors, however, are only part of the picture. The overall structure of the economy sets the conditions and the parameters in which labor markets function. The decline of highly paid, blue-collar manufacturing jobs in the core sector of the economy coincides with a dramatic increase in white-collar occupations and in poorly paid service occupations. This means that many male workers have recently suffered an income loss. To the extent that women shared the incomes of these previously high-paid workers, they too have suffered an income loss. Some women have been moving out of heavily female-dominated occupations and into administrative and managerial jobs as well as some technical and professional occupations in the peripheral sector. Occupational sex segregation is declining slightly, but only in the peripheral sector of the economy, where firms pay lower wages for all occupations than do firms in the core sector of the economy. Meanwhile, the sex segregation of industries has been increasing. Women have shown particular movement into the real estate, finance, and insurance industries operating primarily in the peripheral sector of the economy.

Comparable-worth policies and the comparable-worth movement have been important strategically for the women's movement; however, the impact of these policies has been limited primarily to the public sector. This should not be underestimated, as 25 percent of working women work in the public sector. Progress has been primarily at the state and local levels where the female-to-male wage ratio is already 9 percent higher than it is at the federal level and about 16 percent higher than it is in the private sector.

Labor-market policies and the feminization of poverty

As is clear from the above analysis, a number of factors are responsible for the "feminization of poverty." Very low Third World wages undercut the wages of many manufacturing and production jobs in the United States and have motivated firms to move their production abroad. This has been true for textiles, steel, autos, electronics, and a variety of other manufacturing industries. Technological innovations have further reduced the need for what used to be fairly high-paying jobs. The result has been a major shift in the structure of the U.S. labor force out of manufacturing and into the lower-paying service sector. Most employed women (84%) work in the service sector. Only 16 percent work in the goods-producing sector of the economy.

All of this means that more women are entering the labor force at a time when the number of high-paying jobs for all workers is shrinking. Women increase the pool of workers who have the intellectual and organizational skills for top jobs, thereby providing the nation with a higher level of worker at these levels and making the top jobs more competitive, more demanding, and more time-consuming for both men and women in the peripheral sector of the economy. Firms in the core sector seem to be excluding women from top positions by maintaining occupational sex segregation and by controlling internal labor markets. Because they must accept the double burden of motherhood and employment, many women do not find it possible to compete for these demanding top-level jobs. At the lower skill levels in the labor force, some working women have available to them either clerical or operative jobs in core-economy firms where wages are relatively high and benefits are good. Most women, however, work in the peripheral sector of the economy where demand is high and new jobs are being created. In general, these jobs are with small-to-medium sized firms, firms that are operating in a competitive environment and consequently do not offer the job stability, routinized personnel procedures, or the benefits that larger firms in the core economy can offer. Wages for many of these jobs are not far above the poverty level. Because the nation does not provide a "safety net" for individuals in these jobs in terms of comprehensive health insurance, childcare facilities, and pregnancy leave, working women in this environment are very likely to fall into poverty. Another way of stating this situation is to argue that a great proportion of the jobs in the peripheral sector of the economy do not pay enough to provide for adequate housing and nutrition if the workers who fill these jobs are expected to reproduce and to care for themselves and their young children.

Policy proposal: a Third World minimum wage

A variety of proposals and policies are needed to address the problem of female impoverishment. From the perspective of the United States in a global economy, Mead (1987) argues that the poverty level in the

United States cannot be reduced until some sort of floor is placed under Third World wages. As long as cheaper labor is available elsewhere, U.S. firms will move their production plants out of the United States. As the middle class declines in the United States, markets for consumer goods will also shrink. Workers in the United States will no longer have the money to buy new automobiles, television sets, microwave ovens, and the like. Unless counteracted, this shrinking of consumer demand cannot help but cause the economy to stagnate and ultimately to shrink into recession or depression.

The workers in Third World countries who are filling the new jobs created by the exodus of manufacturing firms from the United States and other industrial countries will have higher incomes and will generate some market demand if their numbers are substantially greater. However, the distribution of wealth from a number of workers in one part of the world who earn over $12 an hour to a similar number of workers in another part of the world who earn less than $1.50 an hour will not generate new consumer markets for the global economy as a whole. Unless some international agreement can be reached to set an international minimum wage (which is extremely unlikely at this point in history), downward pressures on the U.S. labor force will continue. This is context within which U.S. policies must operate. The major dilemma of this age for economic policymakers is that the U.S. economy is inextricably linked to the global political economy, yet political jurisdiction and sovereignty are confined to limited geographical territories. An understanding of the interdependence between the U.S. poverty level and the operation of the global political economy is essential.

Policy proposal: comparable worth

Comparable-worth policies, as described above, assume that men are paid more than women because men have more human capital than women, and because men are not crowded into certain culturally defined, low-paying, sex-segregated occupations. By asserting that female and male sex-segregated occupations having similar skill, responsibility, and educational requirements, and similar working conditions, should have equal wages, the comparable-worth movement is making a quite radical and at the same time a quite conservative argument. Comparable-worth policies are radical in that they challenge the idea that labor is a commodity like any other and that free-market forces of supply and demand should determine wage rates. Advocates note that competitive labor markets do *not* operate in most core-economy firms, where internal labor markets and administrative mechanisms generally set wage and salary levels. Neither do competitive labor markets operate in the public sector. Furthermore, comparable-worth policies, which are an extension of the pay-equity movement, argue that equal pay should go to jobs of comparable worth regardless of marketplace worth. Comparable-worth policies are rather conservative if viewed in relation to the above analysis of the causes of the sex/wage gap. They do not address the causes of occupational sex segregation. If the wages of certain heavily female-dominated occupations were raised, men might be attracted to those occupations; but comparable-worth policies say nothing about how women are to move into predominantly male-dominated occupations.

When it comes to providing long-term, deep structural gains for women in the labor markets of the United States, comparable-worth policies do not seem to be the answer. Differences in pay within occupational categories that crosscut the core and peripheral sectors of the economy are often more significant than differences in pay between men and women in similar but different occupations in firms in the peripheral sector of the economy. Comparable-worth policies address the latter but not the former situation.

Policy proposal: encourage more women to enter capital-intensive, core-economy industries and firms

The exact form of a policy proposal to encourage women to enter different industries is not yet clear. The problem is one of both demand and supply. As the above analysis indicates, the supply of jobs in the core-sector firms is dwindling. Women need to be encouraged through education and socialization to compete for the relatively small number of top jobs that exist. Because most of these jobs operate in internal labor markets, women have to pay much closer attention to the planning of their careers throughout their life cycles. They need to make more investments in their own human capital in terms of education, training, and experience. They also must apply political pressure to open up more job opportunities for women in a variety of occupations within the core-economy industries. It is in these industries that the relatively high-paying jobs exist at all levels.

In order to compete with men in this arena, women need help with the double burden imposed by childbearing and childrearing functions. To make the competition equal, either men in these more desirable jobs must assume an equal role in the reproductive functions of the society, or some provision must be made to provide quality childcare for children and to require equal parenting leaves from work for both sexes. Enormous socialization changes would have to be made for this kind of strategy to work.

Policy proposal: a national family policy

The above analysis of the wage gap clearly identifies the work histories of women as being a major factor in suppressing women's wages. Differences between the sexes in education and age account for very small amounts of the wage differential. Numerous studies using different analytical methods and different data sets identify the time commitments of motherhood as a major contributing factor to the sex/wage gap. Not only would family policies that provided for paid parental leaves, child allowances, and quality childcare help narrow the wage gap, they would also provide a badly needed safety net that could keep many women from falling below the poverty line.

Policy proposal: health insurance, retirement security, and equitable tax treatment for women

In 1981 and in every succeeding year, an Economic Equity bill has been introduced in Congress. The 1985 Economic Equity bill had five major titles: (1) retirement security for women as workers and as divorced or surviving spouses; (2) childcare for low-income working families; (3) sex equity in health insurance; (4) equal employment opportunity and pay equity in the federal government for women; and (5) equitable tax treatment for women. Taken as a package, the Economic Equity Act is hardly a comprehensive piece of legislation. Rather, it is a somewhat motley assortment of bills packaged together as an omnibus bill. In 1985 it was introduced in the House both as an omnibus bill and as separate bills, while in the Senate it was introduced as an omnibus bill with some titles also introduced as separate bills. Each year, some parts of the bill have been passed. As certain provisions become law, they are replaced by new titles that often deal with quite different aspects of the problem. The Economic Equity Act thereby becomes a way of linking a variety of economic and equity issues together to emphasize the interrelationship of these issues as they affect women. The dual introduction is a strategy designed to facilitate the passage of individual parts of the bill while still maintaining an ongoing pressure for legislation to address the many other aspects of the problem. Usually the separate titles are incorporated into other, broader pieces of legislation.

In the Ninety-ninth Congress, six parts of the Economic Equity bill became law. Three others passed one or both houses of Congress. The Economic Equity Act itself was introduced into the House and the Senate in May 1985. In the House, the bill was referred jointly to committees on Education and Labor, Ways and Means, Armed Services, Banking, Finance and Urban Affairs, Energy and Commerce, Post Office and Civil Service, House Administration, and Small Business. In the Senate, the bill was referred to the Finance Committee. To date, the bill as a whole has not been reported out of committee (Gladstone 1987).

Meanwhile, parts of the Economic Equity Act have been enacted into law. These are interesting to review, as they illustrate the kind of activity in this policy area that is occurring and not occurring in Congress. One of the provisions pertains to health insurance, three to tax and pension matters, one to military survivor benefits for former and surviving spouses, one to childcare for low-income students. Another law that was passed relates to the provision of health care for poor pregnant women but was not originally a part of the Economic Equity Act (Gladstone 1987).

"The Consolidated Omnibus Budget Reconciliation Act of 1985" (P.L. 99–272) signed into law on April 7, 1986, included the provision in the Economic Equity Act that required businesses with more than 20 employees that offer group health insurance to continue coverage for up to 3 years to widows, divorced spouses, and their dependents. This act also included a provision that was not in the Economic Equity Act which requires states to provide Medicaid coverage for pregnant and postpartum women in two-parent families that meet AFDC income and resource standards, even if the principal breadwinner is employed. Previously, Medicaid coverage had not been available unless the principal breadwinner was absent (Gladstone 1987).

The "Tax Reform Act of 1986" (P.S. 99–514) signed into law on October 22, 1986, included several provisions from the Economic Equity Act. One provision increased and indexed the earned-income tax credit and made the standard deduction for single heads of household more equitable. A second mandated 100 percent vesting for single-employer pensions after 5 years on the job, or vesting at 20 percent after 3 years, rising to 100 percent after 7 years. A third proposal taken from the Economic Equity Act provides for a reduction in the allowable integration of pension and Social Security payments to enable an employee to retain at least 50 percent of the pension amount due before integration (Gladstone 1987).

The "Reauthorization of the Higher Education Act of 1965" (P.L-99–498) signed into law on October 17, 1986, provides that grants be given to postsecondary institutions to establish on-site childcare for low-income students who are the first in their families to go to college (Gladstone 1987).

The "FY 87 Department of Defense Military Functions and Personnel Levels Authorization" (P.S. 99–661) signed into law on November 14, 1986, improved the access that former spouses and survivors can have to survivor's benefits (Gladstone 1987).

Measures in the Economic Equity Act introduced in the Ninety-ninth Congress that passed one or both houses of Congress but have not become law include a provision to make grants to public housing agencies to contract for lower-income childcare facilities in public housing projects. A second proposal required a study of wage differentials within the federal government. Still a third unsuccessful measure called for the provision of education and training for single AFDC mothers (Gladstone 1987).

A measure that was first introduced in the Ninety-ninth Congress is the "Family and Medical Leave Act." This legislation would establish parental leave benefits for employees. Although the bill made its way through committee and cleared the Rules Committee, Congress adjourned before taking any action (Gladstone 1987).

Overall, the political climate for an economic-equity policy in Congress is an embattled one. The enormous budget deficit and the Reagan Administration's commitment to cutting government spending in all areas except the military have in the 1980s been powerful deterrents to progressive legislation in this area. A common argument advanced to oppose each of the proposals mentioned above is cost. Because of this unwelcoming climate, many women's groups have turned their attention toward state and local arenas. Yet, on the national level, pressure for economic equity for women persists. Women's groups, unions, and politicians press for seemingly small pieces of economic-equity legislation that can be absorbed in other, more comprehensive and politically palatable proposals.

Meanwhile, major questions are not being addressed. The "feminization of poverty" and the resultant growing impoverishment of children is very much like an economic time bomb threatening the future human resources of the nation. Widespread poverty among women and children means widespread hunger, malnutrition, sickness, high infant-mortality rates, and high incidence of learning disabilities among children. How can the United States compete as a high-technology economy when a larger and larger proportion of the nation's brainpower is being crippled at birth or in childhood by poor nutrition? It is vital to the nation's economy (not to mention its political stability) that the safety net of nutritional programs that has been eroded during the 1980s be rebuilt. At a time when the average worker's earning power is declining, a national health-insurance program, quality childcare programs, and parental medical leaves become essential if the ranks of those in poverty are not to grow.

Conclusions

Solving the problem of economic equity for women is not simple or straightforward. The factors contributing to the sex wage/gap are numerous. Some relate to the international economy and the availability of very cheap labor outside of the United States. Some relate to the changing technological character of the U.S. domestic economy and to the duality of its structure. Others relate to the patterns of sex segregation of industries and of occupations in the economy. The lack of comprehensive national policies to provide quality childcare, medical insurance, and parental medical leaves means that women must carry a double burden as long as men do not share equally in the time-consuming duties of parenthood. This places women at a disadvantage in competing for highly desirable jobs, and at the mercy of sickness, divorce, death, unemployment, and lack of adequate childcare arrangements when they are in low-paying jobs. To make the situation equitable, the fathers must share equally in the parenting of their children. Furthermore, a much more effective safety net of nutritional, health, housing, and childcare programs must be made available for the increasing number of workers (and nonworkers) whose incomes are not much above the official poverty level. Affirmative-action programs, comparable-worth programs, consciousness raising, and educational efforts that reach both men and women continue to be extremely important in attacking the discrimination factor which continues to play a role in the sex/wage gap. To improve their economic chances, women need to prepare themselves to participate in the economy and to plan their training and their careers accordingly. Of particular interest for further research and possibly for political activity is the participation of women in relatively high-paying large-scale core industries and firms. The equalization of sexes among occupations does not seem to be happening in these core firms and industries as it is in the peripheral economy.

The comparable-worth movement is extremely important symbolically and ideologically as an extension of the equal-pay movement. However, comparable worth does not address the problem of the sex segregation of occupations or the exclusion of women from top-paying occupations in top-paying industries. Although 25 percent of the female work force is in the public sector and thus likely to benefit from comparable-worth policies once they are implemented, the bulk of the economic activity of the nation continues to reside in the private sector. The comparable worth movement has not yet found a way to make inroads into the private sector where sex discrimination and occupational and industrial sex segregation are the most pronounced.

The problem is enormous in its dimensions. Even if the President and the Congress were willing to make economic equity for women their first priority, it is difficult to see how even a massive governmental program would quickly eliminate the sex/wage gap. Certainly such a program or set of programs could reduce the wage gap considerably. Lacking such a national commitment for change, the advocates for economic-equity policies must work diligently and incrementally in a variety of policy arenas.

References

Averitt, R. (1968). *The Dual Economy: The Dynamics of American Industry Structure*. New York, Norton.

Bayes, J. (1986, May). "Women, Labor Markets, and Comparable Worth." *Policy Studies Review*, 5, 776–799.

Beck, E.M., Horan, P.M., and Tolbert, C.M. II. (1980, December). "Labor Market Discrimination." *Social Problems*, 28, 113–130.

Bianchi, S. M. and Rytina, N. (1986, February). "The Decline in Occupational Sex Segregation During the 1970s: Census and CPS Comparisons." *Demography*, 23, 79–86.

Blau, F. P. and Hendricks, W. E. (1979). "Occupational Segregation by Sex: Trends and Prospects." *Journal of Human Resources*. 14, 197–210.

Bloom, D. E. (1986, September). "Women and Work." *American Demographics*, 8, 25-30.

Bluestone, B. and Harrison, B. (1982). *The Deindustrialization of America: Plant Closings, Community Abandonment, and the Dismantling of Basic Industry*. New York, N.Y. Basic Books.

Brown, J. L. (1987, February). "Hunger in the U.S." *Scientific American*, 256, 37-41.

California Savings and Loan v. Guerra (1986, October). U.S. 85-494.

Chi, K. (1986, May). "Comparable Worth in State Government." *Policy Studies Review*. 5, 800-814.

Corcoran, M. (1979). "Work Experience, Labor Force Withdrawals, and Women's Wages." In C. Lloyd, E. Andrews, and C. Gilroy, eds., *Women in the Labor Market*. N.Y., Columbia University Press.

Doeringer, P.B. & Piore, M.J. (1971). *Internal Labor Markets and Manpower Analysis*. Lexington, Mass., D.C. Heath.

Duncan, G.J. (1984). *Years of Poverty, Years of Plenty: The Changing Economic Fortunes of American Workers and Families*. Ann Arbor, Institute for Social Research, The University of Michigan.

Edwards, R. C. (1979). *Contested Terrain: The Transformation of the Workplace in the Twentieth Century*. New York, N.Y. Basic Books.

Ehrenreich, B. (1987, September 7). "Is the Middle Class Doomed?" *The New York Times Magazine*, pp. 44 and following.

England, P., Chassie, M. and McCormack, L. (1982, January). "Skill Demands and Earnings in Male and Female Occupations." *Sociology and Social Research*, 66, 147-168.

Fuchs, V. R. (1986, April). "Sex Differences in Economic Well-being." *Science*, 232, 459-464.

Gladstone, L. W. (1987, January 12). *The Economic Equity Act Updated*. Washington, D.C. Congressional Research Service.

Hodson, R. and England, P. (1986, Winter). "Industrial Structure and Sex Differences in Earnings." *Industrial Relations*, 25, 16-32.

Kelly, R. M. and Bayes, J. eds. (forthcoming) *Comparable Worth, Pay Equity, and Public Policy*. New York, N.Y. Greenwood.

McGlen, N. and O'Connor, K. (1983). *Women's Rights: the Struggle for Equality in the Nineteenth and Twentieth Centuries*. New York, N.Y. Praeger.

Mead, W. R. (1987, March 1). "Third World Wages Undercut the First World's Way of Life." *Los Angeles Times*., pt. 5, 1.

Mead, W. R. (forthcoming) *Mortal Splendor: The American Empire in Transition*. Boston, Ma., Houghton Mifflin.

Mincer, J. and Ofek. (1982, Winter). "Interrupted Work Careers; Depreciation and Restoration of Human Capital." *Journal of Human Resources*, 17, 3-24.

Mincer, J. and Polachek, S. (1974, March/April). "Family Investments in Human Capital: Earnings of Women." *Journal of Political Economy*, 82, 76-108.

Mincer, J. and Polachek, S. (1978, Winter). "Women's Earnings Reexamined." *Journal of Human Resources*, 13, 119-135.

O'Toole, Peter. (1981). *Making America Work*. New York, N.Y. Continuum.

Reich, M., Gordon, D. M., and Edwards R. C. (1973, May). "A Theory of Labor Market Segmentation." *American Economic Review*. 63, 359-365.

Sidel, R. (1986) *Women and Children Last: The Plight of Poor Women in Affluent America*. New York, N.Y., Viking.

Stallard, D. Ehrenreich, B., and Sklar, H. (1983) *Poverty in the American Dream: Women and Children First*. Boston, Ma., South End Press.

Treiman, D. and Terrell, K. (1975, April). "Sex and the Process of Status attainment: A Comparison of Working Women and Men," *American Sociological Review*. 40, 174–200.

Treadwell, D. and Redburn, T. (1983, April 24). "Workplace: Site of Latest Revolution," *Los Angeles Times*.

Vertz, L.L. (forthcoming). "Pay Inequities and the Political Context of the Comparable Worth Controversy." In R. M. Kelly and J. Bayes, *Comparable Worth, Pay Equity, and Public Policy*. New York, N.Y. Greenwood.

Westoff, C.F. (1986, October). "Fertility in the United States." *Science*, 234, 554–559.

Teenage Parenthood and Poverty

Richard A. Weatherley

The apparent connections between teenage childbearing and poverty make adolescent sexuality a seemingly logical focus for antipoverty strategies. Numerous studies have shown that early childbearing is associated with poor health outcomes for the young mothers and their infants, diminished educational and employment status, marital instability, and increased likelihood of public welfare utilization (Card and Wise 1978; Menken 1980; Moore and Burt 1982; Mott and Marsiglio 1985). One estimate placed the 1985 public welfare costs (i.e., AFDC, Medicaid, and food stamps) attributable to adolescent childbearing at $16.6 billion (Burt 1986).

Both academic and popular accounts have placed teen childbearing "at the very hub of the U.S. poverty cycle" (*Time* 1985, 79). This perception has been heightened by dramatic increases in out-of-wedlock births during the 1960s and 1970s and by the growth of poverty-prone single-parent families. Crossnational comparisons show teen fertility rates in the United States to be much higher than rates in comparably modernized nations as well as many less-developed countries. In 1981 there were 96 pregnancies per 1,000 girls aged 15–19 in the United States. The rates for other developed countries, with comparable levels of adolescent sexual activity, were 45 per 1,000 in England and Wales, 43 in France, 44 in Canada, 35 in Sweden, and 14 in the Netherlands (Jones *et al.* 1985, 55).

Fewer than half of sexually active teenage girls aged 15–19 use any form of contraception. Half of these nonusers become pregnant within two years. According to the latest statistical estimates, 43 percent of all adolescent girls will experience one or more pregnancies before reaching age twenty (Hayes 1987, 51, 74).

Surveys reveal that sexually active teenagers are appallingly ignorant about prevention and the risks of pregnancy. One study found that more than half those girls not using contraception during their last intercourse thought they could not become pregnant. Most often this was because they believed pregnancy could not occur because of time of the month or because they were too young or had intercourse too infrequently (Zelnik and Kanter 1977). Less than half, and as few as 10 percent of adolescent girls could correctly identify when in the menstrual cycle the greatest risk of pregnancy occurs (Presser 1977; Zelnik and Kanter 1980).

These facts would seem to suggest that increased emphasis on sex education and family planning might be an economical and effective way to combat poverty. Unfortunately, it is not so simple. The etiology of poverty and teen childbearing are complex; both defy easy solutions.

Policy discussions of teenage pregnancy have long been characterized by what Frank Furstenberg, Jr. (1976) termed an ''innoculation bias,'' a search for *the* solution. Yet no policy or program is likely by itself to produce a substantial decrease in teen pregnancies and births. Sexual attitudes and behavior are rooted in one's total life circumstances, and are not easily altered. The teenagers at risk are a diverse group in terms of age, race, socioeconomic status, and sexual behavior. A wide range of programs and services is needed for this population.

There is increasing evidence that the relationship between teenage childbearing and poverty is a reciprocal one. Teen parenthood contributes to poverty but, to a large extent, it is also a reflection of poverty and racial separatism. Teenagers who are poor or live in impoverished neighborhoods initiate sexual activity earlier. They are less likely to use effective contraception, and therefore more likely to become pregnant. When pregnant, they are more likely than middle-class teens to carry to term, and they are less likely to marry before the birth of the child. The diminished life chances and poor birth outcomes of many teenage mothers are due not just to their childbearing, but also to their impoverished circumstances and lack of adequate health care. In other words, much of teen childbearing and its adverse consequences is a *reflection* of poverty. Insofar as this is true, it suggests that public policy must address poverty and unemployment if it is to have an impact on teen pregnancy and childbearing among the poor.

This essay examines the causes and consequences of teenage nonmarital childbearing. It first considers the sequence of behaviors that result in out-of-wedlock births. It then examines adolescent fertility in its historical context, and reviews the trends in teen sexual behavior, marriage, and childbearing. The chapter concludes with a discussion of policy alternatives.

Behaviors resulting in adolescent nonmarital childbearing

The National Research Council's Panel on Adolescent Pregnancy and Childbearing recently published a comprehensive analysis of research on adolescent childbearing (Hayes 1987). The panel noted that there are a series of behavioral decision points that may or may not lead to unmarried parenthood. The chain of behaviors includes sexual activity; the nonuse of contraception, or contraceptive failure; pregnancy and the failure to obtain an abortion; failure to marry before the child's birth; and the decision not to relinquish the child for adoption (Chilman, forthcoming; Danziger 1986; Hayes 1987). Each of these points represents a potential area for policy intervention.

Figure 1, taken from the National Research Council study, depicts the behavioral decision points, pregnancy, marriage, and birth outcomes of the cohort of 9.77 million girls aged 15–19 in 1982. About 40 percent initiated intercourse. Of these sexually active girls, only 40 percent used an effective method of contraception. As a result, there were just over one million pregnancies, 897,000 to unmarried women and 180,000 to married women. Nearly 40 percent of the premarital pregnancies were terminated by abortion. An additional 11.6 percent resulted in miscarriages. Of the 445,000 young women who carried their pregnancies to term, 184,000 (41.3%) married before the birth. Only about 12,000 (about 4.6%) of the unmarried women relinquished their babies for adoption. The remaining 249,000 women became single parents (Hayes 1987, 74).

There are several potential points for policy intervention in this chain of events. First, efforts may be made to discourage the initiation of sexual activity. This has been a major emphasis of the Reagan Administration. The 1981 Adolescent Family Life Act (Title XX of the Public Health Services Act) stressed services to avert adolescent sexual relations, thereby earning it the name, "the chastity bill." Voluntary groups including the Urban League and Planned Parenthood as well as more conservative organizations have also advocated or sponsored "say no" campaigns promoting chastity.

Second, some would stress sex education, to encourage the post-

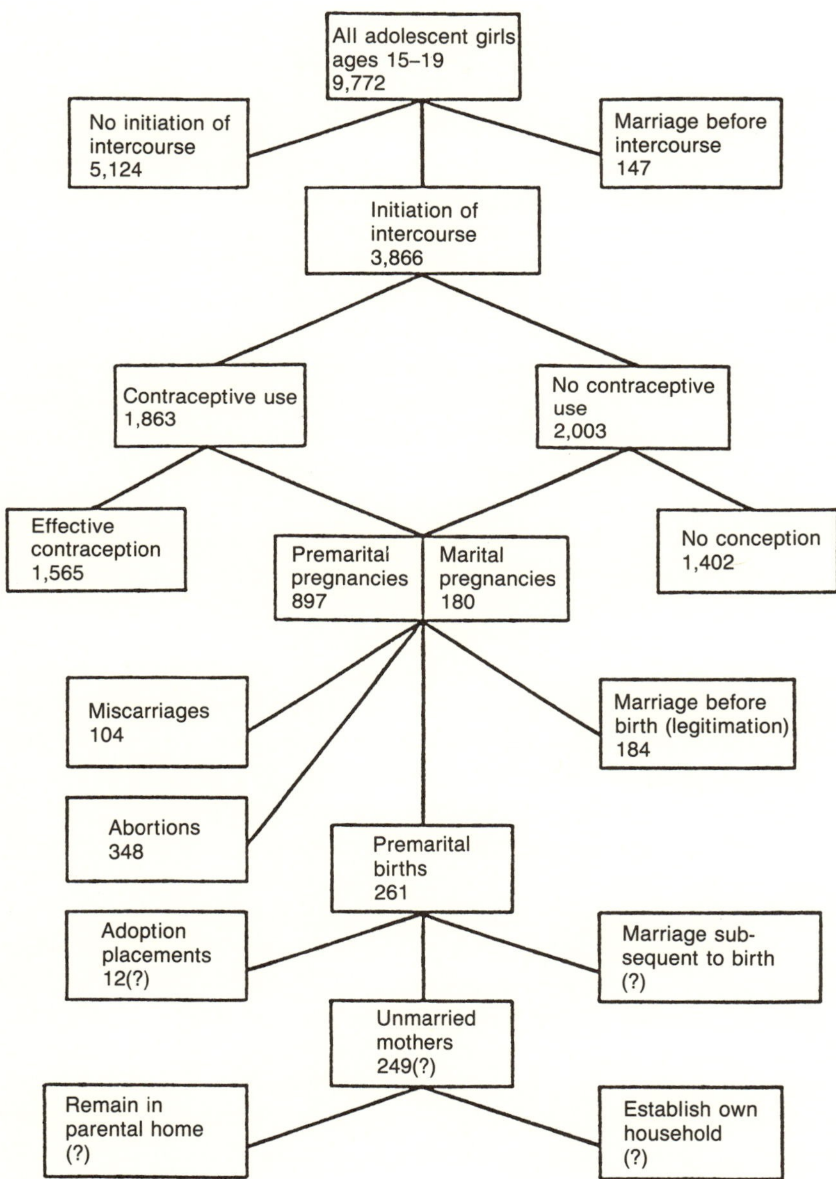

Figure 1 **Sequence of decisions and estimates of population at each step, 1982 (in thousands)**

Source: Cheryl D. Hayes (ed.), *Risking the Future* (Washington, D.C.: National Academy Press, 1987), p. 73. © 1987 by the National Academy of Sciences.

ponement of sexual activity and to provide instruction about birth control, sexual responsibility, and the prevention of sexually transmitted diseases. While the majority of Americans have consistently indicated their approval for providing sex education in the schools, it remains a subject of considerable controversy. Few schools currently offer a comprehensive sex-education curriculum.

Third, efforts may be be undertaken to increase access to and use of contraception. One option is the expansion of the Title X family planning program to fund more clinic services for teenagers. School-based health clinics that provide prescriptions for or dispense contraceptives have attracted much attention. Concern about AIDS has led some to advocate condom promotion and distribution programs for teens, and efforts to bring nonprescription contraceptive advertising to television.

Fourth, access to abortion could be increased. While most would prefer to prevent teen pregnancies, abortion plays a significant, if controversial role in limiting unwanted births to adolescents. While some states continue to provide Medicaid funding for abortions despite the 1977 ban on federal reimbursement, access and costs remain a problem. In addition, a number of states have sought to limit teen abortions through parental consent legislation.

Fifth, some advocate greater promotion of adoption. Title XX, the Adolescent Family Life Act, calls for an emphasis on adoption. Some legislators have introduced bills that would provide financial incentives to encourage teens to relinquish their infants for adoption.

Finally, a wide range of measures could be undertaken to support young single-parent (as well as two-parent) families with a view toward diminishing the adverse effects of early parenthood. These include more accessible health care, nutrition programs for the poor, improved educational and employment opportunities, paid maternity and paternity leaves, daycare, and more adequate levels of public assistance. The United States is unique among western industrialized nations in its lack of family-support services (Kamerman 1984).

This brief look at alternative policy options illustrates the extent to which adolescent pregnancy and childbearing has become politicized. It is an issue that touches upon a number of concerns central to the Reagan Administration's social agenda—the erosion of parental authority, premarital sex, abortion, public assistance for unmarried mothers, and the disappearance of the traditional two-parent family. Many conservatives have sought to limit family planning, sex education and public assistance on grounds—not supported by empirical evidence—

that these services are an inducement to promiscuity and illegitimacy. They advocate sexual abstinence, and more restrictions on access to public assistance, abortion, and family-planning services. Others seek to expand preventive services and access to abortion.

The politicization of teen pregnancy and childbearing has led some to oversimplify the problem. Some advocates have portrayed teen childbearing as responsible for poverty, high infant mortality and morbidity rates, school leaving, unemployment, illegitimacy, and welfare dependency. Were this true, policies to alter adolescent reproductive behavior would have the fortuitous effect of ameliorating a number of social problems at one time.

The exigencies of the political process also encourages policy advocates to portray teen childbearing as a national crisis. This view is reflected in the title of the *Time* cover story cited above, "Teen Pregnancies are Corroding America's Social Fabric" (1985). To capture the attention of policy makers, social issues must be deemed to be of crisis proportions, but also amenable to simple, low-cost, and politically feasible remedies (Kingdon 1984). This helps explain the predominant focus on the behavior of individual teenage girls to the neglect of the structural context of nonmarital adolescent childbearing. A concern about female sexual deviance was a central theme in earlier approaches to adolescent childbearing.

Adolescent childbearing in historical perspective

The current adolescent birthrate is no higher than it was throughout the first half of this century when it ranged between 50 and 60 births per 1,000 females aged 15–19. The adolescent (and adult) birthrate rose sharply during the post–World War II baby boom, peaking at a high of 97 in 1957. It has steadily declined since then to 52 per 1,000 in 1982 (Cutright 1972a; Hayes 1987; Vinovskis 1981).

Teen pregnancy and parenthood first emerged as a national concern in the early 1960s. Before then, premarital pregnancy was considered a private matter (Steiner 1981). Most white teenagers who became pregnant either married before the birth of the child or relinquished their infants for adoption (Cutright 1972a). Black women, aided by extended family networks, generally kept their babies (Stack 1974). Maternity homes, usually operated under religious auspices, offered shelter, concealment, and the possibility of moral rehabilitation for girls who had ''made a mistake'' and were willing to atone for it. It was assumed that the girl would give up her baby for adoption (Rains 1970). The homes provided a key link in the transfer of white infants to middle-class couples seeking to adopt.

The relinquishment for adoption of white babies born out of wedlock was reinforced by social norms, professional authority, and economic circumstances. Historically, attitudes toward illegitimacy, teenage and adult, have been characterized by a condemnation of nonmarital female sexuality (Shur 1984). The stigma of illegitimacy made it most difficult for young white women to consider keeping their babies. Beginning in the 1930s, social work and psychiatry, drawing upon Freudian concepts, attributed unmarried parenthood to neurotic adolescent girls' acting out unresolved childhood conflicts. Some authors attributed this in part to inadequate mothering by domineering women who had rebelled against traditional female roles (Clothier 1943; Young 1954a). These neurotic girls were by definition unfit parents who had to be encouraged, if not coerced, into giving up their babies (Scherz 1947; Young 1947). There were few alternatives available to them. Except for a brief period during World War II, employment and childcare opportunities for young women were limited. Until the late 1950s public assistance was administered so as to deter applications from unmarried mothers (Cutright 1972b; Labarree 1939; Young 1954b).

The 1960s saw a liberalization of attitudes about sexual behavior marked by greater acceptance of premarital sexual activity (Reiss 1980). In addition, the women's and children's rights movements provided sanction for unmarried adolescents to keep their babies, and public assistance became increasingly available to the children of indigent unwed mothers. Cutright (1972b) estimated that only 54 percent of white and 33 percent of black children born out of wedlock were on AFDC in 1961. By 1969 there had been and increase to 87 percent and 60 percent respectively, mostly because of increasing access.

Before 1960 about 95 percent of unmarried adolescent mothers gave up their babies for adoption. By 1982, 93 percent (i.e., 91 percent of whites and 95 percent of blacks) kept their babies (Bachrach 1986), a situation contributing to what has been called the ''baby famine'' (Benet 1976). These developments also heightened concerns about the quality of teen parenting.

In the 1970s, the perception of an ''epidemic'' of teen pregnancies in the face of a declining birth rate was heightened by the increasing *numbers* of teen births, as the baby boom cohort reached childbearing age. Between 1950 and 1970, the number of adolescent girls nearly doubled, from 5.25 million to 10 million (Bolton 1980). Several major changes in adolescent sexual and reproductive behavior also contributed to the perception of a growing problem. While birthrates were declining to prewar levels, adolescent sexual activity was increasing as was reliance on contraception and abortion. The trend toward delaying marriage, however, yielded a rising rate of out-of-wedlock births (Steiner 1981; Vinovskis 1981). Public concerns about teen pregnancy have been responsive to these developments: increasing rates of teen (and especially female) premarital sexual activity, abortion, single parenthood, and a decline in the numbers of white babies available for adoption.

In the 1960s, policy advocates seeking support for interventive programs began conveying a picture of a teen pregnancy crisis. Given public ambivalence about adolescent sexuality, portrayals of teen parenthood as inevitably adverse gained credence. Typical, were characterizations like the following:

> The girl who has an illegitimate child at the age of 16 suddenly has 90 percent of her life script written for her. . . . Her life choices are few, and most of them are bad.
>
> . . . Very young women . . . are biologically too immature for effective childbearing. Prenatal care, no matter how comprehensive, appears to be unable to ensure the same prematurity rates sustained by older women (Alan Guttmacher Institute 1976, 18, 21).

In fact, research has demonstrated that with adequate prenatal health care, adolescents as young as sixteen have as good or better birth outcomes as older mothers (Baldwin and Cain 1980; McAnarney and Thiede 1983). Nor are teen parents any more prone to abusing their children than are older parents (Gelles 1986). Early nonmarital childbearing itself, and many of the adverse consequences associated with it, are related to the poverty and minority-group status of adolescents at risk. The health problems, cognitive deficits, and emotional difficulties identified in children of teenage parents have been found to be related to the social and economic circumstances of their lives (Hayes 1987, 139). While in the aggregate early childbearing does disadvantage adolescent mothers, many older teen mothers (15–19) do well, and even many younger teens manage to overcome the difficulties of early parenthood and achieve productive lives (Chilman, forthcoming; Furstenberg and Brooks-Gunn 1985).

The high rates of adolescent pregnancies, abortions and births in the United States, and the negative consequences associated with them, are indeed cause for concern. However, policies aimed solely at altering adolescent sexual behavior and contraceptive practices may have only limited effect, especially for those in impoverished circumstances. The high incidence of teen childbearing may contribute to poverty, but it is also a consequence of poverty, as may be seen in the data on teen sexual behavior, marriage, and childbearing.

Trends in adolescent sexuality and childbearing

Sexual activity

There was a sharp increase in sexual activity among unmarried adolescent girls during the 1970s. The proportion of girls aged 15–19 who had had intercourse one or more times increased from 28 percent in 1971 to 46 percent in 1979, and then declined to 42 percent in 1982. The net increases between 1971 and 1982 occurred at all ages. While black girls continue to have a higher level of sexual activity than white girls, the gap has narrowed, leaving only a thirteen percent difference in 1982 (Hayes 1987). This increase in sexual activity among unmarried girls brought them closer to adolescent boys' levels of sexual experience. In this way the sexual revolution narrowed the gap between the experience of adolescent boys and girls as it did for older men and women (Ehrenreich, Hess, and Jacobs 1986). Boys initiate sexual activity earlier than girls. However, the gap between male and female sexual experience narrows with age. By age twenty, most (about 83 percent of boys and 73 percent of girls) have become sexually active (Hayes 1987; Zelnik and Kanter 1980).

The changes in sexual behavior that occurred in the 1970s are consistent with earlier trends. Substantial numbers of adolescent boys and girls, married and unmarried, had been sexually active prior to the 1960s and 70s, but it was then more customary to legitimize a premarital pregnancy with marriage (Cutright 1972a). The sexual revolution brought no rampant promiscuity. Most sexually active adolescents engage in intercourse infrequently and with a limited number of partners (Hayes 1987, 42–44).

The age at initiation of intercourse is related to the likelihood of pregnancy during adolescence in two ways. First, the earlier one becomes sexually active, the longer one is at risk of pregnancy. Second, there is an inverse relationship between contraception and age. The younger the individual, the less likely it is that he or she will use any, or one of the more effective contraceptive methods.

A number of related socioeconomic and psychological factors are associated with early nonmarital intercourse. They include poverty, minority-group status, living in a single-parent household, low educational aspiration and achievement, low educational and occupational achievement of parents, residing in a low-income neighborhood, and, for blacks, attending a segregated school (Chilman, forthcoming; Danziger 1986; Hayes,1987; Hogan and Kitagawa 1985; Moore *et al.* 1986; Furstenberg *et al.* 1985).

Contraceptive behavior

The likelihood of pregnancy is significantly related to the use of contraception. About half of women using no contraception, compared to 15 percent of those using a medical method and 25 percent of nonmedical-method users, became pregnant within two years after initiating intercourse (Hayes 1987). Fewer than half of those 19 and under used any method at all at the time of first intercourse, and only about 20 percent used a more reliable prescription method (Zelnik and Shah 1983).

Adolescents' use of contraception increased during the 1970s, reflecting a growing reliance on the condom and withdrawal. The percentage of unmarried sexually active adolescent girls reporting that they had ever used contraception increased from 66 percent in 1976 to 85 percent in 1982 (Hayes 1987, 46). Despite these advances, however, there is much more that could be done to increase the accessibility and use of contraception. Zelnik, Kanter, and Ford (1981) observed: "In terms of their penetration of the market for teenage contraception, the nation's physicians and clinical services can reasonably be regarded as marginal suppliers" (pp. 129–30).

Poverty is associated with a failure to use contraceptives in two ways. First, as noted above, poor and black adolescents initiate sexual activity earlier, and the youngest adolescents are the poorest users of contraception. This appears to be related to their greater ignorance of fertility and contraception, the infrequency and lack of planning for sexual activity, and limited access to contraception.

Second, youngsters in impoverished circumstances may lack incentives to avoid childbearing. Those who perceive little likelihood of improving their situations through education, employment, and/or marriage are not likely to be motivated to defer childbearing (Chilman, forthcoming; Hogan and Kitagawa 1985; Moore *et al.* 1986). Poverty may engender a sense of fatalism, powerlessness, and alienation that is not conducive to avoiding pregnancy. Furthermore, having a baby may bring some rewards. It may raise the mother's status within her family and among peers, and provide a focus to an otherwise bleak life (Furstenberg 1980; Stack 1974).

Family-planning clinic services are of vital importance to teenagers. Adolescents, much more than older women, rely on clinics rather than private physicians. In 1983, 55 percent of teen family planning visits were to clinics as compared to 36 percent of adult visits. Black teenagers are especially dependent on clinic services. About 75 percent of their family-planning visits, compared to about half of white teenagers' visits, were to clinics (Zelnik *et al.* 1984).

Federally funded family-planning services first became available under the Economic Opportunity Act in 1964. Services expanded rapidly with the enactment in 1970 of the Family Planning Services and Population Research Act, Title X of the Public Health Services Act. In 1968 only about 14 percent of women living below the poverty line in need of family-planning services participated in public or private programs (Cutright 1972b). The number of women under 20 served by family-planning clinics increased from 214,000 in 1969 to 1.6 million in 1983 (Dryfoos and Heisler 1978; Torres and Forrest 1985).

Some conservatives have attacked family-planning programs for allegedly encouraging promiscuity. Senator Jesse Helms has charged that Title X "repudiates parental rights, family responsibility, and traditional morality . . . [and] directly and positively increases the incidence of venereal disease, teenage pregnancy and abortion." According to Helms, "one and a half billion dollars given to terrorists could not have inflicted the long-term harm to our society that Title X expenditures has" (Rosoff and Kenney 1984, 114, 115). But, contrary to such assertions, there is no empirical evidence that the availability of family-planning services induces adolescents to become sexually active. There is considerable evidence, however, that access to contraceptive services does enable sexually active adolescents to avoid pregnancy (Hayes 1987).

Several characteristics of family-planning clinics have been found to be associated with use by adolescents: free services, an absence of parental notification requirements, convenient hours and accessible locations, walk-in services, and a warm and caring staff (Moore *et al.*

1986, 58–59). Obstacles to reliance on private physicians include concerns about confidentiality, high fees, and difficulties finding physicians who will accept Medicaid reimbursement (Chamie *et al.* 1982; Orr and Forest 1985).

Abortion

Abortion has been a major factor in limiting the number of births to teenagers during the past fifteen years. From 1972 to 1984 the percentage of teen (ages 15–19) pregnancies terminated by abortion doubled, from 20 to 40 percent. Adolescents account for about a third of all abortions (Hayes 1987).

Teens account for a disproportionate share of the more traumatic second-trimester abortions. They tend to postpone verification of pregnancy and delay seeking an abortion. Utilization of abortion services by teenagers is also constrained by parental-consent requirements, fees, and geographical distance (Alan Guttmacher Institute 1981). The adolescent abortion rate has been found to vary widely, from a low of 1 per 1,000 adolescent girls in Mississippi, to 57 per 1,000 in California, reflecting differences in attitudes and access (Dryfoos and Heisler 1978).

The choice of abortion, like the initiation of sexual activity and use of contraception, is also related to socioeconomic status. Girls from poor families, especially those receiving AFDC, are less likely to have an abortion than girls from families with higher socioeconomic status (Zelnik *et al.* 1981). Those who are doing poorly in school, do not have high educational and employment aspirations, and whose parents have a limited education are less likely to have an abortion than high achievers with educated parents and a strong future orientation (Hayes 1987).

Nonmarital births

The dramatic rise in births to unmarried adolescents over the past several decades has heightened concerns about adolescent childbearing. In 1940 there were 7.4 births per 1,000 unmarried women aged 15–19; by 1984 there were 30.2, a more than fourfold increase (Bolton 1980; Hayes 1987). More than half of all births to adolescents now occur outside of marriage (Hayes 1987). The rate of nonmarital childbearing has been consistently much higher among blacks, but the gap has narrowed significantly in the past 15 years due to an increase among white teenagers and a slight decline in the rate of black nonmarital childbearing. Nonetheless, the proportion of nonmarital births to black adolescent girls (89% in 1984) is still more than twice that for white girls (41.5%) (Hayes 1987).

As startling as these statistics are, the nonmarital birth rates for older women have increased even more. Women aged 15–19 comprise two-thirds of the unmarried female population, but contribute less than half the out-of-wedlock births (Bolton 1980).

It is important to bear in mind that the nonmarital birthrate is a function of both births and marriages. There was a sharp rise in the rate of adolescent marriage immediately after World War II and continuing through the 1950s. Since the 1960s, the teen marriage rate has steadily declined (Bolton 1980). Consequently, more of the births to teen parents have been out of wedlock. In 1960 the average age at first marriage was 20 for women and 23 for men. Sixteen percent of women were married by age 20. By 1983 the average age at marriage had risen to 23 for women and 25 for men; only 7 percent of women were married by age 20 (Hayes 1987). This trend toward later marriages has been even more pronounced among blacks. The percentage of black women who had married by age twenty dropped from 16.2 in 1960 to 1.6. in 1984 (Hayes 1987).

A study conducted in the early 1970s attributed half the differential between black and white out-of-wedlock birth rates to the higher proportion of blacks who were poor. Nonmarital births occur disproportionately among the poorest teenagers for two reasons. First, poor women are more likely to become pregnant, and when pregnant, to carry to term. Second, they are less likely to marry during pregnancy.

Three structural factors are associated with the trend toward delayed marriage: youth unemployment, prolonged high-school and college education, and a skewed sex ratio reflecting a shortage of marriageable males, especially between the ages of 18–35. The impact of unemployment and the declining pool of available males has been most severe for blacks.

The percentage of men who have ever married varies directly with their income at every age and educational level. The employment and income picture for adolescents and young adults has been bleak since the 1960s. This is due to economic stagnation compounded by the entry of the baby-boom cohort and an increasing percentage of women into the labor market. Youth unemployment rates have remained consistently high, especially for black males, even in periods of recovery. The declining purchasing power of entry-level wages has also eroded the economic foundation for marriage and family formation (Bell 1983; Bolton 1980).

Especially in black communities, there is a shortage of marriageable males, leading among other things to debates among black women about "man-sharing." Males between 15 and 35 have high death rates from accidents, murder, and suicide, and a substantial percentage become incapacitated or incarcerated. Violent death and incarceration take an especially high toll among black males, and with the high rate of unemployment, there is a dearth of potential marriage candidates available to black women (Bell 1983; Wilson 1981).

The lingering stigmatization of illegitimacy fosters the presumption that marriage is necessarily more desirable than single parenthood. It should be noted that adolescent marriages tend to be unstable and have a high rate of dissolution. Furthermore, girls who, when pregnant, marry and leave their families of origin have more children more closely spaced than those who remain at home (Furstenberg 1980).

Current policy approaches

In contrast to many industrialized nations, the United States has no explicit national policy with respect to adolescent sexuality, pregnancy and childbearing (Jones *et al.* 1985). These matters are left to state and local jurisdictions to address if they choose. Many adolescents do benefit from national programs such as Title X (family planning), Title XIX (Medicaid), and the Maternal and Child Health block grant that provide funds for family planning and prenatal and perinatal care. However, coverage is limited by funding constraints and variations in implementation from state to state. The proportion of high-risk teenage, minority, and low-income women receiving prenatal care has always been far below that for older, more economically secure white women, and is well below recommended levels. It declined even further between 1980 and 1982 (Hayes 1987).

Despite the absence of a national policy, several approaches have attracted attention from those concerned about teen pregnancy. Three of these approaches are discussed below: comprehensive service programs, school-based clinics, and sex education.

Comprehensive service programs

Beginning in the early 1960s, the U.S. Children's Bureau, and later several national foundations and advocacy groups, pushed the concept of local comprehensive-service programs for adolescent girls who were pregnant or had babies. Drawing upon the model of the neighborhood multiservice center promulgated by the Office of Economic Opportunity, the Bureau urged local communities to establish programs that would offer a variety of services at one site or through referral. Ideally, the comprehensive programs would provide pregnancy testing, sex education, family-planning services, screening and treatment for sexually transmitted diseases, prenatal and perinatal care, nutrition information, and education and vocational services. By the mid–1970s more than a thousand local programs had been initiated under the sponsorship of schools, health providers, and social-service agencies.

A prime factor in the initiation of comprehensive services was the availability of support from a variety of Great Society and other federal grant programs—among them, The Elementary and Secondary Education Act, Headstart, Community Action, Model Cities, Comprehensive Employment and Training Act (CETA), Law Enforcement Assistance Act, and federal revenue sharing. The model became the centerpiece of President Carter's 1978 teen pregnancy initiative, his "alternatives to abortion," enacted as the Adolescent Health Services and Pregnancy Prevention Act, and continued in 1981 under the Adolescent Family Life Act.

More than twenty years' experience with comprehensive service programs has revealed many shortcomings. Lacking a firm funding base, local providers have found it difficult to initiate and sustain programs. Many of the federal grant sources that were used to develop services in the 1960s and 1970s have been curtailed or terminated. The federal Office of Adolescent Family Life Programs (formerly the Office of Adolescent Pregnancy Programs) funded only a few demonstration projects each year in hopes that other communities would launch programs on their own. However, only a few exceptional communities have succeeded in maintaining comprehensive programs.

A basic assumption made by proponents of comprehensive programs was that most of the services already existed, and needed only to be organized more efficiently. This proved to be unrealistic (Weatherley *et al.* 1986). A national survey found that only 4.8 percent (54) of the 1,132 programs nationwide provided a comprehensive array of health, education, and social services; and even among these "comprehensive" programs, more than a third did not offer contraceptive information to the young mothers, and two-thirds offered no infant care or vocational assistance (JRB Associates 1981). The major benefit of comprehensive programs seems to be the support they provide the participants and the assistance they offer in securing access to social and health services (Weatherley and Cartoof, forthcoming).

In addition to the difficulties in implementing the model, a fundamental limitation was its narrow focus on already-pregnant girls and young mothers. Evaluations have shown that while some programs had short-term success in temporarily reducing repeat pregnancies and helping young mothers to remain in school, the long-term results were disappointing. In follow-up studies, program participants had educational outcomes and repeat pregnancy rates comparable to matched groups of nonparticipants (Polit and Kahn 1985; Quint and Riccio 1985).

School-based clinics

The apparent success of the St. Paul, Minnesota clinic and the Self Center in Baltimore, Maryland in lowering birthrates has generated considerable enthusiasm for school-based (or school-linked) clinic programs. By 1985 there were 40 programs in existence and 50 reported to be under development. The clinics provide physical exams for team sports, treatment for minor illnesses and accidents, nutrition and weight-reduction counseling as well as pregnancy testing and family-planning services (Center For Population Options 1986).

By offering a range of health services in a familiar setting, school-based clinics have the advantages of convenience and effective outreach. They serve a high proportion of males, something that family-planning clinics have not succeeded in doing. Among their disadvantages is their failure to serve dropouts, or students during vacation periods. In addition, they face the same kinds of implementation constraints as comprehensive service programs, including the absence of a firm funding base and their vulnerability to local opposition.

Sex education

Opinion polls show consistent and wide public support for sex education, including information about contraception, in public schools

(Kirby and Scales 1981). Sex education is already being carried out extensively. About three-quarters of the public schools provide some form of sex education. However, this typically involves no more than about ten hours per year and is generally offered in the later grades. Only about a fourth of the school districts offering programs have as a goal the reduction of sexual activity or the prevention of pregnancy (Alan Guttmacher Institute 1981; Hayes 1987). Fewer than 10 percent of all students take comprehensive sex-education courses of more than 40 hours (Kirby 1984).

Evaluations of sex-education programs have shown them to be effective in increasing students' knowledge about sexuality, and in some cases their use of effective contraception, especially when the education is linked to birth-control services. The programs had little effect on sexual activity, and their impact on pregnancy rates is unknown (Kirby, Alter, and Scales 1979; Scales 1983).

Other approaches

Researchers and local service providers have tried or advocated a number of other approaches to reduce adolescent fertility. Among them are mentoring programs, assertiveness-training and life-planning programs, and family communications enhancement. None of these approaches, however, has demonstrated a direct impact on pregnancy rates, although assertiveness training has been found to produce more reported use of contraception. However, it has been firmly established that the provision of family-planning and abortion services prevents unwanted pregnancies and births. Prenatal and pediatric care and nutrition services can produce favorable birth outcomes, reduce the incidence of low birth weight, and improve child health (Hayes 1987).

Conclusions

Teen pregnancy and childbearing is firmly rooted in the social and economic conditions of contemporary American society. The numbers of births to adolescents will continue to decline due to declining overall birthrates and decreasing numbers of teenagers reaching childbearing years. Nonetheless, the numbers and rates of nonmarital adolescent childbearing remain unacceptably high. More and improved services are necessary to help teens prevent unwanted pregnancies and have healthy babies, and to provide for the needs of young families.

There is a clear but complex relationship between poverty and teen parenthood. Early childbearing does impose lasting hardships on young mothers and their children, though many are able to overcome these hardships to live productive lives. On the other hand, the evidence suggests that impoverished circumstances provide the conditions that lead to teenage childbearing and many of the adverse consequences associated with it. It is not only poor and minority teens who have babies; however, they are more likely to have children and are at greater risk for the problems associated with early childbearing. This suggests the need to direct special attention to the poor.

Based on what is known about teenage childbearing, there are three complementary measures that should be taken. First, efforts should be directed toward altering adolescents' sexual, contraceptive, and reproductive behavior. Federally funded family-planning services have had an enormous impact in reducing teen pregnancies. However, much more could be done in making such services more widely available to teens, and educating adolescents about sexuality and sexual responsibility. The availability of abortion has made it possible for many teenagers to terminate unwanted pregnancies. While most would agree that pregnancy prevention should be a first priority, access to abortion should be maintained.

Second, better support services for young mothers and their children are needed. Even with improved prevention services, many teens will continue to have children. A few exemplary programs have yielded vastly improved health outcomes by offering high quality prenatal and perinatal care. Such services ought to be more universally available.

Third, and most important, efforts must be made to improve the social and economic conditions associated with early childbearing. This would entail a direct attack on poverty through income redistribution, full-employment policies, and expanded welfare-state services. As the National Research Council observed, "Pregnancy prevention strategies must provide teenagers the necessary support and encouragement to strive for fulfilling, productive adult roles in addition to parenthood" (Hayes 1987, 265). The key to pregnancy prevention would seem to be education, preventive services, and opportunities that will motivate young people to defer childbearing. That would require a reversal of tax, wage, and welfare policies that have contributed to increasing poverty and inequality in recent years.

References

Alan Guttmacher Institute. 1976. "11 Million Teenagers: What Can Be Done About The Epidemic of Adolescent Pregnancies in the United States?" New York.

Alan Guttmacher Institute. 1981. "Teenage Pregnancy: The Problem That Hasn't Gone Away." New York.

Baldwin, W., and Cain, V. 1980. "The Children of Teenage Parents." *Family Planning Perspectives* 12 (1):34–43.

Bell. W. 1983. *Contemporary Social Welfare.* New York: Macmillan Publishing Co.

Bolton, F. G., Jr. 1980. *The Pregnant Adolescent: Problems of Premature Parenthood.* Beverley Hills, CA: Sage Publications.

Burt, M. 1986. "Estimates of Public Costs for Teenage Childbearing." Unpublished paper prepared for the Center for Population Options, Washington, D.C.

Card, J.J. and Wise, L.L. 1978. "Teenage Mothers and Teenage Fathers: The Impact of Early Childbearing on the Parents' Personal and Professional Lives." *Family Planning Perspectives* 10 (4):199–205.

Chilman, C. S. forthcoming. "Never Married, Single Adolescent Parents." In Chilman, C. S., *Families Experiencing Problems Related to Family Structure.* Beverly Hills, CA: Sage Publications.

Chamie, M., Eisman, S. Forrest, J. D., Orr, M. T., and Torres, A. 1982. "Factors Affecting Adolescents' Use of Family Planning Clinics." *Family Planning Perspectives* 14 (May/June).

Clothier, F. 1943. "Psychological Implications of Unmarried Parenthood." *American Journal of Orthopsychiatry* 13 (3).

Cutright, P. 1972a. "The Teenage Sexual Revolution and the Myth of an Abstinent Past." *Family Planning Perspectives* 4 (January).

Cutright, P. 1972b. "Illegitimacy in the United States 1920–1968." In Westoff, C. F. and Parke, R. Jr., (eds.), Commission of Population Growth and The American Future, Research Reports Volume l, *Demographic and Social Aspects of Population Growth.* Washington, D.C.: U.S. Government Printing Office.

Danziger, S. K. 1986. "Breaking the Chains: From Teenage Girls to Welfare Mothers, Or, Can Social Policy Increase Options?" Discussion Paper No. 825–86. Madison, WI: Institute for Research on Poverty.

Dryfoos, J. G., and Heisler, T. 1978. "Contraceptive Services For Adolescents: An Overview." *Family Planning Perspectives* 10 (July/August).

Ehrenreich, B., Hess, E, and Jacobs, G. 1986. *Remaking Love: The Feminization of Sex.* Garden City, N.Y.: Anchor Press/Doubleday.

Furstenberg, F. F. Jr. 1976. *Unplanned Parenthood: The Social Consequences of Teenage Childbearing.* New York: Free Press.

Furstenberg, F. F. Jr. 1980. "The Social Consequences of Teenage Parenthood." In C. Chilman (ed.), *Adolescent Pregnancy and Childbearing: Findings From Research.* NIH Publication No. 81-2077 267–308. Washington, D. C.: U. S. Department of Health and Human Services.

Furstenberg, F. F., Jr., and Brooks-Gunn, J. 1985. "Adolescent Fertility: Causes, Consequences and Remedies." In Aiken, L. and Mechanic, D. (eds.), *Applications of Social Science to Clinical Medicine and Health Policy.* New Brunswick, N. J.: Rutgers University Press.

Furstenberg, F. F., Jr., Morgan, S. P., Moore, K. A., and Peterson, J. 1985. "Exploring Race Differences in the Timing of Intercourse." Unpublished manuscript. University of Pennsylvania.

Gelles, R. J. 1986. "School-Age Parents and Child Abuse." In Lancaster, J. B. and Hamburg, B. A. *School-Age Pregnancy & Parenthood: Biosocial Dimensions.*

New York: Aldine De Gruyter.

Hayes, C., ed. 1987. *Risking the Future: Adolescent Sexuality, Pregnancy, and Childbearing.* Washington, D.C.: National Academy Press.

Hogan, D. P., and Kitagawa, E. M. 1985. "The Impact of Social Status, Family Structure, and Neighborhood on the Fertility of Black Adolescents." *American Journal of Sociology* 90 (4): 825–855.

Jones, E. F., Forest, J. D., Goldman, N., Henshaw, S. K., Lincoln, R., Rosoff, J., Westoff, C. F., and Wulf, D. 1985. "Teenage Pregnancy in Developed Countries: Determinants and Policy Implications." *Family Planning Perspectives* 17 (March/April): 53–63.

JRB Associates, Inc. 1981. "Final Report on National Study of Teenage Pregnancy." Washington, D.C.: Department of Health and Human Services, Office of Adolescent Pregnancy Programs (August 15).

Kamerman, S. B. 1984. "Women, Children and Poverty: Public Policies and Female-headed Families in Industrialized Countries." *Signs: Journal of Women in Culture and Society* 10, 21: 249–71.

Kirby, D., Alter, J., and Scales, P. 1979. "An Analysis of U. S. Sex Education Programs and Evaluation Methods". U.S. DHEW, National Institute of Education, Report No. CDC-2021-79-DK-FR. (July).

Labarree, M. S. 1939. "Unmarried Parenthood Under the Social Security Act." *Proceedings, National Conference on Social Work.*

Levine, M. D. and Adams, G. C. 1985. "Trends in Adolescent Pregnancy and Parenthood." Paper prepared for the Conference on Adolescent Pregnancy: State Policies and Programs.

McAnarney, E. R., and Thiede, H. A. 1983. "Adolescent Pregnancy and Childbearing: What We Learned During the 1970's and What Remains to be Learned." In E. McAnarney (ed.), *Premature Adolescent Pregnancy and Parenthood.* New York: Grune and Stratton.

Menken, J. 1980. "The Health and Demographic Consequences of Adolescent Pregnancy and Childbearing," In C. Chilman (ed.), Adolescent Pregnancy and Childbearing: Findings From Research. Washington, D.C.: U.S. Department of Health and Human Services.

Moore, K. A., and Burt, B. R. 1982. *Private Crisis, Public Costs: Policy Perspectives on Teenage Childbearing.* Washington, D.C.: The Urban Institute.

Moore, K. A., Simms, M. C. and Betsey, C. L. 1986. *Choice and Circumstance: Racial Differences in Adolescent Sexuality and Fertility.* New Brunswick, NJ: Transaction Books.

Mott, F. L., and Marsiglio, W. 1985. "Early Childbearing and Completion of High School." *Family Planning Perspectives* 17 (September/October):234–237.

Orr, M., and Forrest, J. D. 1985. "The Availability of Reproductive Health Services From U.S. Private Physicians." *Family Planning Perspectives* 17 (March/April: 63–69.

Presser, H. B. 1977. "Pregnancy and Misinformation About Pregnancy Risk Among Urban Mothers." *Family Planning Perspectives* 9: 111–115.

Rains, P. M. 1970. "Moral Reinstatement: The Characteristics of Maternity Homes." *The American Behavioral Scientist* 14:219–235.

Reiss, I. 1980. *Family Systems in America.* New York: Holt Reinhart and Winston.

Rossof, J. I., and Kenney, A. M. 1984. "Title X and Its Critics." *Family Planning Perspectives* 16 (May/June).

Scales, P. 1983. "Adolescent Sexuality and Education: Principles, Approaches, and Resources." In C. S. Chilman (ed.), *Adolescent Sexuality in a Changing American Society.* New York: John Wiley & Sons, 207–229.

Scherz, F. H. 1947. "'Taking Sides' in the Unmarried Mother's Conflict." *Social Casework* 32: 57–61.

Schur, E. 1984. *Labeling Women Deviant: Gender Based Stigma as Social Control.* Philadelphia: Temple University Press.

Stack, C. 1974. *All Our Kin: Strategies for Survival in The Black Community.* New York: Harper and Row.

Steiner, G. Y. 1981. *The Futility of Family Policy.* Washington, D. C.: The Brookings Institution.

Time. 1985. "Children Having Children: Teen Pregnancies Are Corroding America's Social Fabric." (December 9).

Torres, A., and Forrest, J. D. 1985. "Family Planning Clinic Services in the United States, 1983." *Family Planning Perspectives* 17 (January/February): 30–35.

Weatherley, R. A., Perlman, S. B., Levine, M. H. and Klerman, L. V. 1986. "Comprehensive Programs for Pregnant Teenagers and Teenage Parents: How Successful Have They Been?" *Family Planning Perspectives* 18 (2) (March/April): 73–78.

Weatherley, R. A., and Cartoof, V. forthcoming. "Helping Single Adolescent Parents." In C. S. Chilman (ed), *Families Experiencing Problems Related To Family Structure.* Beverley Hills, CA: Sage Publications.

Wilson, W. J. 1981. "The Black Community in the 1980's: Questions of Race, Class, and Public Policy." *Annals of the American Academy of Political and Social Sciences*. 454 (March): 26–41.

Young, L. R. 1947. "The Unmarried Mother's Decision About Her Baby." *Journal of Social Casework* 28.

Young, L. R. 1954. *Out of Wedlock*. New York: McGraw-Hill.

Zelnik, M., and Shah, F. K. 1983. "First Intercourse Among Young Americans." *Family Planning Perspectives* 15: 64–72.

Zelnik, M., and Kanter, J. F. 1977. "Sexual and Contraceptive Experience of Young Unmarried Women in the United States, 1976 and 1971." *Family Planning Perspectives* 9: 55–71.

Zelnik, M., and Kanter, J. F. 1980. "Sexual Activity, Contraceptive Use, and Pregnancy Among Metropolitan-Area Teenagers." *Family Planning Perspectives* 12 (5), (September/October).

Zelnik, M., Kanter, J. F., and Ford, K. 1981. *Sex and Pregnancy in Adolescence.* Beverly Hills, CA.: Sage Publications.

Zelnik, M., Koenig, M. A., and Kim, Y. J. 1984. "Source of Prescription Contraceptives and Subsequent Pregnancy Among Women." *Family Planning Perspectives* 16 (January/February): 6–13.

Educational Programs

Indirect Linkages and Unfulfilled Expectations

Margaret D. LeCompte and
Anthony Gary Dworkin

The task of this essay is to detail ways in which education can alleviate poverty. What we shall do is describe the history of direct attempts to use education to alleviate poverty, and apply a rather unconventional analysis to show where these attempts have been effective, where they have not worked, and why. In so doing, we shall try to outline the extent to which education can do anything at all to reduce poverty, and whether or not it can indeed bring people "beyond welfare."

We assume a structural and systems perspective. That is, we begin any search for the causes of a social problem—in this case poverty—by examining societal contradictions, strains, and tensions, and the failure of organizations and institutions to accommodate the changing demography of the populations they are designed to serve. We do not blame victims for their poverty by assuming that the poor are disadvantaged by choice, lack of ambition, or lack of intelligence. Systematic poverty is created when the political system deprives a certain segment of the population of resources, including education, that people need to get jobs that will lead to economic self-sufficiency, as well as failure of the economic system to provide adequately paying jobs to portions of the population desiring them.

Nevertheless, it must be acknowledged that the linkage of education with jobs and an exit from poverty is indirect and at times tenuous. That is, schools can only reduce poverty to the extent that they link large numbers of disadvantaged students to long-term, viable employment. This is because the linkages between affluence and educational achievement, or grades and test scores (as opposed to attainment, or years of schooling completed) are indirect at best (see, for example, Jencks *et al.* 1983; Persell 1977; and Hurn 1985). Education can only lead to economic well-being to the extent that it facilitates employment in a well-paying job or connection with a well-heeled spouse. In either case, many other factors, including motivation, discrimination, associations, and opportunities play roles that are as important as that of education in an individual's ultimate achievement of affluence (see especially Persell 1977, 153–171). Thus, we do not believe that education alone can ameliorate poverty, even though it may be a necessary prior condition for most people. In this paper, we look closely at the historical, economic, and political context of contemporary education for linkages *through* schooling to employment and mobility.

Second, given the indirect link between education and poverty, we believe that a significant measure of the success of an educational innovation, whether enriching or compensatory, is not whether student test scores rise, but whether it improves the retention of an entire cohort of students and faculty. Thus, the key indicators of system health are dropout rates and teacher turnover, or the extent to which students complete their studies and teachers stay on the job. It matters little how successful programs may have been in the short run in raising test scores of disadvantaged students, reducing violence and absenteeism in schools, or making teachers feel competent, if students and teachers ultimately become so alienated that they drop out of school.

This is what we believe has happened in American schools. While much effort has gone into improving school performance, educational innovation during the past twenty-five years has not closed the gap between the greatly disadvantaged underclass and the privileged, though it has seemed to keep those who are moderately disadvantaged from dropping still farther behind their more fortunate peers (Carter 1984, 7). Dropout rates have not fallen below 25 percent of the cohort for the past twenty years, and 20 percent of the teaching force still quits each year (Darling-Hammond 1984; Duke 1984). Increasing evidence suggests that this attrition includes the most creative and able of teachers and many bright students (Vance and Schlecty 1982; LeCompte and Goebel 1987; and Dworkin 1987).

The other side of the coin is that education is a necessity; individuals find it hard to acquire economic well-being unless they possess minimal skills, whether in terms of cognition—reading, writing, and mathematics—or connections sufficient to get them socially promoted despite educational deficits. We feel that programs can be considered to be successful if, over the long run, they maintain a competent and motivated teaching staff, help to bring disadvantaged students closer to stable cognitive parity with their non-disadvantaged peers, decrease dropout rates or increase cohort survival, and in this way facilitate viable employment for young people.

Characteristics and varieties of educational innovation

Rather than highlight individual educational success stories touted by specific districts or schools, we shall focus upon the generic types of educational innovation that constitute innovative programs. Most innovations represent variations on one of the several approaches to educational reform that we shall discuss. Years of evaluation have proved that program success is often idiosyncratic and particular to settings, selection of site and participants, implementation strategies, congruity of goals, treatment and measures of success, and appropriateness of research design (Borman and Spring 1984). As a consequence, policymakers and educators repeatedly witness ''washing out'' of treatment effects when dissemination of programs occurs (Scimecca 1980). Evaluation results have been so dismal that some noted educational researchers have given up on experimental research design, redefined their roles as evaluators, and stated flatly that causal effects from educational treatments cannot be determined (Stake 1985; Eash 1985; Shapiro 1985).

Great variation in program design across sites is also a problem. Some large-scale programs, like Headstart, Follow-Through, and the Teacher Corps specifically encouraged ''planned variation,'' even permitting variation in the socioeconomic status, ethnicity, and age of the children served, measures of success, and goals of the program (McDaniels 1975). In fact, it often is a misnomer to refer to these as programs, when in fact they are multiple programs subsumed under a general funding rubric, and are best evaluated as multiple discrete case studies (an approach most often *not* used). For these reasons, we have chosen to discuss only the specific instructional content of the programs.

When people talk about education to reduce poverty, and then describe a program as ''working,'' they usually mean that they (or participants) are satisfied with the project and agree with its objectives, and that the project has improved the performance of students as measured on standardized-norm-referenced or criterion-referenced tests. In fact, standardized test scores have become the only really legitimate measure of program success, largely because they are the only relatively reliable and easily obtainable measures *for short-run evaluation*. All educational programs have operated in the short run—usually a maximum of three years. Long-term effects, such as improvement in student cohort survival, generally have not been examined, though teacher turnover has.

A program also is considered to be "working" if it reduces poverty. However, this can occur only if validity is posited for the following set of assumptions. Program success means better performance of students; this leads to greater educational attainment, or higher rates of graduation; and this, in turn, leads to better jobs.

People also assume that a great deal of money has been spent on educational innovation over the past years, and that most of the funding of education to reduce poverty over the years has been directed at improving the performance of students and disbursed to those for whom it was intended—the poorest and lowest achievers. This is why the public is so dismayed when it becomes apparent that poverty still exists, perhaps to an even greater extent than when the War on Poverty began. An examination of some misconceptions about and characteristics of educational reform will elucidate why the disillusion came about.

Inappropriate standards

Abt and Magidson (1980) describe a trap evaluators, educators, and policy makers fall into that has wreaked havoc with attempts to determine program effects. They called it the "all good things go together" phenomenon, in which "a favorable change in one educational outcome is assumed to result from or at least be regularly correlated with desirable shifts in all of the others" (p. 100). Thus, if a program is good for parents, teachers, school staff, and/or students, it must also improve achievement. What the "all good things go together" trap has done is to cause any and all programs, regardless of their goals or designs, to be judged successful only if they raised pupil achievement or standardized test scores.

Construct validity, however, has proved to be a problem when the goals of a program cannot be measured well by available standardized tests, whether norm- or criterion-referenced. Only where the purpose of educational innovations was specifically to effect cognitive change in students and where they set up instructional treatments linked to those desired changes, were tests appropriate measures of the changes. Even where the treatments were instructional, district-wide tests of basic skills often were the only measures available to evaluators. These were not always appropriate for the program under consideration. For example, LeCompte found that these tests did not have items which mapped to objectives for programs designed to teach inferential reasoning and critical thinking. When basic skills inventories were used anyway because of the absence of more suitable ones, and under pressure from results-seeking policy-makers and administrators, the consequences were disappointing, since even stellar programs may not show positive results on tests which do not assess the constructs covered in the innovation (LeCompte and Goebel 1984).

Multiple and noncognitive goals

Only a few of the federally funded programs for educational innovation were specifically directed at instructional programs. Most funds were spent for hiring teachers, aides, and ancillary staff, especially in Title I and Chapter I, programs for the handicapped (PL 94–142), and bilingual education. Many programs stressed developing parent involvement, desegregation, teacher training and in-service programs. Title III sought to build linkages between community social and cultural agencies and the educational system. Title IV was directed at research and development, and set up the system of university-based labs and centers. Title V gave funds to state agencies for staff and improved planning, statistical maintenance, and evaluation. Programs aimed at children varied; while many stressed cognitive outcomes, others emphasized the development of self-concept and satisfaction with school. Others sought indirect effects on student achievement by teaching parents to be more effective in helping their children with homework and other school-assigned tasks.

It is important to bear in mind that, despite the many efforts to improve the context, climate, and support systems of the schools, the only programs shown to have any *direct* effect on student achievement are those that directly link instruction to desired outcomes. The only programs that provided this sort of instruction were those devoted to compensatory education, and in some cases, to enrichment. Further complicating the picture is that separating out direct program effects, even of instructional programs is difficult since eligible students often participated in multiple programs simultaneously (McDaniels 1975, 9).

Funding: how much and to whom?

Over the past several decades it has been asserted in the media, press, popular opinion, and conservative political philosophy that immense sums of money have been spent on educational programs to help the poor and disadvantaged. We submit, however, that not only did a great deal of the money go only indirectly to children, but the funds did not constitute a major portion of the schooling budget. Furthermore, much of the funding did not go to those for whom it was really intended. Even in the peak year of federal funding (1975), the programs subsumed under the various titles of the Elementary and Secondary Education Act (ESEA), the largest of the federal educational programs, constituted only 3 percent of the total public-school budget. In only 11 percent of the nation's school districts did ESEA ever contribute more than 7 percent of the budget. Per capita, ESEA contributed only $40 per year per student overall, and only $175–$200 per year for each of the five to six million students deemed to be disadvantaged (Halperin 1975, 5). In 1987 Secretary of Labor Brock reported that this percentage had remained constant. Furthermore, because of the way funds were dispersed, a majority (60%) of the students deemed to be poor and low-achieving did not benefit from any compensatory education (Title I) funds at all. Significant numbers of nonpoor (21%) and normally achieving (19%) students did receive Title I benefits (Carter 1984, 6). This is because under Title I, the primary source of compensatory education funding, monies were often disbursed to designated schools, not to students. In this way, students who were not Title I–eligible, but who attended Title I–designated schools, benefit from the funds, while Title I–eligible students in nondesignated schools did not.

It also is to be noted that the pattern of not providing the greatest amount of aid to those most in need has persisted through the new Chapter II, or "block grant" consolidation of federal aid to education. In 1981 Chapter II consolidated 32 former categorical programs into a "block" of money to be disbursed to all state educational agencies, which were to provide them to individual districts for the specified programs. These programs included funds for library support (ESEA Title IV–B), innovative practices (Title IV–C), desegregation assistance (ESAA), career education, Title II Basic Skills Improvement,

Teacher Corps, gifted and talented education (Title IX, part A), and Teacher Centers. The impact of this shift was a "massive redistribution of federal funds away from [urbanized] states serving large numbers of poor and nonwhite children and toward more sparsely populated states with fewer minorities and healthier economies. . . . Large urban districts lost most with consolidation" (Knapp and Cooperstein 1986, 129–130).

Characteristics of compensatory education

We have suggested that much educational innovation did not directly affect instruction to students. The category called "compensatory education" or "enrichment education" did. Among these programs was bilingual education, for which there were three models: intense immersion in English with supplementary English-as-a-second-language (ESL) instruction; dual language instruction; or transitional bilingual education, wherein content area subjects were taught in the native language of the children, along with ESL, until children could make the switch to all-English instruction. Other programs included some special education for handicapped children, enrichment or remedial education for low achievers, and some supplementary education for gifted and talented students.

The characteristics of compensatory education, regardless of the program name within which it was embedded, included the following:

—smaller classes;

—teachers who were less experienced than regular teachers, but who had had more coursework and in-service training than regular teachers;

—less time in the regular classroom and more time in pullout programs;

—greater use of audio-visual materials;

—considerably more instruction in reading and mathematics than provided in the regular classroom, but less in social sciences, language arts, science, art, and physical education;

—instruction congruent with that offered in regular instruction in the early primary grades, but diverging further and further from regular instruction as grade levels increased. By sixth grade, the types of instruction most used with Title I students were those least used with regular students (Carter 1984).

One important implication of these findings is that the progressive divergence in type of instruction between grades 1–2 and grade 6 may be related not only to the fact that Title I students made the most gains in the early grades, but to the often-noted fact that very disadvantaged students fall further and further behind their more privileged peers the longer they stay in school (i.e., the "fan effect," as noted by Coleman *et al.* 1966; Murnane 1975; and Dworkin 1987). First, we have noted that while some educators view learning as a spiralling process wherein material missed at one point in time can be picked up the next time around, most teachers are reluctant to skip over rough spots and move on to new material when they feel that students have not thoroughly mastered the old. Unfortunately, this means that students may get stuck in very elementary material, and, as Bennett (1986) notes, be remanded to remedial or low-track instruction as early as first grade. There, they receive instruction that is both quantitatively less and qualitatively different from that received by more advanced students.

If our hunch is correct, compensatory-education curricula consist largely of drill on basic skills, in such things as decoding, sounds, word recognition, memory and recall, as well as simpler mathematical operations (Murnane [1975] had the same hunch). They almost never stress the development of inferential reasoning, comprehension, evaluation, and synthesis, which begin to be introduced in grades 4–6. Thus, students who remain in compensatory education may not receive the same exposure to the more advanced cognitive skills that are critical for success in the higher grades and that are taught to students in regular education. Students never instructed in these skills may never acquire them, and subsequently may fail to make the transition out of remedial status. A corollary is that students in compensatory education receive their extra hours of instruction in reading and math at the expense of science, social studies, art, and other material in the regular curriculum. This, too, creates a progressive deficit and lacunae in their knowledge base.

Which approaches help children to learn?

Below we have listed approaches to instruction that have proven to facilitate student achievement—as measured on standardized tests.

Teaching to the test. While teaching the material that is covered on tests is sometimes considered to be "cheating," it does improve the construct validity and general fairness of tests to children. Programs that had a high degree of overlap between curriculum content and test items demonstrated improved achievement for children (Carter 1984, 9).

Increasing opportunities to learn. Practices that increased the amount of time that children spent in learning, rather than in management activities, housekeeping, and the like, increased student achievement. These practices usually are referred to as increasing "time on task;" they are necessary but not always sufficient to increase achievement. They include getting teachers to spend more time in direct instruction, using time in the classroom more efficiently, lengthening the school day or year, and offering supplementary instruction (Jordan 1985; Tharp and Gallimore 1976; Stallings 1980; Carter 1984). An indication of the importance of learning time is the fact that low-achieving junior-high students spent 40 percent of their time in academic activities, as compared with 85 percent of the time for high-achieving students (Evertson 1980).

Spending time on hard subjects that use textbooks. Time spent on mathematics, reading, and academic verbal interaction was related to achievement in those subjects; so was time spent using textbooks, as opposed to puzzles, games, and toys. By contrast, time spent in more exploratory activities was positively related to lower student absenteeism, which may be a consequence of greater satisfaction with school. (Stallings 1980).

Greater interaction. Interaction, whether with teachers or students, pays off in terms of higher achievement. More direct teaching, discussion, and reading aloud, and less unreviewed seatwork and time spent by the teacher grading papers and maintaining records during class time, all were associated with improved student performance (Stallings 1980). Ironically, the education of minorities and the educationally disadvantaged is often associated with more limited teacher interaction (Entwisle and Hayduk 1981; United States Commission on Civil Rights 1973; Bennett 1986).

Individualized educational plans (IEPs). IEPs were initiated to provide coherent, consistent, and comprehensive educational planning among members of the multidisciplinary teams that worked with handicapped children. They do not involve individualized instruction, because they may in fact prescribe large doses of group work for students. However, they require that the educational needs of each child be diagnosed consciously, and that a plan be worked out that best suits the students. IEPs have been used with dropouts, gifted children, and students in regular instruction, and where adhered to, improve student performance (Klausmeier 1982).

Early intervention. The earlier intervention begins, the greater the improvement shown by students. We already have indicated curricular reasons why this may be so; compensatory education may tend to repeat itself year after year rather than permitting children to progress to more difficult material. Group improvement in the earlier grades may also be an artifact of testing residual populations in remedial classes; as the brighter and more able students "graduate" from remedial education, only those who can be expected to show little or no gain remain in the program. However, these considerations notwithstanding, evidence points to the efficacy of early intervention, especially as it prevents the despair attendant to cumulative deficit and years of failure (Carter 1984, 7).

Structured instruction. Programs like Mastery Learning (Bloom 1971) and DISTAR, especially in the early grades where straightforward objective-based teaching is easiest, have proven effective. They make each task clear to students and teacher, break it up into comprehensible steps, and test specifically the material taught.

Bilingual instruction. While bilingual instruction is still controversial, and most evaluation results are mixed, substantial evidence from *well-implemented* programs, whether they stress English-as-a-second-language, dual language instruction, or transitional and supportive dual language instruction until students are competent in English, indicates that extra support for the student with limited proficiency in English pays off in improved later performance. Further, students who acquire basic cognitive skills in their native language first, and then make the switch to English-language instruction, fare better in school. These children do not have to learn both the cognitive skills, and the language with which to acquire them, simultaneously.

There are some problems with these approaches. Perhaps the most important is that they seek answers to educational problems only *within* schools and classrooms, rather than in conditions that, though they might be external to the schools, affect them profoundly nonetheless. The approaches we have outlined also require certain perspectives and characteristics of the relationship between teachers and students, schools and the community, parents and administrators. They require competent, caring, committed teachers. Second, they require students who believe in the efficacy of learning. Third, they require that parents, teachers, and students understand each other culturally and linguistically. Fourth, they require hope that students *can* learn and *will* succeed.

Unfortunately, in increasing numbers of communities, these conditions do not prevail.

We now move to a discussion of contemporary schools, the measure of their problems, and how the hopes pinned upon them for reducing poverty have run into trouble.

Problems facing contemporary schools

The combined effects of a high student dropout rate, social promotion (in which students are passed from grade to grade without becoming literate), and a burned-out, demoralized teaching staff interact to mitigate the capacity of school systems to affect the level of poverty in America. Yet, the belief that persists schools facilitate social and economic mobility. This notion draws from the experience of selected individuals, not groups, and is immortalized in the Horatio Alger stories so beloved in American cultural ideology. It is fueled by a cultural mythology about paths to mobility that is held by the general population and acted upon by school policymakers and educators as they shape programs and curricula for students.

Cultural myths about education

1. Schooling leads to moral virtue and intellectual enlightenment, occupational success, and social mobility.
2. The system works pretty well; if individuals experience failure, then it is their responsibility for failing to fit in well enough.
3. People who do not take advantage of schooling are lazy and undeserving. If this is not the case, then they must be handicapped by unfortunate circumstances, which, with a modicum of effort, can be compensated for by a benevolent society—which then expects the recipient to join the mainstream.
4. People who do not participate in the advantages of education constitute a small group of marginal people, who are generally irrelevant to society's overall productivity.
5. Conformity to middle-class Anglo standards is the most effective way to achieve success.
6. Social (and educational) problems can be solved quickly and at low cost.
7. Use of technology can both accelerate the speed and lower the cost at which solutions can be found.

8. Continuous technological progress means that survival in the future will require that the schools transmit ever-higher levels of cognitive skills to the general population.

Under these myths, educational programs have been set up that are doomed to failure. In part this is because of the weak actual linkages between education and the acquisition of affluence. The myths pertain most genuinely to the experience of individuals from the privileged and dominant cultural groups, and when they are used to structure a set of rules by which individuals from an underclass that has systematically been disadvantaged in the system must operate, they begin to look like a stacked game. Their continued existence in the context of economic, demographic, and political shifts that obviate their validity may be the reason why many young people find that their schools have little promise, and why, as a consequence, they cease to take them seriously. Teachers, who find that they must operate as if the myths were true when they know they are fraudulent for the students they teach, also become disillusioned (Dworkin 1987).

Schools and the failure of students

The dropout rate from schools is perhaps the most critical symptom of bigger problems in an ailing social and economic system. Educators, policymakers, and legislative bodies have made heroic attempts to reduce dropout rates in the past thirty years. However, not only has the dropout rate failed to decrease appreciably, but some efforts to improve the quality of education, such as upgrading standards of minimum competency for students, may in fact accelerate dropout rates (Archer and Dresden 1987). Yet, policy makers continue to try to use the schools as a means to solve social problems. Let us examine why this has been so.

The success of public schools today is determined by:

1. overall scores on standardized tests
2. the number of students who graduate in four years
3. the number of students, whether graduates or not, who find jobs
4. the number of students who go on to attend college, whether or not they graduate from college

On all four of these standards, public schools in the 1980s must be seen as inadequate. Test scores have been declining over the past decades in ways that cannot be explained in terms of changes in the characteristics of the student body or of the tests (O'Neill and Sepielli

1985). Rates of dropping out and teenage unemployment indicate that students are neither graduating nor attaining employment in desirable numbers. Finally, and most important, comprehensive high schools did not have as their original goal the preparation of all students for university. While pressure for parity of esteem with the private academies of the nineteenth century did lead to efforts to make the high-school curriculum resemble the liberal-arts orientation of private academies, and while there was great pressure to convince educators that the education appropriate for life also befitted one for college (see the recommendations of the NEA Committee on Secondary School Studies 1893), the high schools clearly were not articulated with university preparation. Then, it was clearly stated that college training was not appropriate for all students; today, a college education may not lead to professional white-collar employment even for those who do attain it. In fact, a college education may only add $1700 per year to the income of a graduate (Goodman 1979). Especially in the liberal arts, a surplus of graduates and inflation of credentials may mean that college and high-school graduates compete for the same types of jobs.

Defining school failure in terms of dropping out

Dropping out can best be seen as a problem of perspective. Prior to the 1950s, dropout levels that exceeded 25 percent of the cohort were not considered to be as serious a problem as they are now. This is because employment, at least at some level, required cognitive skill levels no higher than those acquired in eight of nine years of schooling. Military service, the primary sector (i.e., mining, agriculture, forestry, fishing), and a labor-intensive economy could absorb those who did not finish high school. Since then, however, not only has the surplus of labor created by the post–World War II baby boom induced inflation of educational degrees, but the high-school diploma has come to represent not so much acquisition of cognitive skills but a "conformity certificate" attesting to the fact that the holder has learned how to survive in an institution long enough to assure good behavior in similar organizations such as factories, offices, and other work places. In addition, higher levels of literacy are needed for effective functioning in the 1980s. Although these circumstances have made completion of high school more critical to the future well-being of young people, they seem to lack persuasive power to an increasingly large and diverse group of people.

While theoretical and analytic linkages between schools and the societies in which they are located have long been drawn (Dewey 1916; Durkheim 1973; Carnoy 1974; Bowles and Gintis 1976; Collins 1977; and Ogbu 1978, to name only a few), practical solutions to problems seldom have been sought in these linkages. Rather, the prescriptions have been limited to "damage control," or manipulations of the curriculum, clients, and staff of educational institutions themselves, such as those described earlier in this paper. These do not and cannot address a more fundamental question: Are the schools really linked organically to the generation of individual wealth and power? Have they also ceased performing the fundamental purposes for which public schools were established—transmitting a civic culture and imparting basic cognitive skills? Perhaps the failure is in the American cultural experiment, which, in the interests of promoting egalitarianism, attempted to force one institution both to promote equality and to support the economic needs of a stratified social system. To understand the dropout problem in such a context, it is necessary to examine the linkages of schooling to jobs and cultural aspirations in an historical perspective.

When most people do not need to go to school at all, either because they can survive economically without being literate, because literacy can be acquired without going to school, because high levels of literacy are not required for employment, or because there is no pressing civil or ecclesiastical body of knowledge that people must be compelled to master, then the percentage of the population that fails to acquire a terminal degree from school is not critical. In fact, dropping out as an educational problem is a relatively new phenomenon; in 1940 only 38 percent of the young adults in America between the ages of 25 and 29 had achieved educational levels equal to or exceeding a high-school diploma (O'Neill and Sepielli 1985). However, in a society that requires literacy for economic well-being, and that postulates that literacy be acquired in a formal, governmentally supervised or sanctioned school, it becomes critical that as large a portion of the population as possible attend school and complete the required course of studies. People who do not achieve at least this minimum standard have little hope of acquiring and maintaining a satisfactory standard of living.

When, as has become the case in the past quarter-century, the possession of a certification of completion of studies is equated with literacy skills themselves and required for employment, graduation becomes imperative for the entire school-aged cohort. By 1984, 85.9 percent of all adults between the ages of 25 and 29 had a high-school education (Statistical Abstract of the United States 1986, 133). When this does not occur—that is, when people drop out—it is indicative that the institution somehow is out of synchrony with its cultural and structural context. It also means that as the numbers of dropouts grow, the size of the impoverished underclass increases. In the Western world, the existence of such a problem is demonstrated by the following conditions:

1. Levels of graduation, or school completion, required for employment have continued to rise beyond those basic primary-school-level skills of literacy and computation required for most employment.
2. Acquisition of the given level of certification no longer guarantees acquisition of a commensurate job.
3. The level of skill an individual demonstrates no longer is commensurate with the level of certification acquired.
4. The levels of skill and certification acquired by the population are distributed differentially by ascriptive characteristics such as race, gender, ethnicity, religion, or place of residence or origin.
5. Significant segments of the society no longer feel that participation in schooling is congruent with their philosophical goals for themselves or their children.

These are the conditions that indicate there is a major problem with the functioning of the system of education and training. They invalidate the deeply held cultural myths about schooling, and make visible the social-stratification function of schooling.

Two new wrinkles in contemporary society make this obvious. First, those disadvantaged in, and dropping out of, the system no longer are limited to poor minority populations (LeCompte and Goebel 1987). Second, because increasing concentration of poverty and segregation in the inner cores of large metropolitan areas (Wilson 1987) has brought about a radical change in the fabric of city life, all social problems, including those of education, have become less amenable to traditional solutions.

Education and the failure of the system

Public and political pressure has grown for amelioration of these problems without radical change in underlying social and economic structure. Under these conditions, the educational system—the colleges, universities, and public school systems—are called upon to engage in "damage control," organizing programs and policies that are ameliorative and reformist in an attempt to cope not only with changes wrought by the scientific, cultural, and technological revolution, but by those forms of inequity and prejudice not eliminated in reform and practice. We will argue that educational reform efforts do in fact stave off the problems for a while because they appear to treat the symptoms such as teacher burn-out, student drop out, and poor health care and hygiene of children. However, in the long run, they neither really change the schools nor solve the problems. In fact, many of them act to create bigger problems in the long run. Additionally, educational reformers have attempted to construct "model schools," often around portraits of effective suburban, middle-class schools, or around their recollections of what worked in the 1950s. In ignoring the fact that the schools of the 1940s and 1950s really were the products of successful educational reform designed to make schools meet the human-capital and ideological needs of an industrial, labor-intensive, capitalistic society (Carnoy 1976a), reformers have attempted to transform schooling by patching up the system and repairing the myths, rather than by profound examination of the system and the social conditions that made it possible.

Some of the most important determinants of school success in that era were external to the school system, but affected it profoundly nonetheless. They included the following:

1. Restricted encapsulated roles for women (Chafetz and Dworkin 1986);

2. A cadre of well-educated females for whom teaching offered the only professional career outlet;

3. Families characterized by the presence of two parents, one of whom did not work or worked only when the children were in school or otherwise not present in the home;

4. An expanding market for schools, which was, in fact, produced by the post–World War II baby boom;

5. Affluence, which was produced by high employment during the Korean War;

6. A labor-intensive economy with a large unskilled sector and an equally large middle sector that did not require more than a high-school diploma for employment;

7. Racially and economically homogenous neighborhoods, which produced equally homogenous neighborhood schools;

8. A native minority population that was politically irrelevant and an immigrant minority population assumed to be desirous and capable

of rapid assimilation;

9. Relatively high levels of education and affluence;

10. Cultural aspirations and expectations for children that were shared by both teachers and parents.

While this is not a bad model, what Chafetz and Dworkin (1986) call ''global factors'' external to the schools since 1957 have irrevocably changed the socioeconomic and cultural circumstances of most schools so dramatically that in most cases, the 1950s model is impossible to implement because the societal supports for it simply are no longer present.

Sociocultural changes invalidating the model

It is important to realize that the world described above no longer exists. In the first place, society has become increasingly urbanized, and minorities are no longer segregated in the cities. One out of every three children enrolled in the American schools by the year 2000 will belong to nonwhite minority groups (Hodgkinson 1985). Moreover, communities are increasingly stratified by race, class, and geography, concentrating the poor in the cities where their problems are even more intractable. Classrooms and the teaching force no longer are homogenous and oriented to the neighborhood. The reforms of the 1960s and 1970s mandated programs of desegregation; these plus major demographic changes in the U.S. population have meant that even in suburbia, school enrollments include groups of children these teachers never had to cope with before. Mainstreamed handicapped children, children who cannot speak English, children of all races and every economic condition now crowd even elementary classrooms. Teachers find that many of their colleagues are not from their own race or background. Most teachers and many children do not live anywhere near the schools they attend, and find it difficult to participate in after-school programs. Exacerbating the friction are patterns of remaining prejudice which make it difficult for teachers and pupils of different races to communicate with each other (Orfield 1975; Dworkin 1980).

Perhaps most important, as Janes Bayes points out in her essay in this volume, the nature of work required of the labor force is changing. While we still need good mechanics, artisans and technicians, as well as a professional elite, the number of such jobs relative to the overall size of the work force is diminishing. Based upon current projections, it appears that few new jobs in the coming decades will be created in highly paid sectors; the vast majority will be middle- and low-wage jobs in the service and temporary-contract sectors.

Second, schools are organized on the assumption that children live in two-parent families with a full-time caretaker at home, but often this is not the case. Despite the fact that teachers assume the support of mothers to help with homework, serve as teacher aides, and attend conferences with school officials on matters of their children's achievement and deportment, 1985 figures indicate that 60 percent of the women who have children between ages three and five now are in the work force full-time. More will go to work as soon as their children are old enough to attend school. Asking fathers to fill in is of no avail: 22.9 percent of all mothers of school-aged children are single parents, and among black mothers of school-aged children 55.9 percent are single parents (Statistical Abstract of the United States 1986, 63). They are not available for the sort of educational support activity teachers have come to expect of "concerned" parents. Even dropout programs that try to engage increased parental support must face the reality that the structure of families has changed and parents have less time for their children.

Third, much of the incentive system for school achievement has been predicated upon the ability and desire of high-school students to participate in extracurricular activities sponsored by the schools. Students had to have reasonably good grades in order to be eligible to participate. Homework was a part of the program, since achievement in school correlates directly with the amount of homework students do outside of school. However, by 1980, 70 percent of all teenagers worked during the school year. They have no time for sports or clubs, and often are too tired to do homework. The structure of their social life has changed as well; rather than spend time in extracurricular activities at school or hanging out with friends at the local hamburger stand, teenagers now hang out at the regional malls where they can see friends from school who may live too far away for convenient visiting. As schools lose their centrality in the lives of children, they also lose their capacity to hold them until graduation (see Biddle *et al.* 1981).

Fourth, a vital part of the schooling experience once took place on school-sponsored field trips to zoos, concerts, museums, and the like. These no longer are possible for most students. Mothers are not available for car pools, schools cannot afford the liability insurance necessary to permit busing of children for such activities, and in some states, like Texas, state-mandated time allocations for instruction in basic subjects preempt all time. Schools, as a consequence, have fewer opportunities to build interest-catching activities into the curriculum.

Fifth, while the size of individual classrooms has not changed dramatically, the size of schools has. In the 1950s elementary schools averaged 200–300 children, and a very large high school had 1,500 students. Now, elementary schools that have fewer than 200 students are candidates for consolidation; some have enrollments as large as 1,500–2,000 students. High schools average 1500 and up; some reach 5,000 students. While size alone seems to be a rather simple variable, it dramatically alters the daily experience of life in an institution. Studies of small groups and schools indicate that as the size of a group increases, the number of people who are active participants decreases; levels of dissatisfaction increase. In addition, size leads to specialization and stratification. This means that people have less access to a variety of roles to play and fewer close associates (Kelley and Thibaut 1954; Bales and Borgatta 1955; Barker and Barker 1961; Barker and Gump 1964). These findings are of particular importance for schools, where decisions on size are made for reasons of efficiency, convenience, aggregation of resources, and a variety of other reasons, none of which consider the impact of size on the social setting in which children learn and teachers teach.

As schools become very large, it becomes impossible to know all of one's classmates or even one's colleagues. The percentage of students who hold key positions in extracurricular activities plummets. The number of administrators needed rises. There also is evidence that dropout rates are higher in larger institutions, perhaps at least partly because alienation grows and the extracurricular networks that, other things being equal, make schools attractive to children are more difficult to maintain (Barker and Gump 1964; Tinto 1975; Hess 1986).

Finally, the characteristics of life and instruction in schools has changed. Attending school in the 1980s may be more frustrating, inane, and boring than ever before in history. Whatever intellectual quality there was in the schools has attenuated; students—even those in college-preparatory tracks—take easier courses, and they take fewer of them (Resnick and Resnick 1985). Fear of controversy has watered down texts till neither liberals nor conservatives find much in them to challenge thought. As Resnick and Resnick (1985) have noted, several decades of accommodation to the poor performance of low-income and minority subgroups have led to less rigorous courses of study; students read less well, know less math, and often cannot construct a meaningful paragraph. Even some of the attempts to raise standards have backfired; concern with acquisition of minimum competency in the basic skills has pegged school performance to achievement on machine-scored tests of basic skills and little else.

Teachers, themselves trained in the same system, are poorly prepared and in turn teach their students poorly. They give little individual attention to students, and complain of being "burned out" (Hess *et al.* 1986; Dworkin 1987). Attempts at remediation spawn so many rules and so much paperwork that even good and dedicated teachers quit in disgust. It is no wonder that dropout programs dedicated to bringing students "back home" to such conditions are not notably successful, and that teachers often find the costs of other innovations to be far greater than the benefits deriving from the extra effort they must expend. Changes like these put people subject to them under intense strain, because the organizations in which they live and work no longer fit the conditions that spawned them originally, and the roles that people occupied and the skills they had to demonstrate within them no longer achieve the desired results. Immense psychosocial strain results from pressure to succeed in terms of an old formula that cannot be followed because the ingredients no longer are available. Teachers find that their students are unteachable; students find that life in school has become untenable. In effect, both are put at risk for dropping out. The impact on future prospects of students is obvious. If schools continue to be terrible places, the best teachers—those who have options—will leave, and if the best teachers leave, then no one will be available who can teach at the levels needed to bring students up to the new and rising standards of excellence. The consequence will be increasing numbers of students with substandard skills who drop out and join the ranks of the permanently impoverished.

The consequence of these changes reflects a new kind of Social Darwinism. In the 1980s, compensatory education and financial support to the schools has been replaced by a move toward character education and what is called "excellence." Roughly, this means to increase the number of courses that are required for high-school graduation; raise the cut scores at which students are permitted to pass competency tests: and eliminate all forms of social promotion, so that students will be retained in grade until they meet the new standards. These new reforms are primarily hortatory, and they place most of the onus for improvement on the victims—teachers and students. We submit that they will be even less effective in closing the gap between privileged and disadvantaged populations than the reforms attempted earlier. They are generated out of a desire to reform without really tackling the underlying causes of the problems.

The new reforms have generated few programs other than those involving raising standards; character education, which involves preaching the virtues of hard work, ambition, deferred gratification, and abstinence, still is in the talking stages. An approach mentioned earlier, the ''effective schools'' movement, as well as proposals for educational vouchers, may be the only coherent approaches to improving schools generated recently. They are worth discussing in some detail, because discussion will illustrate quite clearly the undeniably good ideas they contain with regard to pedagogy and the administration of schools, but, and the same time, the inefficacy of such approaches in *directly reducing poverty.*

The ''effective schools movement'' as a suburban solution

The ''effective schools'' movement began with a review of the record, to locate schools where students did achieve at high levels (Brookover *et al.* 1978; Brookover and Lezotte 1977; Edmonds 1979; Bridge, Judd, and Moock 1979). Researchers then tried to determine which school characteristics led to high student performance. The effective-schools movement is a response to both the failure of large-scale and costly interventions to achieve the results desired and the concomitant cutbacks in funding for such programs. In avoiding compensatory solutions aimed at changing the characteristics of students, this approach concentrates on manipulation of resources and variables over which schools presumably have control. We submit that the effective-schools movement is a suburban solution to school problems which denies the stratification of the opportunity structure and assumes the truth for all children of the cultural myths outlined earlier. In so doing, it also ignores the variation in types of dropouts, such as the existence of those who are gifted, or of elementary and middle-school age and thus too young for job-training (LeCompte and Goebel 1987), as well as the fact that students from suburbs find schools to be failing them for reasons that often are different from those prevalent in the inner city. Let us examine why this is so.

The effective-schools studies isolated three overall dimensions of effective schools: leadership, efficacy, and efficiency. These general rubrics subsume such things as positive school climate and overall atmosphere, goal-focused activities, teacher-directed classrooms, shared consensus on values and goals, autonomy and flexibility for teachers to implement their teaching strategies, teacher empathy, rapport and personal interaction with students, high and positive expectations for achievement of students and staff, effective use of instructional time, orderly discipline, a lack of stress on strict ability grouping, and school-wide emphasis on higher-order thinking skills (Mackenzie 1983). Reform efforts worked to recreate these characteristics in schools where they did not exist, or where achievement was poor.

There are some obvious problems with this approach. First, placing major emphasis on leadership, both school-wide and in the classroom, involves a strict application of the cultural myth of individual responsibility. While not altogether a bad idea, this approach oversimplifies by ignoring the social-structural and external issues we have detailed earlier. Second, the research (as Hess *et al.* [1986] point out) was carried out primarily in elementary schools, and there are major difficulties in generalizing from it to high schools in urban areas, which is where the most serious educational problems exist. Most important, however, is that the schools lauded in the effective schools literature are those that most closely resemble the 1950s model. While no one would argue that the characteristics subsumed in that body of literature are bad for schools, exhorting schools to improve by imitating them, in a vacuum, produces fairly predictable and disappointing results.

Schools perform functions appropriate to given cultural forms within a society: accordingly,schools must change as the culture changes in order not to become isolated and hence dysfunctional. This has not happened to the schools in the United States. In other words, social and economic change brought about the first transformation of American schooling, from a collection of free elementary schools, but private secondary schools and tutoring, to a system of comprehensive public high schools which made secondary education available to all children. The second transformation made postsecondary education almost as accessible (Trow 1966). However, a third transformation of the schools has not taken place, one that would bring the educational system into congruity with the social, economic, and philosophical reality of today's postindustrial, multiethnic society. The real problem is first, that the society has changed dramatically and the schools have not, and second, that the schools have been expected to bring about a social transformation that they were ill-equipped to carry out.

Educational vouchers

Critics of American education have often argued that as long as minority groups and the poor have limited choice as to the kinds of schools to which they can send their children, the equality of educational opportunity will be unrealized. Thus, another solution offered by reformers is a system of educational vouchers, whereby parents would be issued certificates redeemable for enrollment in and transportation to any public or private school in their city, or even metropolitan area (see Jencks 1970; Itzkoff 1976; and Appleton 1983). In theory, then, the kind of quality education that rich and middle-class parents can purchase for their children could be obtained by the poor for their children.

Vouchers would be issued to parents by an Educational Voucher Agency, a structure similar to a school board, and receiving schools could convert the vouchers into monetary payments if they met the standards established by the agency. Minimal standards would include maintenance of desegregation and a guarantee that no child would be turned down for reasons of race or social class. Even private schools would be eligible for public funds through the redemption of vouchers received from low-income children whose parents elected to send them to those schools. Funds for the voucher system would come from the federal, state, and local government contributions to public education.

Although the voucher system is yet untried, there is a surrogate for vouchers which can test their feasibility. Magnet schools were approved as a mechanism to attain desegregation under 1968 H.E.W. guidelines and endorsed under Green v. New Kent County, Virginia (391 U.S. 440: 1968) and Swann *et al.* v. Charlotte-Mecklenberg Board of Education (402 U.S.1: 1971). A magnet school is one with special programs ranging from enrichment for gifted and talented children and special remedial programs to programs oriented toward specific career goals. Regardless of the school to which a child is zoned for attendance, parents who opt to place their children in a magnet school may do so, even if a district has to provide bus transportation for the child.

Experience with magnet schools has substantiated many of the criticisms tendered by those who doubt that the voucher system will work to alleviate educational inequality. Proponents of both the voucher system and the magnet system assume that all parents have equal access to the informational resources necessary to make an informed choice about the optimal educational choice for their children. However, there is sufficient evidence from magnet schools to suggest that only minority parents with better educations and higher social class status elect to send their children to magnet schools (Borman and Spring 1984). Since communications about school options are often distributed in the form of notes to parents, a substantial percentage never reach their destination. Additionally, poverty means that parents, often single parents, have themselves been educationally disadvantaged. To expect that such parents will have the time, resources, and information to shop around for a school, visiting each and evaluating its curriculum, is unrealistic. If the most frequent minority users of educational vouchers were the better educated and more affluent, then the sending schools would be drained of their most talented parental resources and would likewise experience declines in achievement, a significant criterion for evaluating the success of an educational program (see Borman and Spring [1984] for an elaboration of this critique).

One solution might be to establish another agency that would serve as a brokerage firm, or parents' advocate, which would do the necessary shopping for those parents lacking the resources to make advantageous decisions on their children's behalf. Unfortunately, such a brokerage firm could too easily be subverted into a bureaucracy that seeks only to minimize the amount of shopping it must do, and merely assigns students in a fashion similar to current school-district practices. In fact, a thorough system of advocacy that matched student needs to school programs would devour much of the Educational Voucher Agency's budget in administrative costs.

Scimecca (1980) has warned that placing the control of education in the hands of a locally run Educational Voucher Agency would involve asking the very political structure that has maintained educational inequality to redress that inequality. There are too many vested interests among the memberships of the local political structure to effect much change.

What is to be done?

This analysis seems to offer a rather gloomy assessment of the relationship between schools and aggregate opportunity for the poor. We find that schools do indeed facilitate mobility for individuals; but to look to the schools for an overall improvement in the economic health of all groups within the society is to confuse the correlation between aggregate levels of education in given groups and nations and their relative levels of wealth, with a causal relation between education and individual wealth. This is not to argue that no effort should be made to make schools better places for students and teachers alike. If only because students and teachers spend so much of their time in schools, these should be humane and interesting places. More important, schools are the arena for the acquisition of the social and cognitive skills that are the necessary preconditions for employment, and hence for the economic well-being of individuals. The changes we suggest can, we believe, be implemented even under present conditions of penury of funding in public education. They do not naively require that a new kind of human being be created to staff the schools. They are, in a word, practical because their very modesty renders them doable. They also reflect some of the current best thinking of educators.

A modest proposal

One of the realities of today's education is that few funds are available for dramatic programs of educational innovation. Our modest suggestions require that we loosen the hold which the cultural myths about education have on our thinking about schools, and the degree of anomie and alienation that schools foster in students (and their teachers). We believe that—holding all other factors constant—alienation is the primary reason students and their teachers quit school. Our proposals also address central concerns over student educational achievement since many student dropouts and pushouts have performed at below grade level expectations, thereby experiencing failure and punishment in school. Each of our suggestions comes from what has been shown to work in education.

1. The earlier an intervention strategy is applied, the better its results will be. Thus, prekindergarten programs for the disadvantaged, including school-based academic daycare for children of adolescent mothers are vital.

2. We must expand the amount of "time on task" for students, as an increase in the opportunities for students to learn also increases actual learning. A greater share of this time must be spent on "hard subjects," including mathematics, and reading; emphasis must be placed upon direct, structured instruction and more verbal interaction with teachers. Likewise, we must teach to the tests, especially if standardized tests are assumed to measure significant verbal and quantitative skills that make people more employable.

3. Curricula must be tailored to the needs of individual students, and teaching should occur in groups sufficiently small to permit adequate attention to the needs and wants of all children. In many cases, that may need to be in a bilingual environment.

4. End the predominantly remedial basic-skills focus. Disadvantaged students need to receive remediation in literacy in the broadest sense of the word—a liberal education with emphasis on higher-order thinking skills. This, not a dead-end and deadly boring repetition of elementary school, is the best deterrent to dropping out, unemployment, and hopelessness. Remedial education often makes students hate school. This does not, incidentally, mean teaching straight *Beowulf* to students with fifth-grade reading levels.

5. Change recordkeeping systems so that dropout statistics at least include summer dropouts, transfer students, and dropouts from middle and upper-primary school. In this way we might get a better idea of the actual size of the problem.

6. Provide daycare on middle-school and high-school campuses for students who are parents.

7. Mainstream potential dropouts. End the practice of labeling them and isolating them from other students—instructionally, socially, or geographically.

8. End the vocational orientation of programs for the disadvantaged, except for those few students who need immediate employment to survive. Schools cannot provide up-to-date training for today's rapidly changing job market.

9. Integrate into classrooms the recommendations regarding increasing "opportunities to learn" and construct validity in testing that were outlined earlier in this essay. Teachers can be taught to monitor their own behavior and to implement both direct teaching and more efficient management styles.

10. Reduce the size of all schools to clusters of no more than 300 students in elementary and middle schools and 500 students in high schools. This may require creative scheduling and masterful use of buildings, but it can be done. Permit each cluster to have its own sports programs, clubs, etc.

11. Provide more opportunities for students and teachers to control the destiny of their learning and its environment. Erickson (1984) suggests that learning is increased if it is negotiated jointly by students and the teacher. Similarly, teachers feel more competent when they feel that they have some autonomy in the course of their activities. Schools

must introduce some relatively radical and almost obsolete ideas from the 1960s—or was it the 1930s? Listen to students. Listen to teachers as well. Mandate that there be exit interviews for those students who do say that they are going to drop out, and then make creative concessions to solve their problems and keep them in school, rather than giving them a final push out the door. Do the same for teachers who announce their resignations. Set up some mechanism for letting students identify problems, and then let them solve them. The model of Highlander Folk School is illustrative, though it was used for community organization, rather than for school dropouts. Highlander taught people how to improve their community by helping them identify problems and empowering them to seek solutions. In a very real sense, schools are communities for students; listening to them and letting them take some responsibility for improving the direction of their lives might well produce surprising results.

Annealing a weak link

The success of any program intended to promote the survival of student cohorts, to guarantee a literate graduating class, and to insure the equality of educational opportunity is dependent upon the quality of the delivery of knowledge, support, and caring. Intrinsic to successful education is the quality of service delivered by school personnel. Teachers who are not motivated to help children, who are unable to communicate effectively, and who are ignorant of their subject matter endanger the success of any new program. Unfortunately for American education, especially in the nation's big cities, teachers remain a weak link in the educational chain. A plethora of national studies, including those by the National Commission on Excellence in Education (1986), the Rand Corporation (Darling-Hammond 1984), the Southern Regional Education Board (see Evangelouf 1985), The Holmes Group (1986) and the Carnegie Task Force on Teaching as a Profession (1986) have decried the deteriorating quality of teaching and teachers in American schools.

Each of the commission reports called for drastic changes in the recruitment, training, certification, and hiring of teachers. Ornstein (1981) warned that education majors all too often are drawn from among those students with the lowest achievement scores in a university. Vance and Schlechty (1982), relying upon national longitudinal data, reported that SAT scores were highest for those who were not recruited into colleges of education, and lowest for those who not only enrolled in colleges of education and became teachers, but who planned to stay in teaching beyond age 30. The researchers concluded that "teaching not only fails to attract the most able, but it also attracts a disproportionate share of the least able" (1982, 25).

The National Commission on Excellence in Education (1983), the National Science Foundation (1984), and the Rand Corporation (Darling-Hammond 1984) assailed the fact that in such critical fields as science and mathematics, there is a growing shortage of teachers.

Additionally, the teaching population is aging, with as many as half of all teachers in education today planning retirement by the beginning of the next century. Yet less than five percent of the number of future teachers needed for replacements in math and science education are enrolled in colleges of education today. The National Science Foundation allocated seven million dollars in fiscal year 1985 for research projects designed to locate the needed future math and science teachers (see National Science Foundation 1984; Dworkin 1987).

Even among the current teaching force, there is a severe problem: teacher burnout. Recently, Dworkin (1987) reported that approximately one out of every three teachers in urban schools feels burned out and wants to leave teaching. In a survey conducted by the National Education Association in the early 1960s, 78.0 percent of a sample of teachers indicated that they still would choose teaching as a career if they had it to do over again. By contrast, 46.4 percent of the teachers sampled in 1982 would again select teaching as a career (National Education Association 1982, 74–116). Clearly, today's teachers are less satisfied with their career choices than those sampled twenty years earlier.

There is no reliable evidence that children can learn without teachers. In fact, the logic behind reducing class size in schools, as mandated by Texas's House Bill 72 educational reform package of 1984, was the recognition that greater student–teacher interaction promotes greater student achievement. Yet the prevalence of teacher shortages and demoralized teaching staffs bodes ill for any intervention strategy that makes education a predicate for alleviating poverty.

A significant amount of teacher burnout could be alleviated if school administrators treated teachers as trusted colleagues and involved them in campus decision making. In schools whose principals are collegial, the functional connection between job-related stress and burnout—the teachers' feeling that their work is meaningless and that they are powerless to effect changes to make their work more meaningful—is severed (Dworkin 1985, 1987).

While a better salary structure would not eliminate the burnout problem among teachers, an adequate salary structure might facilitate the recruitment of more competent people into teaching and educational innovation designed to aid the poor. Salaries comparable to those offered to college graduates in other fields must be provided in the field of education. Moreover, the nature of teacher education must change. Teachers should have the same academic majors as other university students, not majors in education and minors in substantive areas. Then, students contemplating careers in education who discovered they were ill-suited for teaching could enter other careers without finding that their prior college training was useless. Currently, most teachers who find that they dislike teaching remain on the job because they have few salable skills demanded by other sectors of the economy (Dworkin 1985; 1987). Of course, with an economically mobile teaching force, the initial turnover rates may rise. On the other hand, those who remain in teaching will then do so by choice, not because they are entrapped.

Finally, if principals were trained in management, and equipped with skills designed to promote employee satisfaction, the level of burnout would decline. Failure to attract a competent teaching staff and to ensure their continued desire to remain in the profession obviates even the best-intentioned plans that schools might have to bring children "beyond welfare."

References

Abt, Wendy Peter and Jay Magidson. *Reforming Schools: Problems in Program Implementation and Evaluation*. Beverly Hills, California: Sage, 1980.

Appleton, Nicholas. *Cultural Pluralism in Education: Theoretical Foundations*. New York: Longman, 1983.

Bales. R. F. and E. F. Borgatta. "Size of group as a factor in the interaction profile." In A. Hare, E. F. Borgatta, and R. Bales, eds., *Small Groups: Studies in Social Interaction*. New York: Knopf, 1955.

Barker, Roger G. and Louise S. Barker. "The psychological ecology of old people in Midwest Kansas and Yoredale." *Journal of Gerontology* 16 (1961):146–149.

Barker, Roger G. and Paul V. Gump. *Big School, Small School*. Stanford, California: Stanford University Press, 1964.

Bennett, Kathleen. "Reading ability grouping and its consequences for urban Appalachian first graders." Unpublished doctoral dissertation, Department of Educational Foundations, University of Cincinnati, 1986.

Biddle, Bruce J., Barbara J. Bank, D. S. Anderson, John A. Keats, and Daphne M. Keats. "The structure of idleness: in-school and dropout adolescent activities in the United States and Australia." *Sociology of Education* 54 (1981):106–119.

Bloom, Benjamin. ''Mastery learning.'' Pp. 47-63 in Benjamin Bloom, *Mastery Learning, Theory and Practice*. New York: Holt, Rinehart, and Winston, 1971.
Borman, Kathryn M. and Joel H. Spring. *Schools in Central Cities: Structure and Process*. New York: Longman, 1984.
Bowles, Samuel and Herbert Gintis. *Schooling in Capitalist America*. New York: Basic Books, 1976.
Bridge, R. , C. Judd, and P. Moock. *The Determinants of Educational Outcomes*. Cambridge, Massachusetts: Ballinger, 1979.
Brookover, W. B. and L. W. Lezotte. *Changes in School Characteristics Coincident with Changes in Student Achievement*. East Lansing, Michigan: Michigan State University, College of Urban Development, 1977.
Brookover, W. B., J. H. Schwitzer, J. M. Schneider, C. H. Beady, P. K. Flood, and J. M. Wisenbaker. ''Elementary school social climate and school achievement.'' *American Educational Research Journal* 15 (1978): 301-318.
Carnegie Task Force on Teaching as a Profession. *A Nation Prepared: Teachers for the 21st Century*. New York: The Carnegie Corporation, 1986.
Carnoy, Martin. *Education as Cultural Imperialism*. New York: David McKay Company, Inc., 1974.
Carter, Launor F. ''The sustaining effects study of compensatory and elementary education.'' *Educational Researcher*, 13 (1984): 4-13.
Center for National Policy Review and National Institute of Education. *Trends in Black School Segregation, 1970-1974, Vol. I*. Washington, D.C.: U. S. Government Printing Office, 1977a.
Center for National Policy Review and National Institute of Education. *Trends in Hispanic Segregation, 1970-1974, Vol. II*. Washington, D. C. : U.S. Government Printing Office, 1977b.
Chafetz, Janet Saltzman and Anthony Gary Dworkin. *Female Revolt: Women's Movements in World and Historical Perspectives*. Totowa, New Jersey: Rowman and Allanheld, 1986.
Coleman, James S., Ernest Q. Campbell, Carol J. Hobson, James McPartland, Alexander M. Mood, Frederick D. Weinfield, and Robert L. York. *The Equality of Educational Opportunity*, 2 vols. Washington, D. C.: U. S. Government Printing Office, 1966.
Collins, Randall. ''Some comparative principals of educational stratification.'' *Harvard Educational Review* 47 (1977): 1-27.
Darling-Hammond, Linda. *Beyond the Commission Reports: The Coming Crisis in Teaching*. Santa Monica, California: Rand Corp.
Dewey, John. *Democracy and Education*. New York: Macmillan, 1916.
Duke, Daniel Linden. *Teaching—The Imperiled Profession*. Albany, New York: State University of New York Press, 1984.
Durkheim, Emile. *Moral Education: A Study in the Theory and Application of the Sociology of Education*. New York: Free Press, 1973.
Dworkin, Anthony Gary. *When Teachers Give Up: Teacher Burnout, Teacher Turnover, and Their Impact on Children*. Austin, Texas: Hogg Foundation for Mental Health and Texas Press, 1985.
Dworkin, Anthony Gary. *Teacher Burnout in the Public Schools: Structural Causes and Consequences for Children*. New York: State University of New York Press, 1987.
Dworkin, Anthony Gary. ''The changing demography of public school teachers: some implications for faculty turnover in urban areas.'' *Sociology of Education* 53 (1980):65-73.

Eash, Maurice J. ''A reformulation of the role of the evaluator.'' *EEPA* 7 (1985): 249–253.

Edmonds, R. ''Effective schools for the urban poor.'' *Educational Leadership* 37 (1979): 15–24.

Entwistle, Doris R. and Leslie Alec Hayduk. ''Academic expectations and the school attainment of young children.'' *Sociology of Education* 47 (1974):301–318.

Evangelauf, Jean. ''Panel analyzes education graduate's transcripts, finds weak grounding in liberal arts, urges 25 reforms.'' *The Chronicle of Higher Education*, June 26:11.

Evertson, Catherine. ''Differences in instructional activities in high and low achieving junior high classes.'' Paper presented at the American Educational Research Association meetings, Boston, April, 1980.

Ginsburg, Mark B. and Katherine K. Newman. ''Social inequalities, schooling, and teacher education.'' *Journal of Teacher Education* 36 (1985):49–54.

Goodman, Jerry D. ''The Economic Returns of Education: An Assessment of Alternative Models. *Social Science Quarterly* 60 (1979):269–283.

Greer, Colin. ''A review of Christopher Jencks' *Inequality.*'' *Society* 11 (1974):92.

Halperin, Samuel L. ''ESEA ten years later.'' *Educational Researcher* 4 (1975): 5–10.

Hauser, Robert M., Shu-Ling Tsai, and William H. Sewell. ''A model of stratification with response error in social and psychological variables.'' *Sociology of Education* 11 (1983):20–46.

Hess, G. Alfred, Jr. ''Educational triage in an urban setting.'' Paper presented at the American Educational Research Association meetings, Philadelphia, Pennsylvania, December, 1986.

Hess, G. Alfred, Jr., Emily Wells, Carol Prindle, Paul Liffman, and Beatrice Kaplan. *Where's Room 185?: How Schools Can Reduce Their Dropout Problem.* Chicago: Chicago Panel on Public School Policy and Finance, 220 S. State Street, Suite 232, December, 1986.

Hodgkinson, Harold L. *All One System: Demographics of Education, Kindergarten through Graduate School.* Institute for Educational Leadership, Inc., Washington, D.C., 1985.

Holmes Group, The. *Tomorrow's Teachers: A Report of The Holmes Group.* East Lansing, Michigan: The Holmes Group, Inc.

Hurn, Christopher J. *The Limits and Possibilities of Schooling, Second Edition.* Newton, Massachusetts: Allyn and Bacon, 1985.

Itzkoff, Seymour W. *A New Public Education.* New York: David McKay, 1976.

Jencks, Christopher. ''Educational vouchers.'' *The New Republic* 163 (July 4, 1970): 19–21.

Jencks, Christopher, James Crouse, and Peter Mueser. ''The Wisconsin model of status attainment: a national replication with improved measures of ability and aspiration.'' *Sociology of Education* 56 (1983):3–19.

Jordan, Cathy. ''Translating Culture: Ethnographic Information to Educational Program.'' *Anthropology and Education Quarterly* 16, No. 2, (1985):105–123.

Kelley, H. H. and J. W. Thibaut. ''Experimental studies of group problem solving and process.'' Pp. 735–785 in G. Lindzey, ed., *Handbook of Social Psychology.* Cambridge, Mass.: Addison-Wesley, 1954.

Klausmeier, Herbert J. ''A research strategy for educational improvement.'' *Educational Researcher* 11 (1980):8–13.

Knapp, Michael S. and Rhonda Cooperstein. ''Early research on the federal education-al block grant: themes and unanswered questions.'' *Educational Evaluation and Policy Analysis* 8 (1986): 121–138.

LeCompte, Margaret D. "Defining differences: cultural subgroups within the educational mainstream." *The Urban Review* 17 (1985): 111-127.

LeCompte, Margaret D. and Stephen D. Goebel. "Can bad data produce good program planning? : an analysis of record-keeping on school dropouts." *Education and Urban Society* (forthcoming, May, 1987).

Mackenzie, Donald E. "Research for school improvement: an appraisal of some recent trends." *Educational Researcher* 12 (1983): 5-17.

Murnane, Richard J. *The Impact of School Resources on the Learning of Inner City Children*. Cambridge, Massachusetts: Ballinger, 1975.

National Commission on Excellence in Education. *A Nation at Risk: The Imperative of Educational Reform*. Washington, D. C.: U. S. Department of Education, 1983.

National Education Association. *Committee Report of the Committee on Secondary School Studies*. Washington, D. C.: United States Government Printing Office, 1893.

National Education Association. *Status of the American Public School Teacher, 1980–1981*. Washington, D.C.: National Education Association—Research, 1982.

National Education Association. *Teacher Supply and Demand in the Public Schools, 1981-1982*. Washington, D.C.: National Education Association—Research, 1983.

National Institute of Education. *The Desegregation Literature: A Critical Approach*. Washington, D.C.: U.S. Government Printing Office, 1976.

National Institute of Education. *Violent Schools—Safe Schools: The Safe School Study Report to Congress, Vol. I*. Washington, D.C.: Department of H.E.W., 1978.

National Science Foundation. "Program announcement: Grants for research on the teaching and learning of science and mathematics." (Pamphlet). Washington, D.C.: National Science Foundation, 84–74, O.M.B. 3145–0058.

Ogbu, John U. *Minority Education and Caste: The American System in Cross-Cultural Perspective*. New York: Academic Press, 1978.

O'Neill, David M. and Peter Sepielli. *Education in the United States: 1940–1983*. U.S. Bureau of the Census, Special Demographic Analysis, CD–85–1. Washington, D.C.: U. S. Government Printing Office, 1985.

Orfield, Gary. "Examining the desegregation process." *Integrated Education* 13 (1981):127–130.

Ornstein, Allan C. "The trend toward increased professionalism for teachers." *Phi Delta Kappan* 63 (1981):196–198.

Percell, Caroline Hodges. *Education and Inequality: The Roots and Results of Stratification in America's Schools*. New York: The Free Press, 1977.

Resnick, Daniel P. and Lauren B. Resnick. "Standards, curriculum, and performance: a historical and comparative perspective." *Educational Researcher* 14 (1985): 5–21.

Resnick, Lauren. "Cognition and the curriculum." Invited address given for Division B of the American Educational Research Association, Chicago, April, 1985.

Rossell, Christine H. "Magnet schools as a desegregation tool." *Urban Education* 14 (1979):303–320.

Ryan, William. *Blaming the Victim*. New York: Pantheon, 1971.

Scimecca, Joseph A. *Education and Society*. New York: Holt, Rinehart, and Winston, 1980.

Shapiro, Jonathan Z. "Evaluation: retrospect and prospect. Where we are and where we need to go." *Educational Evaluation and Policy Analysis* 7 (1985):245.

Stake, Robert E. "Evaluation: retrospect and prospect. A Personal Interpretation." *Educational Evaluation and Policy Analysis* 7 (1985): 243–244.

Stallings, Jane. "Allocated academic learning time revisited, or beyond time on task." *Educational Researcher* 9(1980):11–17.

Tharp, Roland G. and Ronald Gallimore. *The Uses and Limits of Social Reinforcement and Industriousness for Learning to Read*. Technical Report # 60, Kamehameha Center for Development of Early Education, Honolulu, HI, 1976.

Tinto, Vincent. ''Dropouts from higher education: a theoretical synthesis of recent research.'' *Review of Educational Research* 45 (1975):89–126.

Trow, Martin. ''The second transformation of American secondary education.'' Pp. 437–448 in R. Bendix and S. M. Lipset, eds., *Class, Status, and Power*. New York: Free Press, 1966.

U. S. Bureau of the Census. *Statistical Abstract of the United States: 1986* (106th Edition). Washington, D.C.: U. S. Government Printing Office, 1985.

United States Commission on Civil Rights. *Teachers and Students: Differences in Teacher Interaction with Mexican and Anglo Students*. Report V: Mexican American Education Study. Washington, D.C.: U. S. Government Printing Office, 1973.

Vance, Victor S. and Phillip C. Schlechty. ''The distribution of academic ability in the teaching force: policy implications.'' *Phi Delta Kappan* 64 (1982):22–27.

Wilson, William J. ''The ghetto underclass and the social transformation of the inner city.'' Plenary address given at the American Association for the Advancement of Sciences, Chicago, February, 1987.

About the Contributors

JANE BAYES is professor of political science at California State University, Northridge. A specialist on minorities, interest groups, labor markets, and women in the public sector, Bayes is coeditor, with Rita Mae Kelly, of *Comparable Worth and Public Policy* (1987), and the author of "Women, Labor Markets, and Comparable Worth," *Policy Studies Review,* May 1986.

SHELDON DANZIGER is professor of social work, Romnes Faculty Fellow, and Director of the Institute for Research on Poverty at the University of Wisconsin at Madison. He is the coeditor of *Fighting Poverty: What Works and What Doesn't* (1986) and *The Distributional Impacts of Public Policies* (1987), and the author of numerous journal articles. His research focuses on the effects of income maintenance programs on poverty, work effort, and family structure.

ANTHONY GARY DWORKIN is professor of sociology at the University of Houston. He is author of *When Teachers Give Up* (1985), *Female Revolt* (1986) (with Janet S. Chafetz), and *Teacher Burnout in the Public Schools* (1987). His areas of research include minority group relations and the sociology of education. He serves as editor of a book series entitled "The New Inequalities," published by the State University of New York Press. Dworkin is president of the Southwestern Sociological Association.

IRWIN GARFINKEL is a professor and the former director of both the School of Social Work and the Institute for Research on Poverty, University of Wisconsin at Madison. His research focuses on the causes of and remedies for poverty, and in particular the benefits and costs of alternative kinds of government transfers. In conjunction with officials at the Wisconsin Department of Health and Social Services, he developed a proposal for a new child support assurance system that is being tried on a demonstration basis in the state. He is coauthor of *Single Mothers and Their Children: A New American Dilemma* (1987).

MARGARET D. LECOMPTE is an adjunct associate professor of sociology at the University of Houston. She has held faculty positions in anthropology and sociology of education at the University of Houston, University of

Cincinnati, and the University of North Dakota. She is working on a book with Gary Dworkin on the relationship between the teacher burnout and student dropout problems in U.S. schools.

SARA S. MCLANAHAN is professor of sociology in the Institute for Research on Poverty, University of Wisconsin at Madison. She teaches sociology of the family, medical sociology, and sociology of the life courses and has published numerous articles on the feminization of poverty, the intergenerational consequences of family disruption, and the effects of parenthood on psychological well-being. She is the coauthor of *Single Mothers and Their Children: A New American Dilemma* (1987).

HARRELL R. RODGERS. Jr. is professor of political science and Dean of the College of Social Sciences at the University of Houston. He is a policy analyst who specializes in American Poverty. He is author of numerous articles on the poor and author of three recent books on poverty: *Poverty Amid Plenty* (1979); *The Cost of Human Neglect: America's Welfare Failure* (1982); and *Poor Women, Poor Families: The Economic Plight of America's Female-Headed Households* (1986).

MICHAEL WISEMAN is an associate professor of economics at the University of California at Berkeley. His research interests are in the fields of urban and regional economics, public finance, and income distribution policy. He is an Associate Editor of *Regional Science and Urban Economics* and a board member of the National Tax Association. During the 1986–87 academic year he was La Follette Visiting Distinguished Professor of Public Policy at the University of Wisconsin at Madison.

RICHARD WEATHERLEY is an associate professor of social work at the University of Washington and has written extensively on families under stress. He is coauthor of *"Bad Girls": Adolescent Pregnancy and the Policies of Transgression* (1987); *Patchwork Programs: Comprehensive Services for Pregnant and Parenting Adolescents* (1985), and author of *Reforming Special Education: Policy Implementation From State Level to Street Level* (1979).

PATRICK WONG is a doctoral candidate at the School of Social Work, University of Wisconsin at Madison. He has been involved in the Wisconsin child support reform project at the Institute for Research on Poverty, conducting computer simulations and writing on the impact of the reform proposal.